C000179837

HART'S GIRLS

BY

LYNDA REES

Lynda Rees

Hart's Girls

By

Lynda Rees

Email: lyndareesauthor@gmail.com
Website: http://www.lyndareesauthor.com
Original Edition
Copyright © 2020 by
Publisher: Sweetwater Publishing Company
6612 Ky. Hwy. 17 North, DeMossville, KY 41033
http://www.sweetwaterpublishingcompany.wordpress.com

Lynda Rees

DEDICATION:

*This book is dedicated to my
family; my devoted husband,
children and grandchildren.
You are my legacy,
My gift to the universe.
May you forever be blessed with
love and be safe from harm.
This world is a better place
for having the
treasures you are in it.*

*Love you, always,
MomMe*

Lynda Rees

Lynda Rees

CHAPTER 1

Lemon Sage Benton sat in her vehicle in The Roberts Agency's parking lotawaitingFBI Special Agent Reggie Casse's appearance. It was almost six-thirty. Sage had arrived a few minutes early.

A dark, mid-sized sedan pulled into the lot across Second Street. The building faced Main Street and had been vacant for years. The automobile sped into a spot beside a new, black pickup truck. A burly gent in a leather jacket stepped from the car and slammed the door shut. He hastily strutted toward the back steps and took them two-at-a-time, as he raced to the second story landing. A fierce yank opened the door, and it slammed behind the guy disappearing in a huff. What little had been visible of his face from the angle and his manner said he was agitated and rushed.

"That's odd." Sage spoke to herself.

Real estate agentChloe Robertswaltzed from her office side door and gestured to Sage, as she walked toward her SUV. FBI Special Agent Reggie Casse pulled her black, luxury sedan into the spot beside Sage's truck. Both women stepped from their autos at the same time. They hugged and proceeded toward where Chloe waited.

"I'm excited." Reggie griped Sage's hand then opened Chloe's passenger door and jumped in beside their friend.

"Thank you both for helping me. I've never lived in one location long enough to purchase a house before. This will be my first ever, very own home."

Sage climbed into the backseat of Chloe's SUV. "Of course, Reggie; I'm thrilled about you moving back to Sweetwater. Hey, Chloe, how you doing?"

"You're welcome, Reggie. It's what I do. Thanks for choosing me as your agent. Hi, Sage. I'm good. You?" Chloe glanced around with her brows knitted.

"I'm great. Let's do this thing." Sage fastened her seat belt then relaxed into the cozy bench.

Chloe handed a file to Reggie. "We're viewing these properties tonight. Take a look as we drive to the first one." Chloe gunned the engine to life.

As Chloe pulled from the lot onto Second Street, Sage pointed across the street. "Say, what's up with the building across from here?"

"I'm not sure. Why?" Chloe glanced at the neighboring parking facility as she drove away. It wasn't unusual to see overflow parking using the empty lot.

"Some big guy hastily parked and went in through the second, floor back entrance. He looked angry." Sage bit the side of her lip.

"Did you recognize him?" Chloe glanced at her across her shoulder.

"No, didn't get a good look." Sage winced, wishing she'd gotten a better view of the man.

"Maybe someone has bought it. The structure has been closed since the owner died a few years ago. It's beginning to show signs of abandonment. It's a shame. I hate seeing properties go to waste. I wonder if the new owner wants to fix it up to resell. It could bring a tidy profit with a little effort and minimal investment. Maybe I'll contact them to learn what their plans are. If they want to resell, I'd love to list it." Chloe volunteered. "Want me to let you know what I find out?"

"No need. I'm curious. That's all." Sage needed to focus on Reggie, having volunteered to help her view homes.

Chloe got to business at hand. "We're touring three homes tonight. The second needs a furnace. The first is a divorce case, but the guy's living there until it sells. The third is at the top of your price range, but doesn't appear to require updating."

"Sounds good." Reggie shifted through paperwork, reading condition reports divulgingissues and repairs completed.

Chloe pulled into the driveway of a secluded house at the end of a quiet, wooded lane. A single, shabby automobilerested in the driveway. "Probably the owners'; there is no garage.He was supposed to take a drive, so we could have the place to ourselves.He must be running late." Chloe cut the power as they pulled into a spot beside the car.

"I hope he's leaving. I'd hate snooping in nooks and crannies with the owner watching." Reggie and Sage stepped out and closed Chloe's door.

Chloe pointed toward the roof. "It appears to need gutters."

Reggie made a note on the listing sheet. "Thanks, I'll have it checked by a roofer, if I like it. I like that the neighborhood is quiet, and the view is beautiful." They gazed across a rolling field of wildflowers and bluegrass.

Chloe bypassed the lock box hanging on the door knob and knocked, then rang the bell. "He could've ridden with someone else, but I like to make sure no one's here before rushing in. I've seen some strange things, selling real estate." Chloe winked and rolled her eyes. When no answer came, she tried the door. "It's unlocked." She opened it a ways and stuck her head in. "Anyone here? This is Chloe Roberts with

The Roberts Agency, here to show the house." When no answer came, she stepped into the vacant living room.

Reggie followed her inside. "Guess you're right. The seller's gone as promised." Sage trailed Reggie, taking care to inspect everything she saw.

"Yep, let's check this place out." Chloe led them into a large, airy kitchen. "Nice modern appliances and a granite countertop."

"I like windows around the room. It's sunny and bright. Tile looks in good shape and goes well with the cabinets. There seems to be lots of storage." Reggie slid a hand across the counter.

Sage opened and shut several cabinets, mostly bare of contents. The refrigerator held an open six-pack of beer, a pack of cheese, loaf of bread, a plastic container of lunchmeat and a jar of mayonnaise. "Looks like a bachelor's fridge."

"Hell, it looks like my fridge." Reggie snickered, and they laughed.

Chloe led them into a dining room. "They should be motivated. If you like the place put in an aggressive offer. It might not fly, but is worth a try."

Reggie followed. "So far so good."

Sage trailed them. "The living room is large enough for entertaining, along with the ample dining room." Both were vacant, except for a lounge chair and large television in the living area.

Reggie knelt and ran a hand across flooring. "Carpeting looks newer and is neutral like the walls. This might work."

Reggie and Sage shadowed Chloe into a hallway.

Reggie poked her head through a door and laid a hand on the wall. "I like the white and black tile. This guest bathroom is modern and convenient."

Sage nodded. "It's got a linen closet and there's an extra-large clothes closet in the hallway."

Chloe stood in the doorway. "The guest room is empty except for a couple half packed cartons and a stack of cardboard boxes flattened and stacked against a wall."

The women followed Chloe into the slight space. Reggie nodded her head and looked around. Sage opened the closet to find it empty.

"Let's check the master." Chloe opened the closed door. Her face blanched to the same shade aseggs Sage had gathered before leaving the farm.

Sage rushed to her side. Her heart plummeted toward her stomach. Her windpipe froze. She turned away from the gruesome scene. Arms went around her friend's quivering shoulders, as she drew Chloe into the corridor. Finally she gasped. "What the hell happened here?"

Reggie passed them and hastened into the room they'd vacated. "Oh, hell. Don't tell me you've found another one." She gazed at Sage over her shoulder with one brow high.

Sage's shoulders rose and fell.

Chloe huffed out air. "Not again. This is becoming a habit."

Sage patted Chloe's back. Sage and Chloe had acquired a knack for locating dead bodies.

Reggie eyed Chloe critically. "You too?" Reggie rolled her eyes at Choe's nod.

Chloe looked like she might toss her dinner. "It's the second corpse I've discovered since I returned to Sweetwater. I never paid attention when I was a kid. I'm beginning to think this town has as much violence as New York."

Reggie pulled vinyl gloves from a back-pants pocket and donned them. She stepped into the master suite for a few minutes without making a sound. She examined the man without touching him. Blood pool and injury were a dead giveaway. He was beyond help. She gently touched the second victim's throat for pulse, and when she didn't find one, lifted the wrist and checked for one. She returned to her friends and closed the door carefully.

Sage placed hands on Chloe's shoulder. Chloe's attention diverted to her face. Sage's words were soft and soothing, impressively keeping her own cool. "It's not a first for me either. I discovered a friend's body soon after moving here. Sweetwater is an amazing, warm and welcoming community. Wyatt does everything possible to maintain that status. Every town, no matter where, has its share of violence. Don't let this scare you away."

Chloe sniffed and nodded silently, blinking away tears.

Reggie led the way to the kitchen and pulled out chairs for her friends. They gladly slumped into them. "You'd be surprised where I've encountered crimes in my line of work. Bad things happen to good and corrupt people everywhere. There's no hiding from it."

Closing her eyes with a sigh, Chloe shook her head, but remained quivering. "You're right, and I don't scare easily. I'm living in the house where I found a murder victim." She snickered, as if in control of her senses. Her body continued to quake—a natural instinct.

Sage groaned. "Me either. This sort of thing isn't about to frighten me away, though it's going to piss Wyatt off royally. He swears I'm a danger magnet. I'm beginning to believe he's right."

"Want me to phone him? Or you want to? This is his jurisdiction." Reggie placed a hand on Sage's shoulder and found it surprisingly steady.

Sage shook her head. "Thanks. I'll do it." She whipped her phone out of her jeans pocket and dialed her husband. "Hi, Wyatt; yes, I love you too. No, it's not going well. You're not going to believe this." Sage explained the situation to her husband.

Unfortunately, Wyatt would believe it. Reggie took a seat, and the three women sat holding hands, waiting for sirens.

The two-bedroom cottage teemed with activity. The CSI Team marked locations, collected evidence and took photographs. They took finger prints and made impressions of Reggie, Sage and Chloe's shoes. The women remained seated in the dining area. Another crew worked outside doing the same and inspecting the owner's vehicle.

The coroner's voice was easily heard in the small house, as he spoke to Wyatt. "Bodies are warm. Rigor hasn't set in. Time of death is less than three hours ago. This was definitely murder, as you can see. I can tell you more after a thorough examination in my lab. Let's get them ready." His last comment was meant for his crew.

Two men waiting at the door pushed a vacant stretcher into the room. Another empty gurney in the living room awaited the second victim. As men wheeled the first out of the bedroom, Wyatt halted them. "Sage, Chloe and Reggie, please take a look." He waved them forward.

Stepping carefully so they didn't disturb areas investigators had marked, they reluctantly approached the corpse. Wyatt studied reactions, as the women gaped at the dead man. Chloe and Reggie shook their heads. Sage gasped.

"I've only seen the man when I checked him out before you arrived." Reggie's face showed no emotion. She'd gone into professional mode.

Wyatt stepped between Chloe and Sage. A muscular arm draped across each woman's shoulders. He led their return to the kitchen. "Do you know him?"

Sage drew in a slow inhale. Her breath came heavily. "My head's swimming." Her body appeared to weigh more than her legs could support. Good thing Wyatt had a grip on her.

Chloe's face was whiter than before, but she shook her head in answer. Tears streamed down her cheeks in rivulets. "His throat was sliced. No wonder there was so much blood. The bed was soaked with it." She closed her eyes and puffed out a breath. "I've never seen him before. He could be the owner. It's what I assumed—he was . . . nah—"

Wyatt finished for her. "Yep, the dude was partially naked." He helped Chloe into her seat.

"The listing report and tax data says the house is the property of Simon and Carol Ann Bedford." Chloe leaned against the table.

"We'll check it out . . . unless . . . you know him, Sage."
He deliberated Sage's face.

She nodded. "It's Simon Bedford. I . . . ah . . . know him.
He's a customer." Reggie thought she'd seen recognition in
Sage's expression when she'd lost her breath at the sight of
him up close and personally.

Wyatt eased his wife into a seat. "Okay, baby, stay calm;
that's helpful."

The coroner's men moved Bedford's remains to a waiting
vehicle and maneuvered the second cot into the scene of the
gruesome murder, while Wyatt had questioned the women.
They returned with a black bag zipped around the second
stiff.

"Hold up, guys. Let's give the ladies a quick check. I
need to know if they recognize her." The men wheeled their
cargo toward the kitchen and unzipped the body bag.

Reggie, Chloe and Sage stood to get a good look. The
men secured their load and wheeled it out.

Reggie leaned her butt against a counter. "I checked her
pulse before you arrived—never seen her before that." Sage
and Chloe returned to their chairs.

"Wyatt, I don't recognize that poor child." Chloe burst
into waterworks and laid her face in her hands.

"Me either," Sage muttered through sobs of her own.
"She's so young. It's sad. That poor baby died before she got
a start in life."

Reggie crossed her arms and eyed Wyatt. "There's
bruising on her face, neck and arms. She obviously fought
for life. Heavy makeup is smeared. Tears streaked down her
cheeks, leaving muddy trails. Prints on her slim neck appear
to be from strangulation."

"Looks that way. I agree." Wyatt nodded.

"She can't be more than twelve or thirteen. She had a
tattoo on her neck. That seems strange for someone so
young." Sage sagged in her seat. "But of course, so do her

clothes. She's dressed like a tramp—way too seductive for a kid."She winced. "Wyatt I need to tell you something about Mr. Bedford. I had a rousing argument with him a couple days ago at the warehouse where he works. The altercation was witnessed by some of his staff."

Reggie's gut felt as though something inside was trying to chew its way out. She inhaled. How did Sage draw trouble to her? She was the most peaceful soul Reggie knew.

"Okay, wait a sec. Say nothing more." Wyatt's hand went up. He went to the front door. "Leo, can you come in here, please?" Wyatt returned to his seat followed by Deputy Sanders.

Leo took the fourth chair, as Wyatt indicated he should. "Please take charge of this interview and the case. It's important I not be the one to question Sage. My wife and the deceased have a connection."

Leo nodded and pulled out a phone. He turned it to record and laid it on the tabletop in front of Sage. "I need to record this." Sage nodded. "Go on, Mrs. Gordon."

Formal address sounded odd, since Leo and Sage were on first name basis, but this was an official murder investigation. Tapes could be used by the court. Sage was about to disclose information that would likely make her a prime suspect. Wyatt didn't want to be accused of interfering with a crime for personal reasons. He would stay out of it and let Leo run the show.

It was comforting, knowing Wyatt would simply be acting as Sage's husband during the investigation, whether she needed his support or not. It sounded as though Sage was going to be a suspect. She was lucky to have him to surround her with love. Reggie couldn't ignore jealousy welling insider her at the heart-warming exchange between her two best friends, Sage and Wyatt. Would any man ever be there for Reggie like that?

"Simon and Carol Ann Bedford are customers of Parsley, Sage, Rose, Mary & Wine Farm. Carol Ann is a chef who overseas their five restaurants in a tri-county area. She purchases organic produce and cheeses from me. Simon manages their warehouse facility. Carol Ann is professional and pleasant. Simon's rude, gruff and I generally tolerate him because their business is important to me. I've seen him treat his crew disgracefully, cursing them, yelling and calling them names."

Leo nodded and smiled easily. "What was your beef with him?"

"Rose Coldwater delivered a truckload of our products to the warehouse last week. Simon made her wait a long time to unload, and took an unscheduled truck before her, though she arrived at the designated time. When she was finally backed to the dock, there was no oneto unload the shipment. She finally saw a worker in the warehouse and asked him to help. He unloaded the cargo. Before he could move it to proper refrigeration, Simon Bedford waltzed over and berated the guy for helping. He instructed him to get back to his assignment or he'd be fired. Simon told Rose he'dassigned another team to take our pallets to the cooler, but they were told to finish their current work first. They'd be with her in a jiffy. That jiffy turned out to be a full hour."

Wyatt held Sage's quivering hand on the table. His thumb stroked top of it absently. Eyes focused eyes on his trembling wife. His face was strained but encouraging.

Sage's involvement must be eating him alive. Poor guy was a peacemaker and safe-keeper. Sage had killed before, and it was concerning. Reggie and Wyatt knew Sage wasn't capable of such violent, gruesome murder.

Sage took a deep gulp of air as though hoping to suck in courage from Wyatt before continuing. "It was blazing hot. Simon crudely reprimanded Rose for not moving her truck, screaming she was holding up the next van form taking her

11

spot for unloading. It was true, but she ignored the irate buffoon and refused to leave until her delivery was properly stowed away. The cartons sat on the dock for almost an hour before being moved." She hesitated.

Leo tilted his head with a blank expression. "I'll need to question Rose personally, so do not speak with her about this. I don't want you influencing how she responds. So far it sounds as though Rose has more reason to be angry with Simon than you do."

Sage rolled her eyes. "I can't avoid Rose. She's my partner at Parsley, Sage, Rose, Mary & Wine. I will not speak with her before tomorrow when I return to the farm."

Leo nodded. "Fine; I'll go to her home and get her statement after we finish here. Do not contact her. Understand?" When Sage nodded, Leo continued, "Is there more?"

She sighed. "I was livid when my freight was returned later that day. Carol Ann had inspected cargo in the refrigerated locker and deemed it unfit to serve. I checked. She was correct. I had personally handpicked each item before delivery. It was in pristine condition when Rose took it to the warehouse. Simon's inefficiency cost me a bundle. He offended Rose, which pissed me off. That was bad enough. I was livid. He jeopardized my business with his wife. The restaurant chain is a valuable account."

Her shoulders rose and fell with her deep intake. When Leo waited she appeared to get control of her emotions. "I went to the depository and cornered that asshole. I told him in no uncertain terms, he was on thin ice. Their eateries depend on my crop. He not only cost me a bundle. He cost himself by not having ample staples at his establishments, and he insulted my partner. I will not stand for mistreatment of my people."

She only had one—Rose had started as a farmhand and friend and was now a full partner. Rose was more timid than Sage.

"Rose allowed the bastard's words to roll off her shoulders. I wouldn't stand for it."

The truth put Sage in jeopardy, revealing her as having motive for killing the little twerp in the body bag. She didn't appear to be holding anything back.

"I have confidence in the justice system and in Wyatt and his team of enforcement experts. You'll find out who did this." Sage's smile was weak, but her nerves appeared steadier.

Leo's expression showed hatred for having to ask. "Did you kill Mr. Bedford, Sage?"

"I did not. Leo, I have faith you and Jaiden will discover who killed Simon Bedford and that poor girl. Directly or indirectly, Simon is responsible for her death. That miserable man must have many enemies. Surely I'm not the worst of them." Her brows rose and fell.

Wyatt twisted his head, as though releasing a cramp. With his free hand, he scratched the nape of his neck.

Sage winced at his concerned look. She'd put herself in a perilous predicament. He might be right about her being a danger magnet.

CHAPTER 2

Sage parked her delivery van in the lot behind White's Grocery on Main Street. She nuzzled Tuffy's jaw. "Guess you'd like to take a whiz before I unload. Huh, boy?"

Tuffy answered by leaning into her palm and closing his eyes.

"Okay, let's get this done." Sage hopped from the driver's seat, shut the door and rounded the front of the vehicle. Opening the passenger seat door, she held a hand up. "Wait."

As expected, Tuffy sat quietly watching her every move—his specialty. The ex-police, German shepherd was the smartest dog she'd met and the most affectionate. He guarded Sage with his life. Sage pulled the lead from the door pocket and secured it to Tuffy's collar. She backed up.

"Okay."

1

Tuffy hopped to the ground. Sage led him to a wooded area between the dumpster and alley. He quickly did his business and scratched the turf.

Sage walked to the parking area and up two steps to the back door with Tuffy at her side. A knock produced no answer. She tried the knob. It was unlocked. She opened it and leaned into the stock room. It appeared vacant.

"Anyone here?" She softly called. No answer. "Guess Ben's busy out front." She entered the immaculate storage space. "Let's go see." Tuffy obediently stayed close to her heels at her side.

Sage waved as she walked through the dairy department and produce section, around rows of packaged goods to the front. Mr. White was ringing up a customer's purchase at the register.

"Hey, Wally, how are you? Mrs. Simpson, good to see you." Sage smiled at her customer and neighbor.

"I'm fine, Sage. How are you and the family?" Mrs. Simpson smiled over a shoulder.

"We're doing great. Thanks for asking."

Wally White looked up from his chore. "I'm good, Sage. Glad to see you. I'm running low on your goods but swamped with stocking and customers out here." Another patron nodded a greeting to Sage as he stepped to the conveyor belt and started loading items.

"No worries, Wally. I can handle it. I'll unload and stock the back room then fill your shelves."

"Gee, thanks, Sage. I hate to ask you to do all that yourself." Wally sighed.

"It's no bother. I've got plenty of time. I'm happy to do it." She didn't have another delivery for an hour. This meant she wouldn't have time to stop by the station and have lunch with Wyatt, but business came first.

Sage and Tuffy wandered toward the stock room. She didn't recognize a young girl studying pre-made sandwiches with apparent longing. She would be cute if it weren't for mussed makeup, too heavily applied for her age. An extremely short, cheap dress failed at its attempt to make her look older. Instead it played up her unfed, skinny form. Messy spikes of purple, dyed hair reared across her head, giving the child a circus freak appearance.

Why were kids always trying to look older? Nearing forty, Sage had started noticing fine lines around her eyes and mouth. Wyatt called them love lines.

Sage regained control ofmeandering thoughts, as she went into the storeroom. The youngster had stirred a familiar sadness. She'd been used to such sights living in New York. The girl reminded her of a younger Rose when they'd first met. Sage had formed an instant bond with young Rose wearing Gothic garb, a purple streak in her brunette bob and a *'don't get close to me'* attitude.

Sage had secured Tuffy in the van with windows down, unloaded cargo into the storage room and stowed items where they belonged. She had filled a stocking cart with cheeses, fruits and vegetables, and wheeled it into the storefront.

The young girl was still in the store, now looking at the dairy cooler. Sage watched from a distance as she first selected a pint of milk. She pulled something from her pocket, studied it a few seconds and returned it. She swapped the pint for a half-pint of milk, obviously unable to afford the larger size. She moved away with head down and returned to the premade food cooler, stopped to stare.

Sage pushed the cart to the dairy refrigerator and placed precious, gourmet farmers and goat cheeses inside. From the corner of her eye, the girl ran her hand over sandwiches slowly, almost religiously then walked away without taking any.

Sage moved to the produce section. She filled row-after-row of cooler space with her fresh, crisp vegetables and fruits. In peripheral vision, the youngster moved to Sage's side.

The strange female picked up a carton of strawberries. Knowing they smelled delightful, Sage was proud the child had taken notice of her precious crop and would enjoy the treat. Instead, the girl closed her eyes inhaling a whiff of strawberry scent then returned them to the shelf. Disappointment burned in Sage's throat.

Sage finished loading empty spaces with her harvest and returned the cart to the back room. Reentering the store, she selected a couple bottles of water from a refrigerated unit, one for her and one for Tuffy.

The girl still meandered through the store, now gazing wishfully toward a candy rack. Her eyes darted from side-to-side, as though checking if anyone watched. From her vantage point, Sage could see, but clearly the girl didn't notice Sage. The child snatched a chocolate bar from the rack and slipped it into her pocket.

Sage's heart ached for the girl, who was clearly hungry and likely without enough cash to feed her properly. Sage snatched a quart of milk, a chicken salad sandwich, the carton of berries and three candy bars. She took her load to the register where the girl stood in line.

Wally finished with the buyer in front of the child. She moved forward and sat her meager half-pint of milk on the counter then pulled out a small handful of change.

Sage took control. "Thanks, Honey, here's the rest of our purchase. Oh, and I don't want to forget that chocolate bar you put in your pocket for me. Thanks for helping. I appreciate it."

With a baffled look, the youngster eased the candy bar from its hiding place and laid it all on the conveyor belt. She stood statue still, as though fearing to move. Her eyes darted from Wally to Sage and back, without moving her head.

Wally began ringing the groceries. When he finished, he looked at the girl then Sage. Sage handed him a bill, which he made change from, minus cost of foodstuffs. He bagged the lot and handed it to Sage.

Sage slid an arm gently around the girl's shoulders, feeling a slight flinch before acceptance of her touch. "Come on, Honey. Let's go out the front. We can sit on the bench and take in some of this delightful sunshine. Thanks, Wally. See you next week."

She ushered the girl out the front door and to a bench with Chloe's picture and a real estate For Sale sign and phone number on it. "Let's rest here."

The girl looked apprehensive, with bony shoulders hunched, dread in her eyes staring at the sidewalk. Sage ignored her companion's nervousness and opened the bag. She selected the sandwich and handed it to her companion with a smile. "Start with this."

The child's mouth fell open. She warily accepted the food. When she appeared to understand Sage wasn't going to take it back, she ripped it open and stuffed half into her mouth, gobbling it down in two bites. She made quick work of the other half and started to drop the wrapping on the ground.

Sage snatched the cellophane from her gently and tossed it into a garbage receptacle nearby. She handed the girl the strawberry carton without a word and watched with pleasure as she slowly savored one-after-another sweet-smelling fruit with a look of ecstasy on her face.

When the carton was half gone, she closed it and handed it back to Sage. "Thank you." Her voice was as timid as her actions. She openly wasn't sure what Sage had in mind.

Sage stuck the package into the bag in her lap. "My name is Lemon Sage Gordon. What's yours?" Sage pulled out the milk carton and a straw then handed them to the girl.

Again her eyes grew wide and mouth opened without words, only a sigh. She accepted the carton, opened it and inserted the straw. A fearful voice spoke, "Willow." She sipped with eyes closed until the box was empty. Instead of dropping it as before, she handed it to Sage with a shaky hand. "What kind of name is Lemon Sage?"

Sage snickered and threw the empty in the waste can. "I'm the product of two hippies. My flower-child parents named me. Call me Sage, Willow. Are you okay? Feel better?"

Willow avoided eye contact. "Yeah, thank you."

"Are you in some kind of trouble? Do you need help?" Sage laid a gentle hand on Willow's pale one. Her tremble gyrated into Sage's palm. The child evidently needed a friend.

"No." Willow's eyes remained diverted, zooming from side-to-side, as though looking for someone. As she glanced away, a design became visible.

Breath caught in Sage's throat, and she struggled to remain calm. "Are you meeting a friend?"

"Ah, . . . no." Willow continued to avoid Sage's glance.

"I like your tattoo. Does it mean anything special?" Sage tried to form an alliance with the obviously troubled girl. If Willow needed a friend, Sage aimed to be one.

Willow's already pale skin whitened more so. She slapped a hand over the heart branded on the side of her neck. Her words were not much more than a stutter. "Uh . . . no . . . noth—nothing—just a tat."

"You sure you're okay? Are you in danger?" Concern gnawed at Sage's gut. She trusted her gut. It had never done her wrong. Something scared this child.

Willow stood with her voice attempting defiance. "What's it to you?"

Sage also got to her feet. She pulled a card from the back pocket of her frayed, cut-off jeans and dropped it into the sack. Removingwater bottles and a chocolate, shepushed the tote to Willow. "One candy bar for now, another for later. Enjoy the rest of the berries."

Willow accepted it. Shock was replaced with gratitude. Willow huffed out air. "Wow, thank you, Sage." She snuggled the bag close to her middle.

"Willow, I know you're in some kind of jam. I want to help you. Let me." Sage's chest contracted with concern.

"No." Willow looked over her shoulder as though a boogieman might grab her from behind.

Sage's heart ached to grab Willow and nestle her tight, then take her home where she'd be safe with Sage, Ty, Tuffy and Wyatt. She had no right to impose on the unwilling kid's privacy, if Willow didn't want Sage's aid.

"Okay, fine. I put my card in the bag. Keep it. If you need anything at all, I'm here for you. Call; I'll come—no matter what. Understand. I want to help you."

Willow stared at her as though Sage was speaking Greek then darted around the corner and disappeared, treasures clutched to her barely budding chest.

Sage's face fell. Her belly rumbled, not with emptiness, but with grief. Desperation and terror were familiar emotions. Sage had experienced both more than once. Being alone and in danger was a horrible experience. Sage had lost everything she lived for alone on a New York City sidewalk one night.

She wasn't about to leave Willow alone if she help it. If Willow would accept assistance, Sage would do everything in her power to protect her.

She walked into the store. Wally stood ringing up yet another shopper. After greeting the buyer, Sage turned to the shop keep. "Wally, if that child I was with earlier comes in, give her whatever she wants to eat. Put it on my tab."

He nodded with a knowing look. "She work for you?"

"Not yet." *Maybe someday.* "Thanks, Wally. See you next week." Sage exited through the stockroom and locked the back door behind her, returning to her van and Tuffy.

"Tuffy, I hope I made us a new friend." She backed out of the lot and caught a glimpse of Willow disappearing around a stand of trees and bushes creating a barrier between the store lot and alley.

Wherever Willow's staying, it's within walking distance.

CHAPTER 3

U. S. MarshalShae Montgomery propped his ass against Deputy Leo Sanders' desk in the Sweetwater, Kentucky police precinct bullpen. "Thanks, Leo, Jaiden; it's always a pleasure working with you."

Sheriff Wyatt Gordon had asked Shae to update deputies Leo and Jaiden Coldwater on his assignment. "I support the National Center for Missing and Exploited Children anddirect federal investigations into sex offender crimes in the region. I'm leader of national investigations in the area. The FBI assigned a Suit to the taskforce to work with me and your team. It seems the mid-west is a hotbed for child snatching and human trafficking."

Jaiden's head tilted. "Surprising. Are we looking at sex offenders?"

Shae nodded. "Sure but normally they're simply perverts we'll put away. We focus mainly on serious trafficking operations more sophisticated than you can imagine. They require substantial manpower and resources to make a dent in them. We aim to locate and apprehend head honchos, as well as their network of criminals. Your assistance is essential to make that happen."

1

"Only scums of the earth exploit women and children." Jaiden stood feet apart, hands on hips with a defiant aura. Her exuberance for defending the innocent was well known. She was a welcome resource. The part-Choctaw, ex-Texas Ranger stood tall for her petite height of around five-foot-two. Jaiden's uniform cinched a slim waist and hugged pert breasts. Obsidian black locks were secured into a bun at the nape of her horse-tattooed neck.

Shae's heart jolted at the sparkler glistening from Jaiden's ring finger. His *ex* had ripped hers off, not caring she'd left Shae in fragments, with no clue how to patch himself together. *No time.* Self-pity was reserved for sleepless nights with a tumbler of bourbon in hand.

Leo Sanders was a father and experienced lawman, whose fierce devotion to the force would be a major asset at Shae's disposal. Sheriff Gordon was known for managing a crack team.

The bullpen door swung open. A raven beauty in a navy pants suit strutted in from the lobby acting as though she owned the place. Spotting Wyatt, a brilliant grin swept across her stunning face.Spiked heels didn't deter progress. The gal sped toward the sheriff.

Wyatt appeared at his office door. His arms opened. His smile showed off perfect pearly whites.

The woman leapt into the sheriff's arms. It looked to be a feat, given her approximate height of aroundfive-foot-four with Wyatt standing a tall six-six. Slim legs enfoldedWyatt's waist. Arms seized his shoulders. With a shake of dark curls, she planted an amorous *smackeroo* on the married man's lips.

Shae's opinion of the wedded lawman plummeted. Wyatt didn't attempt to resist the rambunctious female, who obviously adored him. A few minutes previously, Wyatt had proudly showed Shae a photo of his wife and child. This gal was not Wyatt Gordon's precious wife.

You'd think a man of his stature living in a busy-body town wouldn't welcome passion with a lover in public, especially not in front of a room full of his employees.

Sheriff Gordon was top-notch when it came to the law. Shae had mistakenly assumed Wyatt's personal ethics to be up there with the best.

"I'll be in touch." Shae made a quick escape, as Wyatt and his bimbo closed the door.

A last glance provided a view through glass walls. The frisky female sat cross-legged on Wyatt's desk. Morals aside, her image grinning at her lover stuck irritatingly in Shae's brain.

FBI Special Agent ReggieCasse sat atop Wyatt's desk. He eased his long, lanky frame into the guest chair facing her. "I'll be damned if it ain't good seeing you, Reggie. It's been too long. What's this I hear about you moving to Sweetwater?"

"It's true." Reggie went on to explain her role in the task force. "When I was asked for a strategic location for the new regional office, Irecommended Sweetwater. Being a stone's throw to Missouri, Illinois, Indiana, Arkansas, Tennessee and Ohio makes it a perfect shipping hub for legitimate distribution—and illegal as well. Preying on children, especially teenagers and women burns my ass. I asked for this assignment. I'm determined to put those suckers in the slammer."

"I talked with the lead U. S. Marshal heading up the task force earlier today. You just missed him. I've assigned Jaiden and Leo to work with the team. It's good knowing you're the FBI's link to the operation. U. S. Marshal Shae Montgomery is going to enjoy working with you." He winked.

"We'll see. I've not met the marshal." She waggled eyebrows. "Now tell me the down and dirty about that sweet woman and child of yours. I've been missing you all."

"Honey, that gal will be the death of me. Sage has calmed down a bit since giving birth to our son, but she's a magnet for trouble."

She chuckled. "Sage can handle herself. She saved my ass more than once. I understand she's working for you."

Wyatt's hands flipped upward, showing surrender. "I finally gave up trying to keep her out of police business. I assigned her as Liaison to the Cyber Crimes Unit the state Attorney General set up. Cut her teeth on Dovie Fuller's case—stalker went after her. With the unit processing digital forensic evidence from cell phones and computers in the lab in Louisville, Sage helped identify and convict he culprit. Did a good job. Bastard took a couple potshots at Sage. She was carrying our baby. I could've lost both of them in one round." Knowing the sheriff well, Reggie recognized pain in his eyes for a brief instance before he shut it down.

"That's our Sage. Is motherhood treating her well? Can she keep up with Ty and the farm too? Organic farming has been her dream. The business was doing extremely well when she got pregnant." Reggie leaned into her palms against the desktop.

4

He snickered. "She's strong with a will to survive. Sometimes I believe Sage is invincible. She's still the same headstrong, impetuous, independent filly I married. Her farm is running on top cylinders, with the aid of a young woman she hired. Do you remember Rose Casson—now Coldwater. Rose worked at the convenient store when Sage moved to Sweetwater? Rose and her husband, Cal Coldwater, live in Sage's log house on the farm. Rose knows the operation as well as Sage does. She's crazy about little Ty. He follows the two gals around all the time."

"Yeah, I remember Rose. Nice gal. Sage is lucky to have her. Listen. Sage volunteered to help me find a house. I should be on this assignment a couple years, maybe longer. It's the perfect opportunity to invest."

"Good timing. The market is ripe. There are lots of homes available. Sweetwater is the perfect place to call home."

"Don't I know it? I don't want to take advantage of Sage. She's got a lot on her plate."

"Don't be silly. If Sage wants to help, you might as well let her. She'll do it anyway, with or without permission. You know how she is about people she loves. You, Riley, Corrie and now Rose, are like sisters to her. Don't worry about Sage's workload. Rose is a blessing, and Sage has the energy ofmost toddlers."

"Okay, then. It's settled." She chuckled.

"What's this I hear about you staying in a hotel?"

"Well, sure. You and Sage don't have space for me. Your guest room is now Ty's nursery. I'd never dream of camping out in your daughter's room. Hailey needs to know she can come home anytime she needs a break. Senior year in college isn't all fun and games, especially for someone as driven as your little genius."

Wyatt beamed proud. "I've got to admit. That girl surpasses everything I'd hoped for her—on the Dean's List

5

at Stanford. She does like to come home frequently to check on her old Pa, little bro and Sage. We love having her."

"Cal and Rose are living in the log house. So a hotel it is for me. I don't mind. Living in hotels is the norm in my line of work."

"Riley called earlier and said I should advise you to check out of *that damned hotel* and bring your bags to Mane Lane Farm. She and Levi want you to stay with them."

She pushed down envy.Her friends had found partners in life, some sprouting infants. Reggie was the last single gal in the group. Would she ever be lucky enough to meet a guy who would love her—maybe have a kid or two of her own?
What the hell?

At least they continued including her in their lives. Good to be settling down near those she loved. "That's generous. Mane Lane is huge and luxurious; but honestly, I'm fine."

"If you think those gals are going to settle for you shacking up in a day room, you're nuts. Grab your things. Otherwise, Riley, Sage and Corrie will do it for you." Wyatt stood and stretched his lengthy form.

Reggie hopped to her feet. "You're right. Once they get an idea in their heads, there's no stopping them." She smoothed her slacks and side-hugged Wyatt's trim waist as he opened the door and guided her into the bullpen.

Familiar faces nodded and greeted Reggie as they passed through to the lobby door. She casually answered each greeting.

"Hi, ya, Reggie; how are you doing?" Leo shouted.

"Welcome back to Sweetwater." Jaiden waved cordially.

"Thanks, Leo, Jaiden. I'm happy to be back, this time for as close to permanent as I've had since I was a kid. I'll tell you more, later. Right now, I've got an appointment to keep." She waved a hand in their direction.

"Dinner tonight at our place?" Wyatt brow cocked.

"Wouldn't miss it." Reggie gave his middle a final squeeze, released her old friend and exited the station.

Reggie hadn't considered anyplace home since high school. She'd grown up at her grandpa's farm in Sweetwater, with Levi and Corrie Madison, Wyatt Gordon and others she could hardly wait to see again.

Her residence in New York was a place to light between assignments or when working in the city or DC. The swanky uptown condo had been little more than a storage facility for clothing and her few possessions.

The idea of planting roots near people she loved settled warmly in her heart. Much as Reggie thrived on excitement of her career, she'd begun craving permanence. This assignment was a good first step.

CHAPTER4

Shae settled onto a barstool at The Ten Mile House. He could use a cold one after a grueling day helping his WITSEC enlistee find a job worthy of the guy's criminal experience, managing a productive weed and drug production facility.

Shae wished his work was, as the public envisioned the witness protection game, guarding innocent beings who'd observed a major crime. In reality, it was mostly watching out for career lawbreakers willing to shoot off their mouths in court about illegal operations, in order to escape heavy prison sentences for themselves.

The program required enrollees endure extensive training on staying in the wind. Regardless, sometimes these guys ended up doing what they knew best—breaking the law. Rehabilitation wasn't the assignment, but Shae's job was satisfying, especially when he managed to deter an enrollee from reverting to crime.

He'd finally set the man up in a gardener position working for a landscaping firm. Mr. X, as Shae referred to them all in his mind, would happily prune rose gardens, trim hedges and mow lawns for wealthy around the county. Hopefully, the dude wasn't an action junkie and would grow to enjoy ruralKentucky's slower pace. When it came to

9

excitement, Sweetwater couldn't compete with New York City.

Shae appreciated the quieter life. He'd spent most of his adult career in Chicago and Denver. When this assignment came up, he'd jumped on it.

Of course, far as local lawmen knew, Shae's business was strictly to head up the Human Traffic Operation, working in conjunction with Wyatt Gordon's team and whatever support the FBI deemed to send him. They'd offered a Special Agent assigned to the task force, but the *Suit* had yet to show up. Against his wishes, Shae was bound to accept the assistance.

Shae took a sip of the icy brew owner, Justin Henderson, put in front of him. Justin's wife, Corrie Madison-Henderson was helping Justin bartend for the evening. Corrie sat beside Justin, since the crowd was light for now. The short, dark man tenderly stroked his wife's hand, as it lay on his thigh.

Justin gazed proudly at his wife. "Corrie is CEO of her family's multi-company business. The Adelle Corporation is named after her mother. Her father and mother are currently living in Washington, DC."

The lengthy blonde smiled casually. "I'll introduce you to my brother, Levi, and his wife Riley. They should be in later. Levi runs the family equestrian operation, Mane Lane Farm." She said it like it was a little piece of crop dust.

Shae had frequented the race track a few times. Mane Lane Farm was a world-renowned, multi-billion-dollar horse breeding and racing operation. "I've heard of it."

"Levi's wife, Riley Powers-Madison, is a major player in the ad biz. She owns The Powers Agency in Cincinnati but works from the farm, to spend more time with Levi."

"You sound close." Shae had lost his only brother in Iraq and had no other family. He envied the casual way Corrie spoke of her obviously close-knit clan.

"Oh, we are. In fact, we had a double wedding a couple years ago." The door swung open, and with it went Shae's wish to be in the barroom vanished.

"Oh, Hon, there's Reggie. I've got to sit with her and catch up." Corrie pecked Justin's cheek.

"Sure, Doll, go talk girl stuff." Justin walked with a limp, as he hopped to his feet and strolled to the newcomer. "Give us a kiss, Sweet Thang." His arms opened.

The female who had entered rushed into them. She hugged Justin with a tight grip. He lifted her off her feet by leaning back a tad. She kissed Justin's cheeks, and he sat her on her feet. She slapped his slim ass with a crack.

Corrie watched the shocking scene with arms crossed and a smirk. As the feline released her husband, Corrie grabbed the woman with both arms. Instead of knocking her block off, Corrie gave the brunette a major bear hug.

"Good to see you. What's this I hear about you making Sweetwater home, after all these years?" Corrie, the sultry, blonde-bombshell, led the frisky brunette to an empty table in a far corner.

Justin returned behind the bar and popped tops off two sweating, amber bottles. He walked crookedly toward the gals and placed bottles on the table between them. After a quick thank you, they returned to their chatter. Justin limped with a practiced gait to his station with the barest hint of discomfort in the wince on his face. Whatever produced the expression was causing the barkeep pain. He didn't give it credence, but ignored it as though a normal part of his life— which it evidently was.

Why did Wyatt pick tonight to introduce Shae to his friends? Shae dreaded bearing witness to the sheriff's wife and girlfriend jointly partying in the same barroom. The Ten Mile House wasn't a large facility, one good-sized room in the ancient log building. It seemed unlikely Sage Gordon

11

would stand for Wyatt's affair to be flaunted in her face. Old Wyatt was in for a rude awakening. Horse manure was about to hit the pitch fork, and Shae didn't want to be in the line of fire.

Lemon Sage Gordon was a knockout, and from what he'd heard, well liked. The sheriff and his wife had a toddler together. If Shae had a woman like that who loved him, he'd—

Respect for Gordon kept plummeting lower as time went by. The sheriff wasn't the man Shae had heard him to be. Shae would finish a drink with Wyatt, meet his wife and come up with an excuse to leave early.

Thankfully, the Gordon's didn't make him wait long. Before Shae swallowed the last sip, they arrived. Heads turned toward the seemingly loving couple.

Wyatt's arm draped possessively across straight shoulders of a slim female sporting a dark ponytail that would be the envy of many a horse. Shorts exposed what appeared to be runner's legs. Her charming face lit with delight. She greeted friends with a brilliant smile that sparkled in deep pools of her dark eyes. Wyatt guided the striking female to Shae's stool.

"Howdy, Shae, I'm glad you decided to join us." Wyatt friendly manner didn't show nervousness at having his wife and bimbo in the same room. He slapped Shae on the shoulder.

"I appreciate the invite, but I can't stay long." Shae took the large mitt Wyatt extended.

"Sage, this is the fella I told you about. Meet U. S. Marshal Shae Montgomery." Turning to Shae, Wyatt grinned. "This is my incredible wife, Lemon Sage Gordon."

The gorgeous lady was worthy of pride puffing out Wyatt's chest. Sage deserved an ardent lover, not one that catted around town in public with a floozy.

Shae hopped to his feet and took the hand Sage extended. Surprisingly the slim fingers sported slick callouses on their pads. He'd been wrong about Sage Gordon. He'd envisioned a gentlewoman farmer giving direction from a desk, not a hands-on type. This fine woman did manual labor.

"It's my pleasure Mrs. Gordon." Shae stood.

"Please, call me Sage. Everyone does." She shook his hand heartily then waved him to return to his seat. "Wyatt has wonderful things to say about you, Marshal Montgomery." From her easy manner, she seemed oblivious to her husband's philandering.

"Good to hear; Shae, please. Wyatt and I will be working together considerably, it appears."

"Awesome. He's a fierce lawman and will be a great advantage to your work." She gazed adoringly at her tall husband.

"Hey, Sage, join us when you can." Corrie called from the table with acasual smile.

"Yeah, girl, get your sweet ass over here." Wyatt's girl-toy shouted, wearing a sly grin on her much too gorgeous face. Apparently Sage and the arresting bimbo were acquainted.

Why did it bother Shae, knowing the beauty was wasted on a married man; and why did Shae's gut rile at picturing her naked beneath the handsome, silver-haired sheriff? The loose and easy type didn't normally appeal to Shae.

Shae had no stake in this race. He recently met Wyatt, had barely been introduced to Sage and didn't know Wyatt's dazzling concubine from Adam. Yep, he needed to get his butt out of this scene and quick.

"I see you've met Justin and Corrie." Wyatt had observed Shae and Justin chatting as he entered and assumed correctly.

"Sure have." He nodded toward where Justin stood across the counter from the threesome.

"Would you guys mind terribly if I went to sit with them?" Sage's friendly face eyed Shae then turned toward her husband. Love glowed in her eyes for the man who didn't deserve her.

"Not at all," Shae returned Sage's smile.

"Sure, Babe, go play with the gals—love you." He bent and met her lips.

She tiptoed to reach them for a quick peck. "We'll talk later, Shae. It was good meeting you." Sage trotted toward her friends.

Shae needed to get out of the joint now. The women might know each other, but blood could flow hot any second. As he considered escape, another couple entered.

The towering, slim, shaggy, fair-haired fella wore fine, understated clothing and reeked of big money. His jeans and tee shirt probably cost as much as Shae made in a week. Scuffed, polished cowboy boots peeked from beneath lengthy legs of pricydenims. His woman's bronze curls bounced animatedly as she strolled. His arm flexed enough to clearly show muscle definition as he cradled her beneath it.

"Great." Wyatt turned and grinned at the newcomers. "Shae, I'd like you to meet Riley and Levi Madison. Levi's Corrie's brother. Riley, Levi, meet U. S. Marshal Shae Montgomery." Wyatt waved first at the couple then at Shae and stood back to allow them closer.

Levi's arm shot out in greeting. A broad smile graced the blonde man's face, closely resembling his dazzling sister, in a more masculine way.

Shae gripped the surprisingly calloused hand. Though wealthy, Levi obviously did more than sit on his ass in a fine home.

Madison? Where had Shae heard the name? He'd researched the area when selecting a location for the field office. Madison rang a bell for some reason.

The brunette extended a hand with a brilliant smile. "Nice meeting you, Marshal Montgomery." The slim, silky hand she offered had a strong grip.

He took it, accepting her hearty shake.

"Riley owns The Power Agency in Cincinnati. It's one of the country's best advertising firms," Wyatt boasted.

"Thank you, Wyatt. We give it our all. It's a team effort." Riley didn't blush, receiving the praise. "Nice meeting you, Marshal Montgomery. I hope we'll be seeing a lot of you, now you're settled."

"Thank you, Mrs. Morgan."

"Please, we're neighbors and hopefully will be friends. You might as well call me Riley."

The women turned. Sage spoke in a friendly tone. "Riley, join us."

"Do you mind?" Riley eyed Shae then her husband.

"Not at all." Shae took his stool, as Riley left the men. "It's impressive how beautiful local women are. That table could be a tourist flyer extolling charms of life in Sweetwater. Single men reading it would rush to live here." Shae chuckled.

Justin refreshed his empty bottle with a new one, as he served his buddies. *Great.* He needed to down it and get the hell out of Dodge.

"Yeah, but they're mostly transplants. Riley was born in Hazard, Kentucky and grew up near Cincinnati, in Northern Kentucky." Levi took the stool on one side of Shae.

Wyatt grinned. "Sage is from New York. Corrie was born and raised here, but Reggie moved from Denver as a child, when her parents went to Africa as Doctors-Without-

Borders. She only now moved back, having lived in DC or New York City after graduating Quantico."

"Whatever; they make an arresting visual." Shae swallowed a gulp of icy liquid.

Like a time bomb ready to explode.

Shae took another long sip. He'd take acouple more then make his escape. "So what do you do, Levi?"

Might as well scope out the guys.

"I breed and train race horses," Levi answered nonchalantly.

"Levi's being modest. Don't let him fool you." Justin cracked tops off Levi's and Wyatt's fresh bottles. "He's world renowned for knowledge in bloodlines and owns some of the best breeding stock on the planet. He hasn't done too shabby at the racing game either. Levi has a couple Derby winners, a Preakness and even a Triple Crown winner. This boy sells a shot of semen for more than I make in a year." Justin plopped on his stool and began massaging his thigh without losing eye contact, as though the act came natural.

It hit him where he'd heard the Madison name. "You're Senator Garrett Madison's son. Right? I've read about you."

"Yeah." Levi nodded. "Dad wanted me to go into politics. He finally realized I'm more at home in the saddle. I run Mane Lane. Mom and Pop spend most of their time in DC, but the farm will always be their home." Levi's attitude clearly displayed love and respect. "Dad tried to get Wyatt to run for Senate, also."

Wyatt snickered and gazed at the table of females. "I appreciated the honor of being considered; but it would've meant giving up what I love, being Sheriff of Sweetwater. The political game isn't for me. Besides, Sage would havetossed my ass to the curb in a second, if I became a Senator."

16

"Seriously? What woman wouldn't want glitz and the Washington social scene?" Shae shook his head in wonder.

"Sage lived the high life with her first husband in the big city. She has no intention of doing it again. She started her organic farm at Parsley, Sage, Rose, Mary & Wine Farm in Sweetwater to get away from it. We're content in our little piece of heaven, with our son Ty."

If the dude is so contented, why does he need a side woman?

Shae stood. "Well, gents. It's been awesome meeting you. It's time for me to call it a night. I've got work to do." He shook Justin's hand, then Levi's and lastly Wyatt's. With a gesture toward the females' table, he headed toward the door. "Goodnight, ladies. It was a pleasure."

The women waved with cheery 'goodbyes,' as the door closed.

Cool night air filled his lungs. Magnolia fragrancedrifted from trees lining front of the ancient log structure and reminded him of the mysterious gal's perfume, which had lodged in his nostrils, and kept her fresh in his mind. She was a looker, and feisty—the kind of woman who normally didn't appeal to Shae. For some reason that baffled him, she'd stay front and center in his mind since he'd first seen her.

She'd even invaded his dreams. Fantasies of her naked fleshagainst his played hell with his sleep, which had come hard enough since his breakup. He could physically feel her soft, perky breasts teasing and pillowing against his chest.Dark curls tickled his shoulders and cheeks, leaving lasting imprints he could feel even now. Baby-soft lips bent to kiss his as she climbed atop him. At least he'd stopped dreaming about Lydia.

No.

That female was Wyatt's—. Best not covet another man's woman, even if Wyatt was a cheater. The gut-stabbing throb returned and with it Shae's desire to dislike the friendly, well-respected sheriff. He couldn't muster the emotion, however. Wyatt was a likable sort, even if the fabulous beauty was wasted on him. Fantasizing about Wyatt making love with the gal left Shae queasy.

Why her?

Shae had long been without a woman, and had no room for one—or so he was told. Lydia should know. Why couldn't he get the tantalizing she-devil out of his mind?

CHAPTER 5

Reggie applied hot pink lipstick and checked makeup and hair in the rearview mirror. Long, curly tresses usually tamed into a ponytail or twist, hung freely draping her shoulders, and ringlets surrounded her face.

She pulled keys from ignition of her 1970 emerald green Chevelle. She'd turned in the company car for one of her own choosing. Admiring sparkle in the paintjob, she locked the door and strutted toward the nondescript facility occupied mostly by doctors.

She'd thought she recognized the sandy-haired guy at the bar last evening but couldn't place him. Usually her memory fired on all cylinders, especially when it came to tasty-looking men.

Tall, clean-cut and slim wasn't overly thin, but less meaty than she liked them. She preferred a bit of brawn. Too short a haircut made him appear on the edge of nerdy—not Reggie's style, but aptly respectable.

The scar beside his right brow added to masculine appeal. *Funny*; men with intriguing experiences under their belt gave off sex appeal like they sweated testosterone. No wonder she'd gotten that vibe from the not-quite-geeky stranger. It made sense now.

Sage had caught her watching him leave. "Hot, isn't he? I'm surprised he didn't come over and say something to you before leaving."

"Why?" She'd faced Sage with a frown.

"Did you talk earlier?" Sage had looked perplexed.

"No, why would we?"

"You do know him; right?" Sage's head had tilted forward.

"Should I?"

"I'd say so. After all, you'll be working with Marshal Shae Montgomery tight as a filly in season and a rutting stud." Sage winked, obviously under the impression an affair would ensue between Reggie and the marshal.

"That was Montgomery?" Had she needed hitting over the head?

Sage had burst out laughing, joined by Corrie and Riley, who had been listening. The old friends had a laugh fest at Reggie's expense. The rest of the crew had arrived. Sage had repeated the story, and they'd poked more fun at Reggie.

She didn't mind being brunt of their teasing. If you couldn't take a joke, you might as well be toes up. She liked to dish it out, so didn't mind taking it.

The office was marked only by a bronze plaque announcing Suite 100. She tried the door. It opened into a large room. Two desks faced what appeared as a waiting room. A handful of uncomfortable leather seats lined the door side wall. A couple of such chairs fronted each of two desks. One was unoccupied. At the other sat her target.

Reggie ambled toward him without a word, chuckling inside at shock on his face and thrilled she received the reaction she wanted. A closer look showed his square jaw and full, kissable lips.

A zip of heat sped through her. This was going to be fun.

She hitched navy slacks, undid the button of her matching blazer and hopped to sit on his desktop. Florescent light from above glistened on her chartreuse, silk, tank top, directing his eyes to her perky, high breasts. She leaned slightly forward, to give him full benefit of the view. She crossed slim legs and dangled a spiked high heel toward him.

He pushed away and snapped his laptop shut.

Electricity zipped through her insides.

"Close your mouth, Montgomery; don't want to catch a fly. Why didn't you stick around last night? The gals told me who you were, but before I could come to the bar to introduce myself, you ran out like your ass was on fire."

Shae shook off disbelief with a twist and roll of his shoulder. "What are you doing here?"

The gal had impressive cojones. She'd befriended her married lover's wife. Now she was hitting on Shae. He couldn't resist seeing what she was up to before he put a stop to it.

"I'm here to work." She clicked her tongue and winked.

Damn, the broad's a hooker—obviously a high class one, but a piece for hire, nonetheless. Shae didn't fancy paying for sex. If she wasn't for hire, he'd consider a roll in the sheets—if she wasn't Wyatt's woman.

Disappointment in Wyatt Gordon plunged once again. How was he to work with the sheriff, when he abhorred Wyatt's lifestyle? Shae's attitude toward Wyatt's personal business shouldn't interfere; but this was Sweetwater, small town of all small towns. The gossip grapevine was notorious. Shae wouldn't be able to hide disappointment in Wyatt for long.

"Sorry, I'm not in the market for a date, a mistress or whatever arrangement you have in mind." He gripped fingers together in his lap.

Her head threw backward, and she gave out the loudest cackle Shae had heard from a lady. This female might look fine and proper in designer garb, but her profession was anything but ladylike.

"What the hell is so funny?" He stood, hands in pockets of dress slacks. "You'd best go." He shook his head. "Is sleeping with local lawmen a ploy to protect your business? Or do you like to live on the edge?"

He whipped out his badge and flashed it, before stowing it back in his pocket. *That ought to send her running.*

She sprang to her feet with a grin, spread her legs in a broad stance continuing to laugh, and pulled a similar leather folder from her back pocket, flashing an FBI badge. "You've got me, Marshal. I do like living dangerously. Call it job security."

Reading her name, his mouth fell open. His tongue went dry. He snapped it shut it before he could say something else ridiculous.

She waltzed toward the vacant desk. "I guess you reserved this station for me. Cozy. We'll get along famously. Don't you think, Loverboy?" She winked with a sparkle in those mesmerizing eyes.She rambled through sparsely furnished drawers.

Shae shook his head and reseated himself facing her. "I assume you have a computer, Special Agent Reggie Casse. There are a few essentials in your desk, not much else."

She shrugged those straight shoulders. "It's fine."

"Tell me; if you knew who I was, why didn't you introduce yourself last night?" He gripped hands between legs, leaning forward.

"I didn't know." She eyed him blankly.

"I had no clue you were my FBI contact." Shae hated being the blunt of a joke. Defending himself was worse.

"I get that. When Sage explained, I figured out where I'd seen you. You were in Wyatt's office when I arrived."

"Yeah, I'd met with him earlier and was going over a couple things with Jaiden and Leo."

"How'd you like our welcome?" She winked again slyly, as though waiting for her chance to pounce.

"Seriously? I thought you were Wyatt's mistress." He felt his face blanching.

She gave him a brilliant smile. "As I figured."

"That's why you played me today?" He was beginning to see humor in the situation.

Pushing out pouty, perfectly delectable lips, she blew him a smooch. "And it worked. You assumed I was a prostitute. You're too easy, Montgomery. Working with you is going to be entertaining." She turned toward the desk. "And yes, I've got a *Company*issued computer and satellite phone. No worries."

He faced his desk and opened his laptop once again. "Good."

What was he going to do with this gal? *A danger-junkie Suit and a spunky female to beat it all.*

"You should've stuck around. After you left, Jaiden and her fiancé, Dr. Clay Barnes, showed up with her brother, Calvin Coldwater and his wife, Rose. Leo and his fiancé, real estate agent, Chloe Barnes came with them. Cal is a retired-Navy Seal turned horse trainer and works for Levi. Clay's a surgeon at Sweetwater General. We had a great time. You missed the fun." She spun her chair to face him.

"Sorry to hear it."*Holy shit,* Shae must be the laughing stock of the whole town.

"Man, I can't believe you'd think Wyatt Gordon would have a bimbo on the side." She seemed less distressed Shae had thought her to be one, than at his assumption of Wyatt. "That man's as straight up as a number two pencil." She chuckled. Her perky breasts bounced beneath her clingy colorful shirt, and Shae's mouth watered.

He swallowed hard. "Apparently a lot of amusement was had at my expense. No chance we can keep this between us, and not share our little misunderstanding with Wyatt?" *Damn,* he hated destroying a relationship with the sheriff before it got off the ground. He had to do something, before this got out of hand.

She sniggered.

Shae snatched his computer, jumped to his feet and headed out the door. As he gunned the engine to life, the passenger door swung open. Reggie hopped inside with some effort. His brows shot up, a question in his eyes.

"I'm not missing this for the world." She inspected the inside of the truck cab. "Leave it to an uptight geek to choose a power vehicle, camouflaged out to beat all." She eyed him with sarcasm in her voice and on her face.

"What do you mean—uptight geek? I'm neither of those things." He shrugged a shoulder and peeled out of the lot.

"Fooled me, city boy." She smirked.

"I'm no city boy. I grew up in rural Florida on a horse ranch."

"Yeah, I read your dossier; but the photo had been redacted." There was a question in there.

Might as well fess up.

"Sorry about that. I went undercover for a case. It's settled, and my cover is clean. I'm surprised they didn't return the photo to thefile."

"So, you're a true, blue, country lad born and bred. What about this enormous truck. You know what they say about guys overcompensating." She chuckled, as they pulled into a parking spot near the Sheriff's Office.

"I'll leave you to speculate on the size of my manhood." He waggled brows toward her, cut the engine and removed keys. "I enjoy a big vehicle. Camo blends into scenery here. Country fellas are into hunting, fishing and the like." He stepped out of the tall ride, clicked the lock mechanism and stowed the fob in his slacks.

His long, legs made quick progress up the few steps to the entrance, but the spirited agent stayed on his tail. Once inside the bullpen, he glanced around looking for Wyatt. He waved at deputies in house, having met them when Gordon had introduced him previously. Jaiden and Leo's desks sat empty, probably out on calls.

A land line phone was attached to Wyatt's ear inside his glass-walled cubical. Shae knocked on the door, as the sheriff disconnected. Wyatt spun toward them and smiled in a friendly manner. No hint of anger or amusement showed. He waved them inside.

Shae opened the door and turned to glare at Reggie. "I'd like a moment with the sheriff, if you don't mind."

She stepped back and placed hands on hips. "I mind but go for it, big boy." Tilting her head to see him, she waved. "Hey, Wyatt, how's it hanging?"

"Wouldn't you like to know? Good to see you, Reggie." Wyatt chuckled. "Come in, Montgomery. What's up?"

Shae entered, pulling the door nearly shut. A glimpse across his shoulder showed Reggie slipping into a nearby swivel chair at an unoccupied desk.

"Sheriff, I made an assumption about you and Special Agent Casse. I thought she was your girlfriendwhen she arrived in town the other day. It was wrong of me to jump to conclusions. I want to apologize. I hope this doesn't stand in the way of our working together." Humility gnawed at Shae's insides and coated his words.

Wyatt burst into a laugh and leaned forward, hands clasped on his desktop. "I should've known and introduced the two of you, but when I looked into the bullpen you were gone. I figured you'd already connected and knew each other. It was as much my fault as yours—and of course, Reggie's. The filly likes to make an entrance. I can imagine what that spectacle looked like to someone unaware of our history. Reggie is a wildcat in a respectable suit. That girl has always been a flirtatious, wacky free-spirit. I assume she figured out your misconception and took full advantage. She likes nothing better than a good prank. I hope you're not offended."

Shae snickered. "I'm beginning to see that." He was dreading having to work with the spectacular woman. Reggie Casse was trouble.

"There was never anything romantic between us. Reggie and I grew up and schooled together, great pals—still are— but were destined for different lives. Sage purchased

Reggie's grandfather's farm. Reggie is one of Sage's best friends. If not for her, I never would have met Sage."

"I see. Wyatt, I can't express how sorry I am. I hope we can put this behind us, and your wife can forgive me." Anxiety had tapered, but Shae regretted misjudging the honorable man. He owed Sage Gordon an amends as well and would make quick work of it next time he saw her.

Wyatt leaned into the oversized chair that amply accommodated his large body. He stood about the same height as Shae, at six-foot-four inches. Where Wyatt was muscular and broad shouldered with a narrow waist for a man his size, Shae was lean and strong. Wyatt linked hands behind his silver mane to rest his head in them.

"No worries, Montgomery. All is well in Sweetwater."

Relief washed through Shae's veins, and he stood to go. "As much as I'd like to think so, if that were the case, I wouldn't be here."

"Well, maybe not all. We have a fresh murder case on our hands; but you and I are square." Wyatt walked beside Shae as they exited the precinct.

Reggie followed the tall men out of the station, quick-stepping to keep up. Wyatt stopped on the top step as the couple strode toward Shae's ride.

"Nice truck." The powerful sheriff chuckled.

"Thanks." Shae grimaced,clicking his fob and unlocking the tall vehicle. He extended a hand to Wyatt. "Reggie has been busting my stones about it."

Wyatt shook Shae's mitt, cackled and slapped a leg. "I'll just bet she is."

Everyone seemed to be getting a giggle out of Shae's situation."Thank you, Sheriff Gordon. I won't waste more of your time. I'll be in touch soon."

Reggie waved at her friend through the open passenger side window. "Catch you later, Stud."

Lynda Rees

"See you, Reggie." Gordon waved.

"Nice save, Montgomery." Her praise rang sincere, as she climbed into his truck cab, waving off Shae's move to help. He laughed and held the passenger door for her, enjoying the way slacks clung to her petite ass during the effort.

Fiery, stubborn, independent and a FED.
He was doomed.

CHAPTER 6

Wyatt's office filled to the brim for a meeting of minds. Deputy Jaiden Coldwater extended her hand, after bringing an extra seat to accommodate her. "Thank you for inviting us to assist in your operation. Missing children and human trafficking are two of the most vile crimes we suffer from today."

U. S. Marshal Shae Montgomery shook it, and Jaiden sat. Deputy Sanders placed his chair beside Jaiden and shook hands with Shae. "Happy to be involved, Montgomery."

Shae released Leo's hand. "I appreciate your participation, Wyatt, Leo and Jaiden. It's good of you to come on board."

"Hi, Jaiden, Leo, thanks for stepping to the plate." Reggie waved from the seat farthest from them, looking enticing in another tailored, navy pants suit accompanied by a lime green, silk tee shirt and navy heels. Unfortunately, Shae had a clear view of his accomplice.

Reggie Casse gave extra spice to the FBI's nickname *Suits*, and did it justice like no agent he'd met. Now he knew how exotic she looked with those dark curls blanketing her shoulders, her tight French twist teased his thoughts,

Lynda Rees

bringing freshly to mind nightly fantasies of her poised naked above him riding his manhood.

Shae shook his head to clear it. Stick with business.

"Good seeing you again, Reggie." Leo nodded her direction.

"Thanks, Reggie; let's talk later. We need to schedule a get-together to catch up." Jaiden smiled sweetly.

"Will do." Reggie saluted her friend and fellow officer.

"I'd like to introduce our liaison with NCMEC. If you haven't worked with them before, that's National Center for Missing and Exploited Children. Meet Ms. Carla Orson. Carla, you've met Reggie and Wyatt. This is Jaiden Coldwater and Leo Sanders, two of the most experienced and skilled law enforcement officers in Kentucky. Carla and her team at NCMEC requested assistance from the U. S. Marshal Services, hence my assignment."

Carla shook their hands with smiles all around. Introductions done and everyone seated, Shae began outlining their roles, goals and plans. Reggie and Carla provided input from their perspective organizations. When the meeting began to break up an officer knocked on Wyatt's door.

Deputy Joe stuck his head inside. "Sheriff, a woman dropped this stack of fliers with the front desk, asking for help to circulate her daughter's photo. Her child has been missing a couple months from Bonnyville. Mom's circulated fliers around that town and worked with the law there with no success. She's expanding search throughout surrounding areas. I told her we'd post information in the precinct. I gave each deputy a copy." He handed Wyatt the papers.

"Thank you, Joe. We're on it." Wyatt began handing copies to those rising to leave. "Here, you go. Keep this poor girl in mind, as you continue efforts. He gave Carla and Shae extras to hang in their facilities.

As people filed out of Wyatt's area, Sage waltzed into the bullpen. Shae greeted her as she entered and he exited.

Wyatt's arms opened to greet her. "Hi, Babe, I didn't expect to see you. What's up?" He pulled his wife into a hug and kissed her lips.

"Reggie texted me an invite to lunch." Sage beamed up at her man.

Reggie envied the brilliant smile on Sage's face, filled with adoration for Wyatt. She didn't begrudge her best pal for finding love with the man who'd been in Reggie's life long as she could remember. They were a perfect match, as Reggie had figured when she introduced them. Would she ever feel that strongly for any man?

"Hey, Sage; thanks for coming. I'm famished." Reggie gave Sage a squeeze.

"I'm hungry myself." The brunette was striking as always with porcelain skin and slim, runner's legs exposed by frayed, cut-off jeans, work boots and a red tank top. "Rose and I have been plowing all morning. She and Ty were having lunch on the deck when I left. He's due for a nap, so she'll get down time while he sleeps."

Sage embraced Jaiden, who stood beside them carrying her copy of the flier. "You had lunch yet? If not, you might as well join Reggie and me at The Royal Diner."

Stepping back, Jaiden grinned. "I'd love too. Who can pass up a shot at Sadie's blackberry cobbler?"

31

Leo's hand went to Jaiden's shoulder. "Partner, how about bringing me a burger and fries when you return? I've got paperwork to catch up on. After I eat, we can do those interviews we've planned." Leo walked toward his station. The two deputies were heavily engaged in the murder investigation of the man Reggie, Chloe and Sage had discovered.

"Sure thing, Leo." Jaiden followed Wyatt toward the Missing Children's Board, where he was hanging the information concerning the missing teenager.

Sage followed, eyeing the flyer. "What's this?" Concern furrowed Sage's brow.

Wyatt frowned with empathy. "A lady dropped these off earlier. She's searching for her missing daughter."

"I know that girl." Sage's face blanched white as the paper she pointed toward. "I mean, I don't exactly know her. I met her . . . here . . . in Sweetwater."

Wyatt's eyes went as wide as Reggie's. "Where, Sage? When?"

"I . . . ah . . . I saw her at White's Grocery when I made deliveries last week. She was searching for something to eat, looking hungry. I got the impression she couldn't afford to buy food. I bought her a sandwich, some milk, fruit and the candy she'd slipped into her pocket. I told Mr. White to put anything she wanted on my tab, if she returned. When I delivered this week, he said she'd returned and was strolling through aisles acting lost. He told her I'd instructed him to pay for her food, so she bought another sandwich, a carton of milk and a pear."

"Where did she go after you fed her?" Jaiden's face scrunched up.

"I don't have a clue. She said her name is Willow, but that's all she told me about herself. I asked if she was in trouble and offered help, but she refused. She kept glancing aroundparanoid, like someone was watching her."

Carla had been quietly listening, but stepped closer. "That's typical of a child who has been inducted into a trafficking organization. They're brainwashed to believe even when they aren't being guarded, someone is trailing them. It helps keep them from trying to escape."

Sage gasped. "You don't think she's mixed up in something like that. Surely there's no child prostitution ring in Sweetwater." She studied her husband's expression, looking like she might burst into tears. "I'm not sure she's been abducted. She was walking around alone."

"If she has been pulled in, it's been a couple months. By now she would've experienced unbelievable horror. Indoctrination is intense in order to control the child, who sees herself a willing participant. She's unaware she's been duped and controlled. She believes she's protected and is usually devoted to the pimp who brought her in. In her eyes, he's her savior. She's willing to do anything for him, including turning tricks, dealing drugs, becoming a drug mule, a transporter or any number of illegal activities he assigns her. A few lucky ones are sold to people willing to pay exorbitant fees to obtain a son or daughter. That's usually babies or toddlers. Others are sold as slaves at high prices, usually shipped out of the States. Most are used by the original pimp, bartered for by another pimp, or cycled back and forth among several. Mostly they become child prostitutes. Many times the pimp hawks them to perverts willing to pay a lot of dough to have sex with a young boy or girl or for a virgin." Carla leaned her behind against a credenza and crossed arms and legs.

"Why would she willingly do that?" Sage's face turned a pale green.

Reggie slid an arm around Sage's shoulder. "If Willow is involved in local trafficking, she is more than likely drugged, scared and confused."

Carla nodded. "It's what happens. Human trafficking targets don't react like victims of other crimes. These guys are masters at what they do. They prey on troubled kids. The guy notices a girl or boy wandering around alone looking miserable, say at a mall, roller rink, bowling alley, movie theatre or anywhere teens frequent. He's probably a nice looking guy, charismatic and kind. He would approach, chat her up about her problems; say something like, '*you're so beautiful, how can a gorgeous chick like you not be happy*?' He'd tell her how he'd treasure her if she were his girl. He'd give her anything—safety, security, nice clothes, food, attention, love, travel—whatever she desires. He finds out what she needs and offers it to her on a silver platter. He's her rescuer, her liberator, her friend and lover. He makes her want what he offers. He takes her someplace where they can be alone, an apartment, house or hotel. Before sex, he makes sure she's high as a kite and won't fight whatever happens next, whether he sells her virginity or takes it himself."

Leo had returned to the group, listening as he stood beside Wyatt. "That's disgusting."

Sage appeared ready to fall, even with Reggie's grip around her shoulders. Wyatt slid a chair beneath her and gently eased her into it. "I'm sick about this. I should've insisted Willow come home with me that day."

"Don't blame yourself, Sage. You couldn't have known." Wyatt caressed her back.

"No, Sage, she wouldn't have gone anyway—not if she's under her pimp's spell." Carla stood. "She's convinced she needs him. Usually these guys swap between being loving and giving to abusive and terrifying, then back to tender and affectionate. She wants to please him because she longs for that gentle side of him. She's his girl. She wants him to love her. She believes she can't leave because she needs him. She's scared at the same time."

"What's she scared of? She should be scared of him, not me." Sage drooped further into the seat.

Reggie patted her shoulder. "Her pimp has her convinced she's the criminal, selling her body, and will be the one to go to jail."

"But she's a child." Tears flowed down Sage's cheeks.

"He's in control of her thoughts. He's not going to allow her to consider she's a juvenile and victim." Clara shook her head.

"Why would a girl or boy be subject to such nonsense?" Leo growled.

Carla bit her lower lip. "Many reasons; oftentimes there's been a death. Someone's missing, and those left are grieving. Repeatedly adults forget children suffer too. Their grief is often overlooked. Perhaps the remaining spouse is left with debt or financial constraints causing stress. Maybe Dad or Mom is forced to work more hours to make up for loss of an income. If a child dies, the surviving sibling feels to blame or they should've been the one to die. They consider they're unloved, watching parents mourn the loss.Schoolwork suffers. Grades plummet. A feeling of isolation is the norm."

She let her words sink in, while taking a breather. Silence roared through the room. Not a soul spoke or moved.

Carla rubbed hands together determinedly. "Perhaps they're abused at home or elsewhere, or feel unsafe in their environment for some reason. He or she could be in a bullying situation and unable to obtain protection from parents or the school system. There are vast and various explanations for youngsters suffering emotionally. The point is these criminals understand causes, target youths in distress and know exactly how to manipulate them into becoming willing victims. We find many times even after asking to be rescuedthey are extremely loyal to a pimp. Severing ties is a difficult, slow process."

"Willow had a strange tattoo on her neck. It was a heart with a star in the middle, similar to the one the dead girl at the murder scene had. Is that significant?"

Reggie closed her eyes and sighed. Opening them, she met Carla's gaze then turned to Sage. "It is. Pimps demand their prizes prove devotion in many ways. One is by marking their bodies with tattoos. The design is a signature proving to those procuring sex from the girl and other pimps, she is his property. Usually, the higher up the girl is, the more she's marked."

"Are you familiar with the heart design?" Sage studied Carla's reaction.

"No, but we've never had much work in this area. Most cases have been near larger cities. Recently the flux of missing children has grown in the tri-county area. It's why we requested help from the U. S. Marshal Services. Thus, Marshal Montgomery has been assigned to the task. He and FBI Special Agent Casse will get to the bottom of this. The heart tattoo might be a prime clue to help end human trafficking in and around Sweetwater Kentucky. What's this about a tattooed murder victim?"

Wyatt winced. "You've heard about the double murder, I'm sure." Carla nodded, so he continued. "One victim was a young girl with a heart-shaped tat on her neck. It seems she might've been a hooker and the mark connects her to the young lady Sage met." Wyatt flinched at his wife's moan. His hand went to her shoulder protectively. "That information has not been released to the press. I trust you will keep this confidential. It could be key to our locating the murderer."

"Of course, and that sounds viable. Let me know if I can be of assistance—with either case." Carla shook hands with everyone. "I need to get to the office. I appreciate your support." To Shae and Reggie, she smiled. "Give me a call with any news. I'll do the same."

"Mrs. Gordon, if you come in contact with your friend Willow again, please, get her away from whoever is holding her. Contact me immediately."

Sage nodded and took a long, cleansing breath, stood and stretched as she looked at the ceiling. "Wyatt, Reggie, Shae, you need to get the son-of-a-bitch who is doing this. One way or another, we're going to save that little girl."

Jaiden patted her arm. "Do you mind if I bug out on you for lunch?"

"No, that's fine. Do what you need to." Sage smiled and glanced at Reggie.

Jaiden eyed her partner. "Can your paperwork wait? Let's go talk to Willow's mother, then we'll get on those murder investigation interviews. Mom's phone number is on the flyer."

"Damn straight." Leo grabbed his hat. He shot the words over his shoulder as the two of them sped out the door. "We'll give you an update later."

Reggie took Sage's hand. "Let's drown our fears in grease and sugar. Wyatt, care to join?"

He slid an arm around each of the women and escorted them toward the exit. "You bet. Sadie's grub puts a better spin on whatever ails you."

Lynda Rees

38

CHAPTER 7

"Babe, I hope you don't mind. I need to go upstairs and meet with the track owner for a few minutes." Levi held Riley's hand at the off-track betting facility.

Seating in the dining room was nicer than the smoke-filled open area, but not much fancier than a neighborhood diner. At least there were tables, instead of them having to spread out at counters or spend the afternoon standing, as many did.

"No problem, Levi. Do what you have to." Riley smiled.

Levi turned to Rose. "I need Cal to join me. Do you mind?"

"Not at all, Levi, Cal. Riley and I are fine. See you when you finish."

Calvin Coldwater gave his wife a peck on the lips before joining his partner and employer. The two men strolled through thick glass doors to the larger arena, then turned right toward an elevator marked *Private*.

The waitress brought drinks the foursome had ordered when they arrived. "Thank you." Riley reached for her purse.

The uniformed woman held up her hand. "Your Mister said to run a tab. He'll take care of it when your party leaves."

"Okay, thanks." Riley smiled, and the lady left them.

The twosome bet a few races. Riley won a couple races and Rose hit a winner. Their men had been gone about an hour.

Rose took a sip of her tea. "That woman over there looks out of place. I've been watching her since we arrived."

Riley glanced to her side. "You mean that young gal with the older men?"

"Yeah, that's the one. She doesn't seem to fit with those fellas. Those men are at least mid-fifties. The balding one could be older. I'd guess she's close to thirty but a bit ragged. Without that dramatic makeup she might be attractive."

"So?" Riley's head tilted in question. "They're conservatively dressed, like most middle-aged guys. Maybe one is her father."

"Maybe, but they don't act like they care much about her. They barely give her time of day. They're drinking coffee. She's sucking beer down like they quit making it. She's had two since we arrived and ordered a third. It's like she's playing catch up or something."

Riley shrugged. "So what? Lots of folks are heavy drinkers."

"The way she's swigging them down, it's like the she's afraid she'll never get another, or it's been an eternity since she's had one."

"The fellas' clothes are good quality, but the girls are cheap and out of style." Riley knew fine clothing. In her business, she had to dress to impress. "I still don't know what you mean."

"Not sure, but something is off about that gal. She was picking tickets off the floor and took a huge stack to the register to check if they were winners. Her companions totally ignored her. Finally a teller approached and told her to stop. She acted appalled and indignant."

Riley snickered. "I heard her spouting off. Everyone in the room must have. She made a huge racket. The guys she's with didn't react in any way. They kept noses buried, studying racing forms in front of them."

"Yes, the only person who has talked to her is the Hispanic-looking man who sat with them for a few minutes. Her chums greeted the guy then ignored them. She bought the guy a drink when she ordered one for herself. They chatted with heads together for a few minutes. Then he left." Rose bit the side of her lip.

"Must've been a friend." Riley turned attention to the tote board. Five minutes until the next race."

Rose shrugged and stood. "I'm going to the Ladies' Room. Be right back."

She walked across the room, down a hallway and into the facilities. When she exited minutes later, the odd acting woman leaned against the corridor wall.

One foot and her butt propped against it. A heart tattoo with several stars in the center caught Rose's eye, easily seen beneath glaring florescent lighting in the otherwise empty space. A strange man rested an arm above his head to her side. His body lounged seductively against the female, invading her personal space.

She didn't appear to mind and gazed artfully at her empty hand between them. Her fingers shuffled, rubbing the palm, as though she held something. "Fifty bucks." She winked.

He grinned cunningly and handed her a bill. She tucked the cash into her breast. He slipped a hand around hers, and she followed him through a doorway into the restroom.

41

Returning to her seat, Rose whispered. "I knew it. I knew there was something fishy about that woman. She's turning a trick in the Men's Room. I'd wager those guys she's with are pimps."

"Seriously?" Riley's eyes went wide, and she glanced sideways at the older men. Rose nodded. "Are you sure? That sounds a bit out there, Rose."

The men picked up racing forms, tucked them under their arms and walked toward the door. Levi and Cal entered, as the two gents exited. The gal in question joined the men outside the glass doors. One took her elbow. The threesome walked through the throng out of sight.

Levi and Cal joined their wives at the table. "You ladies win anything?"

"A little but Rose placed a winning wager."

"I only bet sure things." Rose smiled at her friend.

"You're in the wrong establishment, Rose." Cal slipped an arm across her shoulders.

"You'd think but no." She gave him a peck on the lips, happy he'd returned.

Lynda Rees

CHAPTER 8

Sage and Rose rested on the deck, sipping iced tea after an afternoon of nurturing tender, young plants. It had been a wild couple weeks, and she had allowed nature to heal her spirit. Remorse for Willow continued to eat at her insides the whole time she and Rose had worked. Between finding the dead man and realizing Willow's dangerous situation, her heart had been in turmoil.

Sage was stronger than she had been, since seeing Willow's photo on Wyatt's wall a couple days before. Hard work and creating new life in brilliant sunshine had done the trick. She was exhausted. A much needed respite was called for.

"What's wrong, Sage? You've been in another world for a couple days now." Rose eyed her over a frosty glass of sweet tea.

She snickered. "You know me well, old friend."

"I'm not old. You've got five good years on me, woman." Rose joked.

Sage explained to Rose what she'd learned earlier.

"The missing girl is the one you told me about from Whites?" Rose frowned. "Wow, I'd never suspect such a thing in Sweetwater—not before yesterday."

"It shocked me, too. What happened yesterday?" Sage's head tilted.

"Just something Riley and I saw at the off-track betting facility yesterday." Rose shrugged a shoulder.

"I told Wyatt and Reggie about the heart tattoo on Willow's neck and hope it helps them find her."

"What tattoo?" Rose's brows furrowed.

"Didn't I tell you? Willow had a heart tattooed on her neck. It had a star in the middle. It was similar to one on the dead girl Reggie, Chloe and I found at the Bedford place. By the way, that's not for repeat. The public doesn't know about the tattoo on that poor child."

Rose's eyes widened. "But you thought that girl was a hooker. You didn't mention her tat."

Sage nodded, feeling moisture fill her eyes.

Rose's face fell, and her eyes grew wide. "Damn, Sage, I need to tell you something."

She explained about the young woman she and Riley had watched at the off track betting facility. "We believe she was a prostitute. I saw her enter the Men's Room with some guy, after he handed her a wad of cash. She had a heart tattooed on her neck, with a bunch of stars in the center."

"Oh shit, Reggie said girls higher in the hierarchy have more marks than newer ones. She must be claimed by the same pimp as Willow. You've got to share this with Reggie."

She pushed buttons on her phone. "Reggie, Rose told me something we need to share with you. It's about Willow's . . . situation."

"Let me put the phone on speaker. Shae needs to hear this, too." A click sounded. "Okay, Rose. Let's hear it."

Rose explained what she and Riley had witnessed. "She acted socially awkward, which is fine. I've always been sort of that way myself; but she had absolutely no social graces,

46

no idea how to act in public, like a girl raised in a convent suddenly sprung free. She was cheaply dressed, but not overly sexy. She looked trashy, but I felt sorry for her—until I realized what she was doing. She reminded me of a puppy tossed out of a car on a country road. Like she was lost and looking for someone to feed her. I didn't think she was selling sex at first. She flirted with severalof the men hanging around watching simulcast racing. The older guys she was with appeared to be oblivious to her behavior. I think they were actually watching her the whole while. She lost a ticket and was hunting for it. A manager told her she wasn't supposed to go around picking up receipts. After he left, she was loud and vocal about him insulting her. Her companions didn't crack a smile. I saw her take a paying customer into the restroom." After giving remaining details, Rose sat quietly.

Reggie's voice wafted through the phone. "Thank you, Rose; I believe what you saw was an important break in our case. Did you recognize either man?"

"No, I've never seen them before. I don't go to the racetrack often, only when Cal needs to for business. The guys didn't look like pimps." She described the men. "There was nothing bizarre or odd about them, only the girl who accompanied them. They ushered her out soon after she returned from the Men's Room. I got the impression she'd attracted unwelcome attention from management."

"If that's the case, they won't return, at least not with her." Shae's voice was steady and businesslike. "Thanks, Rose; we'll fill Wyatt and Carla in on this development and check with Riley, in case she saw something you missed."

Sage sighed. Her heart filled with gloom. "So, this means Willow is almost assuredly tangled in a child prostitution ring."

"Afraid so, Sage." Compassion in Reggie's voice did nothing to still anguish gripping Sage's chest.

Reggie hung up the phone and spun her seat to face Shae's. "Riley confirms exactly what Rose saidwith nothing to add. Where do we go from here?"

"I don't know. How about dinner? I'm starved. We can swing by White's grocery on the way to that little joint down the street. You like Chinese food. Right? You're not one of those delicate females who can't stand a little spice. Are you?" He winked and stood, shutting his computer and unplugging it.

Their eyes locked with the challenge, as she did the same. "Who you kidding, Montgomery? The hotter the better, bring it on. I'm game—Mandarin, Szechwan or whatever."

"Nice, Casse, we'll see how hot you like it." His tongue did a click, as he reached the exit and held the door for her.

She slid through into the hallway and hesitated, enjoying how quickly Shae had learned to give as much as he took in the teasing department. He'd grown apt at reading her moods and finding ways to brighten her spirits. Action and good food would help quell the powerless sensation in her bones.

Could he dish it out in the bedroom? It would be fun to find out.

Shae recognized the helpless feeling in his partner. He shared the sentiment.

Funny.

In the short time they'd been working closely, he'd grown to think of Reggie as his *partner.* She thought like him, was equally skilled and knowledgeable; and he had no doubt Reggie would have his back in a dire situation. It wasn't often Shae had dared trust a peer—or anyone with his life. His sixth sense told him he was safe with Special Agent Reggie Casse.

Strange.

He'd never experienced that level of trust with Lydia—on anything—much less putting his life in her hands.

A couple days later Shae and Reggie went to Bistro de'
Fuller, a highly-recommended French cafe. The darkened,
candle-lit room set a seductive scene, though it wasn't
Shae's intention to seduce his lovely, lady peer. After drinks
were set and the waitress took their order, they were alone at
a discrete corner table. Far from other diners, it was perfect
for discussing business.

"It was disappointing Mr. White wasn't able to offer more
information on Willow." Reggie took a sip of water.

"Yeah, but he was happy to cooperate and willing to let
us know if she returned. She's put a couple purchases on
Sage's bill since they met. She'll show up before long."

They quieted when the sommelier arrived with a bottle
and ice bucket. He showed it to Shae, who nodded. The man
pulled the cork, poured a bit into a fresh goblet and offered it
to Shae.

Shae swished it around eyeing the rosy liquid through
candlelight, smelled then tasted the wine. "Good. Thank
you." He nodded to the man. The gent poured more into
Shae's glass then filled another and sat it in front of Reggie.

"Well, this is a step up from the shady Chinese joint we went to." Her browsquirked.

"Yeah, but you've got to admit, food was amazing."

"It was indeed, and it was hot as a scalded dog. Guess the fire killed germs in that nasty place. Otherwise, we might have cases of Ebola." She chuckled deep and low.

"I didn't hear you complain—sweat maybe but not bitch." His brows waggled.

"Me? I never bitch, and a southern lady might glow. She never sweats." She shot him a comical look that sent them cackling.

Over the dinner table they reached to cut a steaming loaf of bread the waitress had placed between them. Their hands made contact. Eyes locked. Seconds passed without either Shae or Reggie moving. Electricity was sparking between them so consistently it's a wonder the tablecloth didn't catch ablaze.

Finally, Reggie withdrew her hand, placed it on the table and stared at it, as though she didn't recognize her own appendage. She appeared to be looking for some permanent mark their magnetic touch had imprinted on her flesh. A self-conscious smile crossed her closed lips.

He checked his skin for blisters from the fiery sensation and withstood the urge to run a thumb lightly across her delicate mouth. *Were those lips soft as they appeared?* He sliced the loaf and, using the knife to serve, laid a piece on her plate.

"Thank you," she muttered quietly, her voice low and husky.

"You're welcome. Umm, smells good. I love the special butter." Sensing intensity in her silence, he gave her time to form whatever idea mulled around in that brilliant brain of hers.

"It's a special blend made in house. Dovie Fuller, the owner and chef, is an old friend. Her French cuisine is world-famous. This is one of my favorite places in the country to eat." Reggie spoke low and casually, but a slight raise of her cheeks gave away the fact she was thinking of something serious.

"You were with your girlfriend for a long time. Right?" She squinted as though studying his reaction.

"Yeah, Lydia and I lived together a couple years. Why?" Where was this going?

A light shrug countered a gleam in Reggie's eyes. "You loved her, lived together as a couple, yet you broke up and parted ways. How did you know you weren't meant for each other?" Those dark pools in her eyes sparkled with attention, as they fixated on his.

"Why the speculation?" He tented fingers and rested elbows on the table.

"I don't know. Something strange has come over me since moving to Sweetwater. I'm shopping for a home—the first I've ever owned. I've moved around since I left Grandpa's farm for college. It's weird. I'm anxious to put down roots."

"That all?" Her actions, expression and tone of voice told him she had more on her mind than a house. He'd experienced longing for permanency since before shaking up with Lydia. Her leaving had left a gap in his life, but not erased his need to belong.

"I've been trying to analyze what makes a relationship work. Reggie and Levi are totally different, but they fit. Sage and Wyatt are polar opposites. Together they're perfection. Dovie and Moggie are the oddest couple of the century, but they're deeply devoted. Rose and Cal hail from completely different backgrounds and have no interests in common. Yet, they're one of the most loving couples I've seen. Leo and

Chloe aren't alike. They've been through hell together, come out strong and are getting married this fall."

"Well for me and Lydia, I assure you, we were not meant for each other. I didn't see it when we were a couple, but recently I've realized our relationship was one-sided. It was all about her—making her happy, ensuring her safety, meeting her expectations. No wonder she left without a quandary. She wasn't invested in the relationship and didn't love me." Why was he comfortable sharing deepest thoughts with his partner? He wasn't the sharing type.

Reggie reached for his hand across the table. "I'm sorry, Shae. I was so into my head, I failed to realize how my comment might affect you. I didn't mean to dredge up bad memories."

Her touch was warm and reassuring, though he didn't need consoling where Lydia was concerned. Reggie's touch felt right, like it should stay there forever, branding her heat into him body and soul. He'd never experienced such attraction to anyone—not even Lydia. Too bad Reggie was a comrade in arms. Fooling around with a peer wasn't wise.

"It's fine. I've finally understand. I didn't love Lydia either. I wanted a lasting, solid relationship, to give love and to be loved. I tried to create it with Lydia, but we never found it together. I'm better off without her." It had been work with Lydia, unlike interactions with Reggie. His FBI liaison had proved to be easy to talk with, trustworthy and a good friend. Best keep it friendly.

Tell it to my dreams.

"Do you think there's a woman out there for you? Someone you can have that with? Or have you given up and soured on the whole lasting love thing?" Her nose squirrelled up in the most adorable way.

Shae had to fight the impulse to lean across the table to kiss her on that sweet nub. Her scent floated through space separating them, intensified by candlelight on the table. He'd grown fond of her fragrance, spending hour-upon-hour combing records and statements, searching for clues on how to attack their assignment.

Work had become a labor of love and fantasy on his part. His burning disgust for crimes they were to solve, were partly the reason. Enjoyment of working intimately with the feisty female agent had spurred longing in Shae that had grown dormant for too long.

He inhaled slowly, savoring the aroma of more than the food."I'm hoping there's someone for me. I've not given up. As for your friends, if you look closely at their pasts and what they've gone through together, you'll be surprised to discover what they have in common that makes them perfect matches." Was he a perfect match to someone?

"You could be right. Sage lost her first husband in a brutal way. She's fiercely independent and capable of taking care of herself and others around her. She resigned from a fantastic career with the F.D.A., sold her belongings and struck out on her own, moving here from New York City to start a business. Wyatt's first wife cheated and married his best friend after their daughter was born. He moved back to Sweetwater from Chicago and took the job he'd always wanted. He's highly protectively. Sage drove him nuts with her inhibitions, impulsiveness and head-strong personality; but she was like sunshine walking into a dreary room to him. He couldn't resist the draw. Now look at them."

"See, and I bet the rest of your buddies have similar examples of why they work as married couples. What about you?" Who would fit his sizzling partner?

"I never gave love and marriage much thought." She smiled at her hands and picked the cuticle of a finger. "I've had affairs but nothing akin to love. Sex mostly for convenience, with men I enjoyed satisfied a need. My career doesn't make long-term affairs possible. No man could put up with my occupation or moving constantly. Let's face it. I'm not an easy person."

"I beg to differ, Ma'am. I find you highly enjoyable and not bad to look at. Nothing worth a damn comes easy. Life's not supposed to be simple. Life is difficult, and love is messy." He winked and did the click-click thing he liked to do with his tongue and cheek.

She sniggered, as though enjoying his compliment then exaggerated her normal Southern twang. "Not bad? My, gracious, Sir, your way with words darn near caused my poor heart to expire from palpitations." Fanning her face with a hand, the other clutched the top of her bosom.

Jealousy of those delicate fingers lying atop the pillowed mounds hit him square in the chest. "Careful; if your condition worsens, I'll be forced to give you mouth-to-mouth." He chuckled, feeling his cheeks pink.

Her eyes fluttered extravagantly. "My, my; would that be a bad thing?" Her lips went into a profound pout.

"Don't pucker those beautiful, peachy lips at me, Lady. I might have to come over there." He snickered.

Damn.

He wanted badly to come through with his threat. It would never do, but he would if she'd invited him. Spending time with the intriguing, spirited female was the most fun he'd had in . . . ; he'd never had so much.

Gazing down, he mused. Trying to keep it light was getting harder by the day—and so was something else.

Lynda Rees

CHAPTER 9

Jaiden and Leo sat across a table in the breakroom of the warehouse where their victim had managed. Across from them was Jeromy Cariday, who had worked at the shipping facility for ten years—longer than the deceased.

"Describe what happened the day you mentioned with your boss and his wife's man friend." Jaiden smiled quietly, pen poised in hand in front of her notebook. Leo clicked the recording device on again.

The nervous man nodded and returned to his story. "I was loading a shipment onto shelving with my forklift. Outside the main office, the boss grabbed ataller, less weighty man by his collar and shoved. The gent's back thudded against the wall. I killed the engine to my loader in order to hear the exchange. The two rutting studs were oblivious to the show they put on. The boss said, 'You lousy son of a bitch, you've been porking my broad. She ain't much, but she's my piece of pussy.'" The dockworker flinched and winced, eyeing Jaiden.

"It's fine. Go ahead. We need to hear this." Jaiden reassured him.

Lynda Rees

"Okay, please realize, I'd never speak this way in front of a lady." At Jaiden's nod, he continued, "The boss said, 'I'll kill you for this, you slimy bastard.' The taller man wore a business suit and didn't appear overly muscular, but he shrugged Bedford off him like a pesky mosquito. 'Get off me you pervert. Carol Anne told me about your little quirks. You're a disgusting pig.' Soon as there was enough clearance for the tall man to wind up his arm, he punched Bedford in the nose.Bedford fell backward grabbing his nose. Blood dripped from swelling nostrils into his hands. 'You asshole,' he shouted. 'I'll sue you for this. You're mine. You hear me?' He searched for a handkerchief from his back pocket and buried his face in it. The other guy said, 'I heard you came to her office yesterday and shoved Carol Anne. You lay another hand on her, and you'll be sorry you were born.' The suited guy grinned at Bedford's discomfort and continued, 'Stay clear of Carol Anne. She's my woman now.'"

Leo studied the man. "What did you think?"

"I couldn't disagree with the guy's assessment of Bedford. I butted heads with the boss more than once. Everyone in the facility did at one time or another. Rumor has it his wife filed for divorce and planned to take everything but Simon's underwear in the settlement."

Jaiden looked up from taking notes. "Was that the end of it?"

"No," Jeromy grimaced. "The boss kept railing at the feller. 'I suppose you only put it to the bitch in Missionary Position. You deserve that squeaky clean slut, asshole.' Simon Bedford was Warehouse Owner/Supervisor, so his nameplate said. He did everything possible to distinguish himself from the work crew. Bedford wore dress kakis instead of a blue uniform. No one liked him. Apparently he wasn't even nice to his own wife. No wonder she was divorcing the bastard for the handsome, black-haired gent. Anyway, they kept arguing. The strange man said, 'It's impossible for Carol Anne to pick up her personal items without running into you. She doesn't wish to see you, so she sent me.' He produced a locker key from his suit jacket. Simon spit a breath as he backed into the office and shouted, 'Huh, get that bitch's things outta my shop before I burn 'em. Never set foot in this building again.' He glanced toward the first row of storage racks where I was working and screamed at me. 'Cariday, get your ass over here. Don't think I don't know you're listening, you SOB. Show this slimy lizard where the lockers are and follow him until you lock his ass out the front door. Understand?' He stomped off toward the back section breathing erratically and loud enough to hear until he disappeared. I wondered if he might have a stroke." Cariday didn't appear to have been seriously concerned about that possibility.

Leo sat back in his seat. "So how did that go?"

Jeromy snickered. "I left my rig and went to the visitor."

"How did he react?" Jaiden glanced up.

"He was casually leaning against a wall with arms crossed. I introduced myself and led him to the locker room. He extended a hand, and I shook it. He was pleasant and easy-going. He called me Mr. Cariday and introduced himself as Carl Black. I hadn't expected the guy to treat me with respect. It comes hard around here."

"Anything else?" Leo clasped hands on the table.

"Nah, he got the lady's stuff and left. I went back to work. When my shift was almost over, I was hearing a *brewski* calling my name and strutting toward the breakroom to stow my gear. Gloves, shoe and head coverings are required. It's a food-grade facility. I was still baffled by the scene I'd witnessed between Simon and his wife's lover. At least, that's who I assumed Carl Black is. The guys on my shift were preparing to go home. I was at mylocker. The door burst open with a bang. Simon held it with one foot, arms crossed across his pudgy belly, feet spread and spitting vinegar. 'You sons-of-bitches, listen up. I know you've been gossiping about me, wondering what the hell will become of you when that bitch gets done with me. I'll have you know, I'm head honcho around here. I intend to stay in the role. That whore be damned. Do as you're told. Keep your mouths shut and your noses clean. Ain't nothing gonna happen to you. I catch you brown-nosing that freaking cunt or her pretty-boy stud muffin, and your ass is grass. Got that?' I'm telling you. You could hear men swallow but not much else. He told everyone to leave and backed against the door, holding it with body weight to let us pass. Workers grabbed belongings and one-by-one filtered past him. I finished at my locker as quickly as possible, tossed mygear inside and shut it without a slam. I turned to leave; but as I reached the doorway, Bedford blocked my exit. 'I don't expect that Jessabelle or her male concubine around no more, but you best not stick your nose up their asses. Remember who writes your checks, you good-for-nothing son-of-a-bitch.'Damn, I hated it when he called me names. The asshole poked me in the gut as he spoke. It was all I could do to keep from popping the little pipsqueak a good one. I need this job. Bedford docked old Hank's pay last week because he came in late. The guy's wife was giving birth to his son, for Christ's Sake. Bedford didn't care. He had no heart. He even hit on Sylvia Morrison. No wonder Mrs. Bedford had tossed the sleaze to the sidewalk for a better model. I could've busted Bedford's chops without breaking a sweat, but I would've been hitting the bricks looking for a job. I figured it was best to grin and take it. Finally after a stare down, Bedford let me pass. I was hopeful the dumbass realized he couldn't bully me." Cariday rolled his shoulders.

Leo pushed the button on the recorder and clasped hands in front of him. "We understand Simon Bedford was not appreciated by employees."

Sylvia Morrisonburst into tears, talking about her abusive supervisor. "Bedford groped my ass," the single mother of four mumbled. "I was afraid to file a grievance against him for sexual harassment. I need this job. I've got four kids, and I'm a widow."

Jaiden's heart went out to the poor woman. "It's understandable you'd hate him. Did you wish him dead?"

She stared into Jaiden's eyes without blinking. "Gone maybe; I'd never consider dead."

Leo clasped hands on the table between them and Mrs. Morrison. "Did you kill him?"

She met Leo's gaze. "I did not."

"Do you know of anyone who would be so disgruntled they'd with him dead?"

Her head shook, indicating she didn't. "Sure, most people working here hated Mr. Bedford. Killing isn't something I figure any of them would do. I don't know anyone I believe could commit murder."

Jaiden contemplated the woman's expression. "Where were you April sixteenth from three to six p.m.?"

Sylvia glanced away and frowned for a second. Then her eyes brightened. "I was at the Hair Hut on Main Street, getting a perm."

It was easy enough to confirm. Leo nodded and waived toward the exit. "Thank you, Mrs. Morrison. That's all we need for today."

They sent Mrs. Morrison on her way then spoke with Hank, who confirmed what Cariday had said about him being docked for attending his child's birth. Hank had been appalled at Bedford's actions, but had a clear alibi, having been seen by witnesses with his wife at the infant's doctor while Bedford was slain.

They finished interviewing staff. Testimony agreed with what Cariday had told them. They got a couple more complaints from women in the shipping office, and one hinted Bedford had falsified records. Warehousemen had similar incidences to Cariday's, but none stood out as special.

"When we speak with Mrs. Bedford, we need her to pinpoint other investors in this enterprise. Once we confirm ownership, we need to subpoena records or insist they hire an independent forensic accountant to audit books. If Bedford was messing with financials or waybills, he could've been up to something illegal here." Jaiden stood up and rolled her shoulders.

"From what I've heard today, I doubt Bedford was smart enough to manage an illegal business." Leo shrugged and stretched his tall frame, ruffling his reddish hair.

Lynda Rees

CHAPTER 10

Real Estate Agent Chloe Roberts hopped into her SUV parked in the lot behind her office. She tossed her briefcase on the passenger seat and laid the presentation packet and her iPad where she could grab them easily as she departed the vehicle upon arrival at her potential listing. She closed her eyes and psyched herself into sales mode.

Screeching wheels interrupted meditation, and she opened her eyes to a nondescript, dark sedan parking in the vacant lot across Second Street. An angry looking, burly man peeled from the car and made a beeline to the back staircase leading to a second floor landing and entrance then disappeared inside. People frequently used that lot as overflow parking for nearby businesses, so she hadn't thought much of the newer model pickup truck already residing there.

It was the first time in years she'd personally seen anyone enter the structure. If she didn't have an appointment to attend, it might be a good time to talk with the new owners, or at least those working on the facility. Maybe they could tell her more about the buyer's intentions.

Too bad; she had to run.

She would ask her mother about it. Real Estate Broker Ava Roberts knew everyone in town. She was active in community affairs and dating Mayor Kenneth Bailey. Mom would know who purchased the eyesore and likely knew what they intended to use it for.

So far the new owner hadn't bothered with signage or visible improvements. Being in the property industry gave Chloe legitimate excuse to snoop.

That was work for another day. Today she had a house to list.

Chloe pushed the massive dude from her mind and focused on her current project, as she maneuvered her automobile onto Second Street.

Chloe returned from listing the house. The office was buzzing with agent activity. Ava spied Chloe and left her glass-walled office to join her daughter in the agent room. The large, open area provided waist-high partitions separating work stations used by The Roberts Real Estate Company employees, of which Chloe was one. Chloe plopped down at her desk, returning greetings from co-workers.

Ava waltzed to the cubical and leaned her slender, designer clothed behind against the vacant adjoining desk in the cube next to Chloe's. "How'd it go?"

"Great." Chloe held up a signed contract with a happy grin.

"That's my girl. Good job. You'll earn a nice commission on that one, especially if you also write the sales contract. It's going to sell quickly. Be prepared. The neighborhood is popular, and the house looks delightful from the outside." Ava toasted her daughter with the coffee cup she'd carried.

Impressing her mother made Chloe almost as happy as knowing she'd be able to pay her own mortgage. As much as Chloe enjoyed the business, she had living expenses. Selling houses paid the bills.

"It's even nicer on the inside." The sellers made impressive upgrades that will make it attractive to buyers. "Hey, Mom, do you know who bought the old storefront across Second Street?"

Ava's brow rose. "No, I didn't realize it had changed hands. Why?"

"Before I left today, I was sitting in my car out back. A strange man parked next to a pickup truck in the lot. He got out and went inside through the backdoor on the second floor. Obviously someone bought it. Wonder if they're getting it ready to sell."

"Research the title. Maybe you can get the listing, if they're preparing it for the market." Ava stood.

Chloe nodded. "Yeah, once I get this listing in the system and set up the marketing plan, I'll do that. I figured you'd have the scoop, since you know everything going on in Sweetwater."

Ava gave her a smirk and headed for her office. "It is strange. Rumors aren't circulating about it. I'll ask Ken what he's heard. Let me know what you learn, once you dig into it." Ava sauntered back toward her desk.

Chloe curled into the crux of Leo's arm, as he settled it around her. They leaned comfortably into her sofa. Leo's five-year-old son played happily with a new toy in the floor of Chloe's living room. She cared deeply for Cy and hoped he would someday be officially her son.

"Cy loves firemen. It was nice of you to buy the firetruck for him." Leo gave her a sweet peck on the lips.

It tingled all the way to her belly. "I know he does. I'm glad he likes it." She laid a hand on a strong shoulder of the man she adored.

"Dinner was amazing. I'm stuffed." He patted his washboard-hard stomach. Leo looked younger than his thirty-two years, given freckles across his cheeks. His Opie Taylor looks and short, red hair were deceiving. The widowed deputy was an experienced lawman and a devoted father.

"You've really made this place a home. It suits you." Leo glanced around Chloe's cottage. "No one would know, seeing what you've done with it, a violent crime happened here." He whispered the last sentence, not wanting Cy to overhear.

"Thanks. I loved it from the minute I toured it, after making my first sale in Sweetwater." She glimpsed around. The comfortable space she'd created fit her tastes. It didn't feel like a house she'd discovered a body in. Bad vibes had been replaced by Chloe's free spirit.

"We've been dating three years and had ups and downs. Thank goodness we've found a way past our differences." Leo captured her eyes with his.

"Sure . . . the lowest point was when you suspected Mom, Grandpa Tony and me of murder." She glared with a snicker.

"I never thought ya'all did it. You know how it looked. I was in charge of the investigation. I had to ensure the case was handled properly, so no one would think I gave you preferential treatment. Besides, you were the least suspect of the three of you, but I dreaded having to haul Ava or Rizzo in."

She chuckled. "You warned me against it, but we're lucky I stuck my nose in where it didn't belong." She couldn't help teasing him, though he had not been happy for her interference.

He tweaked her nose then kissed the tip. "Yeah, and you're lucky you didn't get yourself killed." She couldn't argue the point.

"Your investigation was going nowhere. My family was at stake. I had no choice but to take matters into hand." Looking back, she wasn't sure. Leo didn't need to know that.

He gritted teeth then planted a sugary kiss on her lips. "I'm glad it's over." He hesitated, appearing to have more to say but acting wary. Finally, he looked up at her with an easy smile. "How was your day?" It sounded like a diversion, but she'd been anxious to discuss her findings.

"Interesting; I researched ownership of the property across from our real estate office."

His brows wrinkled. "The old Simpson place? Why?" His head cocked.

She explained what she'd witnessed, that Ava knew nothing about a purchase and told him about the man Sage had seen enter previously.

He shrugged. "Good, I hope they've finally decided to do something with that place. If it sits vacant much longer, it's going to start deteriorating and become an eyesore. I hate to see rundown properties in town. Main Street is a prime location. Pity some awesome store hasn't snapped it up."

"My thoughts, exactly."

"What did you find out?"

"It's odd. I spent a few hours in the courthouse records room and discovered the attorney for the heirs had arranged sale to a Property Consortium headquartered in New York City. Property Consortium's ownership was difficult to trace, being outside of Kentucky. I finally learned it's owned by another holding company in the Cayman Islands called American Property Management. That was a dead end. I have no idea where to go from there." She sighed with exasperation.

"I wouldn't sweat it. Maybe next time you see someone at the building, ask them who you should contact to find out their intentions." Leo pulled her closer. She nuzzled into his warmth, fitting perfectly. His finger lifted her chin, so he could plant another kiss on his target. He fingered her left hand, which sported his grandmother's engagement ring. "We've been engaged a couple years. You think maybe we should set a date? It's about time you made an honest man out of me. Don't 'cha think?" He glimpsed toward his son, whose head popped up, as though his name had been called. "We've discussed it and came to a conclusion. We want you to be a permanent member of our family. Right Cy?" He winked at the boy.

Cy's grin spread across his chirrup face. "Yep; I mean yes, sir. Chloe, would you be my Mommy?" Sunny, orange hair framed the chirrup face. Cy gazed anticipation-filled, green eyes her direction.

Tears filled Chloe's, taking in what the child had asked. She wiped one away with a knuckle and sniffed, swallowing a knot in her throat. She'd long wanted children and had planned them with her previous fiancé, before his mysterious disappearance. "When I came home to Sweetwater to build a new life, falling in love was the last thing on my mind. Then Casey introduced me to you." Her hand stroked Leo's firm jaw.

"Yep, I owe Doc Casey big time."

Chloe laughed, recalling how her best friend had mentioned a guy she had once dated. Fortunate for Chloe, Casey and Leo made better pals than lovers.

"You were in that bowling alley trying to manhandle a ball way too heavy. Those bouncy, bronze curls flopped across your face, as you wiped perspiration from your brow; but you didn't complain. You just did your best."

"You helped me choose an appropriate ball." A laugh rolled from her chest.

"When those gorgeous caramel-colored eyes met mine, I felt like you saw deep into my soul and gently stroked the broken part of my heart. Our immediate connection surprised the heck out of me."

She nodded. "Me too."

"Neither of us was ready for a relationship, but I enjoyed being around you. When we weren't together, I couldn't get you off my mind." Leo wasn't one to talk much about his feelings. Having suffered loss before, he tended to keep his thoughts to himself. His outright profession of love and chatter about the past was out of character. Where was this going?

"For me, also; brokenhearted, after being cheated on then deserted, love was the last thing on my mind. You were mourning Clair and struggling with single parenting. Sparks flew between us from the beginning. It surprised me."

"You were impossible to resist." He continued stroking her hand lovingly.

Time spurred more than friendship between the couple.

"That fiasco we weathered made it clear. I love you beyond what I'd thought myself capable of."

Heat of his fingers warmed her palm and worked up her arm into her chest filling her with emotion bursting to be released. "How could I resist? You made a scene in front of the entire police department professing your love. A man willing to put it on the line in front of his peers is well worth keeping."

"Chloe, I love you so much it hurts. I promise to cherish you as long as I live. Let's set a date. Marry me." Depths of Leo's emerald eyes spoke more than words.

In them, Chloe saw her future. "I agree, but I didn't want to start this conversation. I'm glad you finally did." She swiped tears trailing down her cheeks. Holding her left hand up, light flashed in the stunning, square, solitaire diamond on her left, ring finger. "You inherited your grandfather's excellent taste. Let's put a simple, gold band next to this exquisite sparkler."

"Don't know about jewelry, but I've got superb taste in women." He cupped her chin and kissed her again, sending tingles to her belly and all the way to her toes.

Cy had been watching quietly, until this point. As though it could no longer be contained, he hopped to his feet and aimed his exuberance at Chloe. He bound into her open arms. "Can I call you Mommy?"

"Absolutely, Cy; I'd like nothing more." She lifted the boy to sit on her lap.

Leo's brawny arms circled them. Chloe was finally getting the family she'd long wanted. "How do you boys feel about a Christmas wedding?"

"Will Santa come?" Cy's adorable face beamed up at her.

"He sure will. Santa's going to bring the three of us the best gift we've ever received." She kissed his forehead and held her men close.

Leo strutted into the precinct wearing a brilliant smile and arms outstretched, facing his co-workers. Wyatt turned from filling a cup at the coffee station. Jaiden and other deputies lifted heads in surprise. Leo was usually quiet and unassuming.

"I've an announcement." Leo couldn't help but grin. "Chloe finally set a date. We're getting hitched December 20."

Jaiden and Wyatt rushed toward him, followed by their peers. Jaiden punched him in the arm. "It's about damned time." She snickered, as she tiptoed to plant a kiss on his cheek. Backing away, she made room for Wyatt.

Leo chuckled. "Speak for yourself, partner. Poor Dr. Barnes hasn't dragged your behind to the altar yet, though you've been sporting that sparkler on your hand a couple years now."

She shrugged and winced. "We've got busy schedules."

Leo snickered and rolled eyes ceiling-ward.

Wyatt's forceful arms bear-hugged Leo. "Congratulations. You and Chloe were meant to be. I'm happy for you." He released Leo and stepped back so the others could take turns shaking Leo's hand or hugging him. "We're having a Christmas Wedding."

Commotion ended. Leo asked Jaiden to join him in Wyatt's office. Wyatt kept his door open, so Leo knocked on the glass wall. "You got a minute?"

"Sure, come on in." Wyatt waived at the two visitor's chairs. The deputies seated themselves in them.

"I want to run something by you. It might not be anything, but it is suspicious. I want your take." Leo splayed hands on his thighs.

"Shoot. Let's hear it." Wyatt leaned backward in his cozy chair and linked hands behind his head. Jaiden sat quietly beside Leo.

"You know that property on Main Street across Second Street from The Roberts Real Estate Company?"

"The one that's been vacant for years?" Jaiden frowned.

"That's it." He explained what Chloe had noticed.

"So? Maybe someone bought it and is fixing it up. What's unusual about that?" Jaiden wore a perplexed expression.

Leo shrugged. "Nothing, really, only Chloe thought the same thing." He explained Chloe's interest.

"Smart thinking; did she locate the owners?" Wyatt asked.

"Sort of but not exactly." Leo explained what Chloe told him about her search. "Don't you find that curious?"

Wyatt sat straight in his chair, hands on the desk, biting the side of his bottom lip. "It's curious, alright but not illegal."

"I didn't say it was," Leo defended.

"You've got my attention. Complicated property titles are rare in this rural area. They're generally straight forward. A person, couple, group of folks or a company own a property. That wishy-washy, helter-skelter type proprietorship usually happens with assets in big cities where firms are mostly investors or developers. If expansion is about to happen in Sweetwater, I want to know. I like understanding what the heck is going on in my town. I'll look into it." Wyatt tented his fingers.

"I knew you would, Boss." Leo stood.

Wyatt nodded. "What the status of the murder investigation?"

"Jaiden and I have been interviewing the deceased's acquaintances and following up on leads. No viable suspect stands out at this point. The female victim has been identified on the Missing Children list as a runaway from Eastern Kentucky." Leo zipped open the report from the ME, read it quietly then gave it to Jaiden. Jaiden read it then handed it to Wyatt.

Wyatt gave the report back to Leo after reading it. "So, the girl was apparently strangled by Bedford, since his hands perfectly fit impressions on her throat. A large blade was the murder weapon."

Leo nodded. "Lots of guys in the area are sportsmen, so if it was a hunting knife that did the deed, it doesn't narrow down the suspect pool much. I'll find out if the wife's boyfriend was a hunter."

Jaiden chewed the side of her jaw. "Good; and I'll go to the restaurant to check with the wife. I doubt she's into the sport, so likely doesn't own one; but she's a chef. I imagine there are lots of hefty, sharp tools in her professional kitchens. I'll let you know if I find any suitable enough to confiscate for testing, or if any are missing."

"Sounds like you two have it under control. I'll take the tough job of contacting the female victim's parents."

Jaiden flinched. "I don't envy you. I'd rather face a gunman head on than inform a grieving family they've lost a loved one."

The deputies excused themselves and returned to work.

Wyatt picked up his phone. After his dreaded phone call he rang Reggie Casse. She'd be able to excavation details he wanted.

"Hey, Lover Boy, what's shaking?" The gal never ceased to flirt. It was one of Reggie's charms. The spicy brunette he'd grown up with was like a sister, and exactly what he needed after talking with the runaway's father.

"Good, Reggie; you?"

"I could stand to get laid. Recommend any prospects, Hot Stuff?"

"Umm, can't say I know anyone brave enough to tackle a wildcat like you, Hon. I'll keep it in mind though." He chuckled.

"Did you call to invite me to dinner? I could use some of Sage's gourmet cooking."

"Why? Isn't the cook at Mane Lane Farm feeding you? Levi and Riley hire only the best." Reggie had taken his advice and moved into the apartment above the five-car garage at their friend's horse farm. "Come on over. Sage will be thrilled. I'll alert her you're coming. That's not why I called."

"It's your dime, Baby. Let me have it." She chuckled.

He explained what Leo had shared concerning the vacant shop. "Could you look into it and let me know what you learn?"

"Anything for you, Wyatt."

78

CHAPTER 11

Reggie took a last bite of beef bourgeon and pushed from the table patting her tight gut. "That was awesome, Sage. Thanks for feeding me. I realize Stud didn't give you much notice. He couldn't back out, when I invited myself to dinner." She grinned at her raven haired pal. They were like sisters neither of them had.

Sage took Reggie's hand on the tabletop. "No worries. There's always room at our table for friends. You're the best we've got. Feel free to stop in anytime. No need to call."

"Nah, I wouldn't want to catch Stud and you having a pre-dinner quickie on the countertop." Reggie winked at Wyatt. His eyes rolled heavenward.

Sage chuckled. "That's a bit harder to do since Ty was born. Occasionally, like today, he takes a nap before dinner." Her eyes darted toward her husband. Wyatt's face purpled.

Sage swiped gravy from the face of the toddler seated in his highchair between the loving couple. Ty jerked his head, and dark hair swung with it. "No Mommy, play cars." She gently released the chair's hold on her son and settled him on the floor. He teetered to a pile of tiny automobiles and began making motor sounds.

"It must be bred into them. Every boy baby I've met automatically makes that same silly noise. *Vroom, Vroom*," Reggie mocked. Her chest expanded with a deep intake of air.

Would she ever have luxury of a man who looked at her like Wyatt did Sage and a young one of her own? She glimpsed around the rustic house. Wyatt's bachelor pad had transformed into a home. Photographs of him, Sage, Ty and Hailey claimed wall space and tabletops previously bare.

"Ty's quickly moving toward the end of his infantile stage. Soon he'll be working with me on vehicles, learning to hunt, fish and going to pre-school. I'm anxious to see him grow up but dread losing him at each phase. He's a joy to have around." Wyatt's chest puffed proudly.

"It's good seeing you two happy. You've each been through hell and deserve joy in your lives." Deep in her soul, Reggie ached for what they enjoyed, though she didn't begrudge them the life they'd built.

"Hell," the tiny one spoke quietly.

"See what you've done?" Sage snickered toward Reggie with a mock frown.

Reggie cringed. "Sorry. I'll watch my language around the young'un." Her accent filtered into her speech, as it did every time she returned to Kentucky.

Sage stood and started clearing dishes. She held a hand up in a stop signal, when Reggie attempted to stand.

"What did you want to talk about?" Wyatt eyed Reggie.

"I looked into the firm Chloe found during research. It was difficult, but I traced it to a guy named Sebastian Bryant."

"Why does that name sound familiar?" Sage gazed at Reggie then her husband.

Wyatt bit his lower lip. "Bryant moved to town about a year ago and bought the Magnolia Plantation."

"Oh, that's right. It's a gorgeous old horse farm with an antebellum mansion and a long, magnolia-tree-lined driveway. It's got a spectacular rose garden surrounding a fountain in the center of a circle drive in front of the home and wraps around the wide veranda. It was a bit pricy for me, but Chloe showed it to me before Mr. Bryant bought it."

Wyatt nodded. "Yeah, the guy has been extremely generous. He funded renovation of the Sweetwater Library and has donated generously to several local causes. He's not involved in city or county politics, but has shown his face at major events in town. He appears a legitimate businessman, some sort of property investor or developer. You think Bryant intends to buy real estate on Main Street and turn it into a strip mall? Citizens of Sweetwater would look down on that idea." He groaned.

"Not sure what he's up to. His finances are complex, if not suspicious. He's wealthy beyond your wildest dreams. It's difficult to tell where his fortune stems from. The agent-attorney who handled the purchase eluded the Main Street building is a 'customer service' business." Reggie took another sip of sweet tea.

Sage brought an icy pitcher to refill their glasses. "What kind of service do they provide?"

"Not sure. It's curious. Maybe it's a call center or a nine-hundred number operation. You know, old ladies talking dirty in sultry voices to lonely computer freak types in the middle of the night; or fake psychics giving advice." Reggie waggled her brows toward Wyatt.

His eyes rolled. He shook his head with a smirk. "Could be as ordinary as taking orders for cigars, shoes or clothing."

Reggie shrugged. "Bryant pays taxes on real estate assets but appears to make way more than would be expected, especially from operations like the small service center on Main Street."

Sage wiped the countertop then starting the dishwasher. "I don't think it's a call center. Chloe doesn't work late nights, but she hasn't seen elderly women or the sort of people you'd associate with such a job. There's not been much traffic. A big, fella went in. Once when she was going into her office, she saw a tall, skinny black man, going in. She said he wore slick clothes and dreadlocks in a ponytail. The only other person she's noticed there was a middle-aged man, decently dressed with partially grey hair and a head start on what looked like a beer belly. So far the only vehicles were a couple of non-descript sedans. The older man drove the flashy newer style pickup."

Reggie mulled Sage's input over. "Maybe they're not up and running." Turning to Wyatt, her head tilted. "Tell me more about Sebastian Bryant."

"I don't know much. He shows his face, apparently works from home, doesn't entertain—at least not locals—and doesn't appear to get close and intimate. He's generous with the town and puts on a likable social front. Learn anything else about his finances?"

"Yeah, the holding company he's associated with owns several warehouses in the Tri-State—Kentucky, Ohio and Indiana. Most are large distribution facilities. He has an interest in Logistical Excellence in Sweetwater, a warehouse partially owned by some restaurant chain. They ship foodstuffs."

"Oh, man," Sage groaned. "That's the distribution facility the hothead Bedford managed—the guy who was murdered. The Bedfords were getting divorced and at each other's throats, from what I heard through the Sweetwater grapevine."

"Interesting." Reggie's eyes went wide.

Wyatt grimaced. "Damn, we'd been figuring Bedford's killing was related to the hooker in his bedroom. The asshole was lying on his bed with drawers at his ankles. Maybe he was done in for some other reason. I've got to get this information to Leo and Jaiden. Leo's heading up the murder case."

Sage kissed her son's head and took a seat at the table. She gripped the sweating glass with both hands. It slipped from her hand and broke in the sink. "Damn." She drew a long whiff in and glimpsed her boy to make sure he didn't pick up on her curse word. Sage was still under suspicion, but an unlikely culprit.

Wyatt sat alert at her comment. Reggie snickered to herself, at the protective side of her old beau.

"I was fuming mad at that asshole for how he treated Rose, but I didn't kill him."

"Asshole," Ty muttered to his trucks.

"Damn, I've got to watch it around that boy. He hears everything, even when you think he's not listening." Sage batted her forehead.

"Damn," Ty remarked without looking at the adults.

Reggie couldn't hide her snicker. Sage finally joined her in a released chortle. Wyatt shook his head at his wife fondly. Sage laughed out loud and stepped toward where Wyatt stood. He slid his hand beneath the brunette ponytail resting against her back and cupped her nape.

"It's okay, Baby. Forget that bastard." He turned to Reggie. "Anything else you can tell us about Bryant?"

"Bastard," Ty repeated.

Wyatt's head rocked and he rubbed his square chin, which had started to show a five-o'clock shadow. "It makes a feller wonder what type setup Bryant's running."

"Exactly." Reggie stood to call it a day.

CHAPTER 12

Jaiden and Leo sat across a stylish living room table from Carol Ann Bedford in her penthouse condo atop an elegant residential building in central downtown Sweetwater. Jaiden had inspected each of her restaurants, spoken to personnel and confiscated a few knives to be tested as possible murder weapons.

The chic widow's mourning garments consisted of baby-blue slacks and a matching cashmere sweater, bone colored kid leather loafers. Her sophisticated air was enhanced by a blonde, trendy bob; and her perfectly made up face glowed. Carol Ann Bedford appeared to be anything but grieving.

She handed them crystal goblets of sweet tea from a silver tray she'd placed on the table. "Officers Coldwater and Sanders, I appreciate you meeting me here this evening. As you can imagine, my restaurant chain requires exhausting hours of attention. Bad enough Simon's latest antics and demise put a wrench in my business. I can't afford to neglect my responsibilities. My patrons and staff depend on me. If I fail to follow through, livelihoods of many would suffer."

Carol Ann reclined on the cushy, white, leather sofa and crossed her legs.

Neglect could put a wrench in her extremely lucrative livelihood as well. Jaiden sat her glass down on a marble coaster and leaned elbows on knees. "Not a problem, Mrs. Bedford. We need to record this interview. I assume that's okay with you." Jaiden pointed to the phone Leo placed on the table and clicked to record. The lady nodded and smiled, so Jaiden sat straight. "Thank you. Tell us about Mr. Bedford's antics—specifically the ones that interfered with your business."

"Simon was less than efficient, and his work ethic wasn't stellar. He's neglected stock before, but it nearly cost me my best supplier of organic produce a few weeks ago. He ruined a full shipment of goods I had to turn back."

Leo rubbed his chin. "Are you speaking of the cargo from Parsley, Sage, Rose, Mary & Wine Farm?"

Carol Ann's eyes showed questioning surprise, and her head tilted. "You know about that? I should've realized. I'm well aware of Sweetwater Police Department's thoroughness. Yes, that's the one. The owner, Lemon Sage Benton was more than gracious when she called about the refused produce; but she was understandably riled. I later heard about how she confronted that little weasel in person. I wish I'd been a fly on the wall to witness that scene. That woman takes no prisoners. She shot a man, you know? What am I thinking? Of course you do. You probably showed up at the scene afterward." She smiled casually and sipped her tea.

Leo snickered. "Yes, Ma'am. I was there, but Deputy Coldwater was a Texas Ranger at that time."

She nodded. "Well, that's impressive. We're lucky she moved to Sweetwater."

Jaiden tilted her head. "Thank you, Mrs. Bedford. I hope you take no offense, but you don't appear to be in mourning for your late husband. I realize you were in process of divorce, but you and Mr. Bedford were together for some time."

The blunt question didn't appear to faze the widow. "Yes, Simon and I were together for ten years—two lovely years and eight of the most miserable ones of my life. When we met Simon was good looking, charming, well-built at the time and a good dancer. He's well-educated and well-traveled, though he's never used it to his benefit. He made me believe I was the center of his universe, an affectionate, doting lover and husband. The man didn't look it, but he was dynamite in the sack."

Without showing her surprise, Jaiden looked up from the notepad she was jotting on. "What came between you?"

"Simon became a slob, let himself go and wanted more and more from me, while giving me less and less. We stopped doing things together. Our workloads were heavy; but we could've made time for each other, had he been willing. Instead, he became a sour, grumpy good-for-nothing. To be honest, I was happy duty saved me from spending time with him."

Jaiden figured she'd best broach the subject, rather than making Leo do it. "Did your sex life suffer?"

Carol Ann snickered. "No, it didn't suffer. It became almost nonexistent. It was partially my fault. Simon didn't give up on sex. He enjoyed it regularly, either by himself, with a blow-up doll or paid-sex-toy—after learning I was unwilling to participate in his pathetic inclinations. The man turned into a pervert over the last couple years. Things he wanted me to do and let him do to me were downright disgusting. When I realized he wasn't about to go back to the fantastic lover he'd previously been, it was the last straw. I filed for divorce."

Leo nodded, as though understanding clearly. He was likely dying to know specifics of the larks Simon wanted Carol Ann to perform with him. It wasn't exactly pertinent, so he wouldn't ask.

Jaiden spared him the musing by directing the subject. "Did you begin seeing Mr. Black before or after you decided to divorce Mr. Bedford?"

Carol Ann smiled cordially, unflinching. "After; Carl and I have known each other for years. He's a wine and liquor distributor I purchase from. When he heard I'd filed for divorce, Carl invited me to dinner. One thing led to another, and we've become close."

Leo bit the side of his lip. "You're lovers?" The woman nodded but remained silent. " Are you living together?"

"No, Deputy Sanders; we're not. We are, however, planning to wed later this year. We'd made the decision before Simon's death. Neither of us has reason to wait. We're in love." She said it as though it were the only reason for marriage, making Jaiden wonder why Simon had courted her in the first place. "You probably know Carl and Simon had a run-in at the distribution center. I know you interrogated our warehouse employees."

"Yes, we got that. We are scheduled to talk with Mr. Black later today."

"Good; both Carl and I are eager for you to solve this crime. It's understandable that the wife and lover of a murder victim would naturally be prime suspects in a man's killing. We're anxious for you to collect the facts and clear us—which you will. We're innocent." She spoke with what appeared to be confidence.

Jaiden simply had to ask—for her own curiosity, as much as for the case. "Is Carl Black as good a lover as Simon had been?"

The widow acted flustered for the first time, and a tiny blush showed on her perfectly groomed cheeks. "Carl is an amazing lover. Simon was a louse and depraved, corrupt soul."

Jaiden smiled glad to hear it. "So you married Simon because he was attractive, charming, attentive, doting and a good lover. Why did he marry you?"

Carol Anne's flush blanched. "I've asked myself the same thing."

"Together you have amassed an impressive portfolio. The house Simon inhabited is nice, but small. The grounds are what make it valuable. Your partnership in the shipping facility appears bountiful. Your restaurant chain financials are extraordinary. This condo is pricy. The two of you have done well for yourselves."

She nodded and slid to sit at the edge of the divan. "Yes, we are doing financially well. If you're thinking I killed Mr. Bedford to have it all for myself, you're barking up the wrong tree. We have grown our businesses to success; yes. Money invested in the ventures came from my pockets—not Simon's. After we were married, I discovered Simon was literally penniless when we met, though he'd made me believe he was well-fixed."

Leo clasped hands between knees and slid to sit like she had. "Did you want Simon out of the picture so you wouldn't have to share profits with him or be requiredto pay him alimony in the settlement?"

She chuckled lightly and slid her back against the seat. "Thatwas not a risk. Simon and I had an air-tight pre-nup. It's why he was fighting the divorce. He didn't want me back. He simply wanted to remain married, so he had unlimited credit. The court would only give him his share of profits from our portion of the warehouse business. The restaurant chain he claimed we co-owned was in my name only and purchased before we met. The property we lived at, where he was killed belongs to me alone. I had no motive for wanting him dead.I'd never kill anyone, even for money."

Jaiden gazed into her eyes. "What about Carl Black?"

"Carl despised the little perv but wouldn't hurt a fly. He could've done a job on Simon when he berated Carl at the warehouse, but Carl handled himself like a gentleman. He took no gruff from the pipsqueak but didn't seriously hurt him. Carl isn't that type man." She appeared to believe her words.

Leo linked fingers on his knees. "Ms. Bedford, are you a hunter, or do you own a hunting knife?"

Carol Ann's head tilted and a brow rose. "I am not and do not." She eyed Jaiden. "I understand you took several tools from my restaurant kitchens. Was the murder weapon a knife?"

Leo lifted and re-settled his clasped hands. "We cannot comment on an ongoing investigation. I'm sure you can appreciate that. Rest assured, your equipment will be returned when this case is solved, if not before then."

The widow blinked and nodded her head with a stern expression. She glanced to the side then turned focus to the deputies. "Fine."

Jaiden looked around the room at expensive original paintings and pricy décor. "Who do you think murdered your husband?"

The widow remained quiet for a few minutes before speaking. She met Jaiden's gaze. "I honestly don't know. I have no idea what all Simon was involved with. He was not ethically motivated, from what I've heard. I have a friend among his workers, and she indicated Simon might be involved with something shady, but she had no idea what."

It concurred with what they'd learned from the depository office staff.

Leo stared at the woman. "Were you aware Simon was paying prostitutes?"

"No, but it wouldn't surprise me. The news said a woman was with him when he was discovered. Are you saying she was a prostitute?" Carol Ann's lip curled, and she swallowed hard. Her face appeared strained.

Leo nodded without expression. "We believe she was but have not confirmed it. We'd appreciate it if you kept that to yourself."

"Is that what got him killed?" She frowned, looked down and shuffled her feet then posed them crossed at the ankles.

Jaiden shook her head. "We can't say, at this point anyway. Investigation is in the works. We're not sure why they were killed."

"I hope that bastard didn't hurt that poor girl." Her fists balled at her sides, as they lay on the cushion. Jaw tightened, and teeth clinched.

"Did Simon abuse you?"

The widow shook her head and flicked her brows then met Leo's gaze. "No, Deputy Sanders, he never hurt me."

Leo stood. Jaiden followed Leo's clue. The interview was over. She pocketed her pen and pad. They'd gotten what they came for. Carol Ann stood, as her guest did.

Leo held the phone in hand. "We can't divulge classified facts about the murder scene. I can tell you, someone did more than hurt the girl."

Jaiden waited a second, observing their hostess' reaction then moved away from the sofa so Leo could follow. She turned with hand extended. "Thank you, Mrs. Bedford. We'll be in touch if we have further questions."

The woman shook Jaiden's hand. Her dry palm was warm but not overly so, and there was no quiver in her touch. She shook Leo's hand. "Of course, I'm willing to help and hope you get this over with quickly."

Jaiden and Leo sat across the desk of Carol Anne Bedford's lover, Carl Black. They'd discussed the need to record, so Leo's phone lay on the desk in front of Black. "So, tell us what you know of Simon Bedford."

The man leaned into his desk chair. "I know he's dead, from what I heard on the news. It doesn't surprise me someone killed the asshole. If you're looking at me for it, you're betting on the wrong horse."

Jaiden smiled at the fine looking man in an expensive suit. "You are seeing his wife, Carol Anne Bedford and were before Simon's demise."

He nodded without changing expressions. "I am seeing Carol Ann."

"Tell us about your confrontation with Mr. Bedford." Leo laid a hand on the desktop.

"Bedford shoved Carol Anne one day in front of employees. She slapped him, drawing blood. He threatened her life. When Carol told me about the incident, I was livid.

She insisted she needed to retrieve important personal belongings from the warehouse. I wouldn't hear of her setting foot on the premises again. I went to get them for her. Bedford was confrontational. He attempted to rough me up. It was comical."

Black's broad shoulders rocked back and arm muscles strained against sleeves of his blazer. Clearly, this man could've laid Bedford out cold, if he'd wanted to.

"Did you get physical?" Jaiden looked at her notes.

"He shoved me and bared his fists. I pushed him off me and made sure he knew I wasn't putting up with his nonsense. He backed down and allowed me to get Carol Anne's belongings."

"Witnesses say you threatened Bedford." Leo tapped a finger on the desk.

Black smirked then met Leo's gaze. "I told Bedford never to lay a hand on Carol Anne again, or he'd answer to me."

"Did you kill Simon Bedford?" Jaiden caught his eyes.

"I did not." No expression on Black's face.

Jaiden looked around the room at photos of Black partaking of several active sports—zip lining, hang gliding, parachuting from a small plane and in a team uniform with a bat propped on his shoulder. "You're quite the sportsman. Do you hunt?"

"No, I prefer more thrilling sports requiring no weapons."

"A bat could be used as a weapon." She snickered. "Do you own any weapons—guns, knives, or the like?"

"No, I don't have need for them."

Leo picked up the phone without turning the recording device off. "Where were you Friday, April sixteenth between three and six p.m.?"

Without having to think about it, Carl Black held Leo's stare. "I was working out from three until around six that day. I showered at the gym,bought a coffee and watched news on television in the coffee shop at Bronson's Gym. Feel free to check it out."

The officers stood. Leo clicked off the phone and extended a hand. "Rest assured, we will. Thank you, Mr. Black. That should be all."

Black rose and shook it firmly. He did the same with Jaiden.

"Thank you for your time. We'll be in touch, if we have more questions." Jaiden followed Leo from the room.

Deputies Jaiden and Leo briefed the sheriff the next day. Wyatt wasn't involved in the investigation, but his drive for perfection required he ensure they didn't miss clues or lines of questionings. He was a perfectionist, as were they.

"The widow doesn't appear good for the crime." Leo chewed his lip. "We questioned both her and her Carl Black. Knives from her kitchens were tested, and none were viable murder weapons. We've returned them to the owner. Neither the widow nor her lover had worthwhile reason to kill Bedford and the girl. The widow seemed to mourn the female more than she did Simon. Learning more and more about the deceased, I find that understandable. Of course, we could be wrong."

Jaiden linked fingers in her lap. "We've checked the couple's finances. What Mrs. Bedford told us is accurate. We did the same for Mr. Black. He's affluent and cool as a summer breeze. The two of them act enthusiastic to help with the investigation."

"So they're a dead end. What about employees?"

Leo pursed his lips. "Yeah, we're checking links we hope lead somewhere. Bedford was a hell of a supervisor. His people hated his guts."

Jaiden nodded. "Yes, and he may've been involved in something illegitimate. At the very least, he might've been cooking books for monetary benefit. Maybe he was grafting funds in case he lost the legal battle to get more money from his wife. Wegot a warrant and hired an auditor to check the distribution center's books. We'll follow up with him to determine if everything was legit."

Wyatt laid palms on the desktop. "Where does Sage stand, in the suspect food chain? Answer only if you can share."

Leo scratched his cropped hair. "It's evident Bedford killed the girl. Sage isn't looking good for this. She might've had motive for Bedford's murder, but it's pretty thin. Besides, if she were going to kill the man, she likely wouldn't have gone after him when he was entertaining company. It's rare a woman would use a knife against a man. Bedford might've let himself go, but he could more than likely overpower a woman Sage's size."

Wyatt snickered. "She's pretty stout for a gal—gets it from all the field labor." Pride was clear in his tone, and he stated the obvious, not trying to convince them his wife was a killer.

Leo sneered. "Sure, but Sage would shoot the pervert—not slit his throat."

Wyatt cackled and leaned back. "True that."

Jaiden rolled her eyes and shook her head. "The victim's wound was slick and done with one fell swoop. We're looking for someone strong—stronger than a female. Our murderer was a man." It was obvious from the data, but needed saying. She was glad Sage was cleared, as were Leo and Wyatt. Their cynical clowning was merely them trying to work off some of the tension in the room.

Wyatt went back to business mode. "What about the girl?"

Jaiden's heart sank every time she recalled the dead child's face. "Unfortunately she had to be a prostitute. The tattoo indicates it's a local ring. Each one is slightly different. Varying numberof stars inside the shape are unique identifiers for each person. Working with Shae and Reggie, we've come up blank so far. I'm sure we'll find something soon."

Wyatt restatedfacts. "Bedford's throat was slit, and he bled out. That child was only twelve-years old. She was strangled—by Bedford, who it appears hired her for sex. The coroner confirmed his hand prints fit her wounds perfectly. The dude was a pervert and pedophile."

Jaiden's eyes filled with tears, and her head bent. She nodded. "Most sex buyers don't care if the prostitute is of age, is willing or being forced into the life. Some are willing to pay extra to get a youngster. It's unfortunate but true."

Bedford did the girl in. Who did Bedford—and why?

CHAPTER 13

Surprisingly, over the weeks Reggie and Shae establish a reasonable working relationship, as they tackled their assigned project. Montgomery's work included more than leading their human trafficking task force. He could be called on at any time by the Marshal Services to apprehend or transport a fugitive, protect a WITSEC enrollee, provide judicial security, seize or be custodian for forfeited criminal assets, or to ensure safety or transport of prisoners for the federal judiciary system.

Then again, Reggie could be called away to assist Wyatt with a national impacted case or any number of FBI cases requiring additional help. Her prime reason for being in the region, however, was working the huge and growing list of missing children in the tristate area and shutting down of operations and apprehension of human trafficking criminals.

Shae scratched his jaw and eyed his FBI partner. "I feel like we're chasing our tails and getting nowhere. We've arrested a couple sex offenders and checked every known offender in the tri-county area. Nothing appears to connect them to a slavery sex ring. Seriously, we haven't run into anyone with enough brains and guts to create and manage such an organization."

She nodded and spun her chair to face him. "We have the heart connection, but it's not enough on its own. We need to locate the source and tie it to brains."

After a long dayscouring documents with the marshal, Reggie crossed her legs at the ankles and leaned her head into hands crossed behind her head. "You know, Montgomery, the more time we spend together, the less nerdy you become."

He didn't wear cologne, but neither did Reggie. It could be hazardous in the field. His personal scent was appealing enough. It had tantalized her nostrils and tempted her lungs to breathe deeply, as they worked side-by-side. She'd been tempted to nestle her nose beneath an ear and indulge her latest fantasy. Instead, she'd forced herself to behave like a lady, not wanting to destroy their working relationship before it began.

He chuckled, and shut his computer down, turning toward her. "Thanks. I'm beginning to think you're not the flighty bimbo I'd thought you to be, either. I'm not into the pay-for-sex route to satisfaction."

"I wouldn't go that far. I'm flirty—not flighty. We'll wait and see, concerning satisfaction." She licked her lower lip and bit it, not minding at all visions in her dreams the night before of the slim, muscular lawman lying beneath her, their nude bodies sweating from the erotic encounter.

The semi-uptight hunk had the decency to turn a delightful shade of lavender, as he turned away.

Damn, she needed to get laid.

Standing, he locked his desk, avoiding the woman observing him. "Time to call it a night."

"Yep." She stood and did the same, without taking eyes off Shae, admiring how jumpy he acted. You'd think he was a sixteen-year-old boy, and she'd asked him to the prom. "What's the matter, Montgomery? Cat got your penis?"

He faced her, shaking his head back-and-forth. A broad grin took his face. "I doubt a cat could handle it—maybe a cheetah or tiger."

She let out a bawdy guffaw and picked up her computer. "Good one."

"I'm not used to women coming on so strong. I'm just a small-town boy, you know." He spun and headed toward the door.

She had to skedaddle to stay on his tail, given his height and hers of only five-foot-four. "Did I scare your *wanger* silly?"

"Nice word. Yeah, he's hiding his impressive head right about now." At her chuckle, he eyed her from the side, seeming to enjoy the way she had to two-step to keep up.

They kept a low profile, using the hallway exit near their office. Tenants in the facility thought they were insurance salesmen.

They strutted across the hallway and out the exit door directly across the hallway. They used this exit mostly, and it was one advantage of the site. Another was a second outside door in their suite, which landed them behind the building, where in case of emergency they kept a spare rental car parked beside dumpsters located there.

He glanced down at her, trotting beside him as they stepped onto the sidewalk. Assigned parking spaces were directly in front of the exterior door, and their vehicles sat side-by-side. Every time she saw his massive pickup truck she had to laugh. It dwarfed her classic Chevelle sitting beside it.

"You got dinner plans, Casse?" Nothing in his expression hinted to his being as hot and bothered as she was.

"No, why? I look delicious, and you need something to eat?" She sniggered.

His head wagged one way then the other. "You're a case, Casse. Maybe later, we'll see. Right now I'm in the market for a huge T-bone and a couple beers. You game?" He walked toward his truck.

"I could eat." She wiggled her brows.

"I'll bet you could." He stared across his straight nose.

"We're taking my ride. I'm tired and don't feel like taking a high jump." She keyed her door and hit the release to the lock on the passenger side.

He hesitated a second, as she slid behind the wheel and shut her door. Finally he climbed in beside her. His head came close to hitting the ceiling, and he could barely see ahead for the visor. His legs bent more than natural in the seating position, but they'd not appeared terribly cramped as he seated himself and stretched them out.

Poor guy barely fit.

"For a second there, I thought I'd scared you off. I don't bite, Montgomery." She gunned the engine to life and pulled from the parking spot.

"I don't scare easily, Casse. You'll find that out soon enough. Nice car."

It appeared the flirtation game was okay with him. Whether it would placate her libido was to be seen. "Thanks, Montgomery. I like big, beautiful things."

He expelled a deep sigh.

After a hearty dinner at an upscale restaurant, Reggie drove Shae to their office to retrieve his truck. "I'm glad to learn you're not the stiff I thought when we met." She good-naturedly chuckled. "That stunt you pulled dropping your buttered roll into your lap was hilarious."

"Yeah, I always like a little butter on my buns." He snickered. The appealing, frisky brunette would no doubt pick up on the double innuendo.

Reggie didn't disappoint. "Umm I do love me some buttery meat." Her perky chest jostled as she laughed, beginning to enjoy the not-as-nerdy-as-she-thought marshal.

Were they firm or soft and pillowed?

"You were entertaining as well. It's not every day I watch a gal spew beer out her nose." He smiled with one brow high and chuckled, when she glanced at him with her tongue out.

Expelling a heated breath he shook his head. What did that pink, moist appendage taste like?

Beer, blue cheese and steak? Three of his favorite flavors.

"Glad you enjoyed my super power." Pulling into the parking lot beside his truck, she turned to face him. "I suppose I've provided all the laughs you can handle for the night."

"You'd be surprised what I can handle." He tittered as he opened the door and stepped out reluctantly ending their enjoyable evening.

"We'll see," she shot back. Her tongue snaked out, licked her upper lip and white molars gripped the lip teasingly.

He eased her door shut with an exhale, spun and clicked his door open. Best distance himself, before he attempted to find out if the flirtatious act was merely a game, or if the seductive minx would dish out more than teasing.

His *ex* had never made his heart pound like visions of Reggie Casse naked beneath him, wearing nothing but a smile and those sexy heels.

He'd best watch himself with that tigress, or they'd end up slopping up the sheets. He hadn't realized how horny he'd become, grieving loss of a future with a woman he'd thought right for him.

He's begun questioned whether he'd been wrong about Lydia. The more he was on his own, the more he began to see, he needed more. He needed someone more self-reliant and sure of herself—someone who didn't depend on him for her happiness. Shae wanted a gal who was contented on her own, who wanted him in her life regardless—and someone strong enough to accept him and his career, since it was part of him.

It was time. He wasn't ready to dive into a full-blown love affair, but a fling might settle his aching libido. As much as he'd enjoy it being with the hotter-than-hot female he'd dined with, it was against their best interests to sleep together. They were business associates, and it could put them in danger.

His logical mind might be ready to meet someone new. It didn't stop his subconscious from dwelling n Reggie Casse.

Lynda Rees

CHAPTER 14

Reggie pushed away from the table in Sage and Wyatt Gordon's kitchen and rubbed her taunt stomach. "Lord, Sage, if you don't stop feeding me, I'm going to have to start wearing sweatpants with elastic waists."

Sage's eyes glistened. "Beef stroganoff is one of Wyatt's favorites." She stood and started clearing the table. Reggie stood and took hers, ready to help.

Shae picked up his empty plate. Sage put up a hand. "Sit that cute, little butt of yours down, mister. Reggie and I have got this."

Shae eyed Wyatt quickly then smiled at Sage. "Are you sure? I'm handy in the kitchen."

Reggie winked, taking his plate from his hand. "I'll bet you are." It tickled her how he reddened.

"How about we leave this to the ladies? You game for a beer on the porch?" Wyatt strolled to the refrigerator and selected a couple cold ones.

"Sounds good." Shae followed Wyatt through French doors to the wide, front deck overlooking grounds surrounding the contemporary log home.

"Run while you can, big boy." Reggie leaned against the doorway to the living area, watching them leave. Shae's backside was even more sumptuous in jeans that caressed it

Lynda Rees

tightly and snugged against firm looking, muscular legs. Reggie licked her lips and turned to the kitchen.

Sage leaned her buttocks against the center island. Arms crossed. "What exactly is going on with you and Deputy Montgomery? You sleeping together?" She strolled to the table and removed plates.

Reggie sauntered to the sink and began washing dishes in the soapy pan. "Hell no." Her words came out more vehemently than intended.

"Too bad. He's a looker and seems like a stand-up guy." Sage placed a pot into the suds.

"Surprisingly, Montgomery isn't the tightly wound bore I figured him for. I assumed he'd resent FBI interference and be defensive. He proved me wrong. I'm seeing a new side of Marshal Montgomery. The more we work together, the better I like him. He's the experienced, skilled lawman I read about in his dossier and has an amazing sense of humor— dry but hilarious."

"Like you?" Sage eyed her across her straight nose. "Honey, I can't imagine you getting along with anyone without a sense of humor. Is there more going on? Sexual tension was clouding the room so thick during dinner I thought I'd have to turn the ceiling fan on to see your faces." Sage hip-butted Reggie, drying dishes as Reggie rinsed.

"We haven't soiled the sheets, but electricity is definitely sparking—except when we're working. We joke but keep sensual overtones to a minimum, sticking with business. We're in a serious profession and can't afford to get emotions involved. It could get one of us or someone else killed." Reciting facts and practical excuses did nothing to deter Reggie's humming libido. "Seriously, sister?" Sage put the last dish away.

"I admit it. I'm horny as hell. I wouldn't mind a roll in the hay. If I bedded the skilled U. S. Marshal, our jobs would

106

suffer from it. It's murder trying to find a dude worth doing the horizontal bop with. Every man I meet is married, gay or a criminal."

"Don't you want something more than a one-night stand?" Sage put an arm across Reggie's shoulders.

"Not until recently. Being you and Wyatt, Corrie and Justin, Rose and Cal, Riley and Levi, Jaiden and Clay and Chloe and Leo, avoiding a longing for that type happiness is tough. I've been a loner so long, I don't know how to settle down or be with one man. It's a good thing, since I haven't found a guy willing to take me on for more than a night." She expelled a puff.

"Reggie, you and I both know you've got it bad for Shae. I see it in your eyes. Kid yourself if you want, but you're not fooling me. You and Wyatt have been close as brother and sister your whole lives.I was watching him at dinner. He's not blind either."

"Geez, it's not good for an FBI Special Agent to be so easily read."

Sage swatted Reggie's behind with a towel. "I doubt everyone sees what we do. Wyatt and I know you better than anyone."

Wyatt handed Shae the beer, as they settled into cushy chairs on the deck.Shae was happy for a break from the women. He wasn't used to seeing Reggie in anything other than her usual navy suit.

Reggie in a purple tank top had teased Shae's surging hunger to a steady growl the whole evening. Flesh toned sandals exposed toenails matching her clinging, silky shirt. His urge to slide a palm over those petite, bare feet; slowly up porcelain skin to where her shorts met at the crux was nearly more than Shae could handle. She'd stood to help Sage clear the table. The barest hint of cleavage had turned into a full-blown glimpse of round mounds haunting Shae's dreams of late. He'd caught his mouth, as it dropped open and inserted a stupid comment about the weather.

What a dope.

"So what's on your mind, Montgomery?" The sheriff eyed him critically.

"This farm is spectacular." Shae did another glance around at the property. He'd surveyed it, as he arrived—a habit from the trade. The discussion would help distract him from lusty thoughts fighting for attention in his mind.

"Thanks, we love it. It's a small farm for the area, just over twenty acres. There's a small forest behind, and the wooded barrier surrounding it provides privacy."

"You keep horses?" Shae eyed a board-fenced corral adjoining a small barn to one side. A rambling, gravel driveway cut through the tree stand at roadside.

"Only three, one for each of us."

"Surely the baby doesn't ride." Shae frowned, confused.

"Nah, not yet; he sits in Sage's lap, when we go riding.Give him another year or two."

Shae tried to hidesurprise. "Who's the third one for?"

"Hailey, my daughter; she's in college in Boston and doesn't get to ride much these days. She's working on her doctorate in chemistry. Her workload is tremendous. Hailey visits a week or two at a time, when she can. She splits free time between here and Chicago."

"I see. I didn't realize you and Sage had more children." Shae sipped his brew.

"Oh, no; Hailey isn't Sage's, though she's as close to Sage as she is Izzy. Hailey's from my first marriage. Her mom lives in Chicago."

"Sorry, didn't mean to pry." It wasn't good to get on the bad side of the sheriff. Shae liked Wyatt and wanted them to become friends.

"No problem. It's no secret." Wyatt paused and looked him in the eye. "Since we're talking women, I sense something more than partnership going on with you and Reggie. Am I wrong?" His blunt honesty and limited words were two things Shae admired about the sheriff.

Shae diverted his gaze. He wasn't sure he wanted to discuss feelings—no fantasies—of Reggie with Wyatt. They seemed close. *Hell*, he didn't want to discuss them with himself.

"We're developing a working relationship, moving toward trust needed when your life is in a partner's hands. Casse is a seasoned agent with incredible skills. She's a joker, fun to be around, classy and sassy. She's a smart cookie. I'm not disappointed the Bureau assigned her. I enjoy her company." Shae could stand a roll in the hay. He wouldn't mind taking the flirty FBI Special Agent to bed but wasn't about to tell Wyatt that.

"She's not bad to look at either." Wyatt appeared to study his response.

"No, she's flat out foxy, but I'm not in the market for a fling. I'm getting over my last relationship—not looking for another." That was honest enough and should satisfy Wyatt.

"Yeah, well, if you say so." Wyatt rolled his eyes.

The women stepped onto the deck, ending Wyatt's opportunity to pry further.Shae eased out a sigh of relief. Sage pecked Wyatt on the lips then took a seat beside him.

Reggie carried a yawning toddler. Rumpling his coal-black hair, she cradled him against her breast. Shae's mouth watered, as she sat in the chair to Shae's left. She'd never looked more beautiful.

A look of rapture took Reggie's eyes, shocking Shae. "This little man woke from his nap and wanted to join the party."

He'd never considered she'd react like that to a child.

Reggie snuggled the sweet-smelling youngster in her arms. Ty's soft breath tickled her neck. His tiny, drowsy head rested against her chest. Miniature, chubby hands touched her skin, leaving lasting imprints not visible to the eye.

Something strange was happening inside her. She could barely take in air. She was so filled with awe. The toddler's skin was silkier than any fabric she'd ever touched. He smelled of baby powder and lotion, the most enticing scent on earth.

She couldn't cuddle Ty close enough to satisfy longing rushing through her veins. Each time she held the boy, a previously ignored yearning fought for attention. Her biological clock was chiming loud and clear. Its clack vibrated her ribcage and slowed her breath. She inhaled the scent of the darling boy, and her eyes closed in euphoria.

Would she ever have a little one of her own?

She'd previously avoided asking herself the question. Lately she could hardly get the fantasy off her mind. She diverted her gaze; afraid her robust emotions would disturb the drowsy babe.

Shae had the strangest look on his face. His hand stroked his neck. His face was flushed, and lips parted with a sappy smile.

What's gotten into him?

111

Lynda Rees

Hell, what's gotten into me?

Lynda Rees

CHAPTER 15

Reggie spun in her seat, shut her computer and studied Shae. He ignored her stare for a moment then tilted his head that way and gazed across his nose at the fabulous woman watching him. Having grown used to working with her, he'd grown more than fond of Special Agent Casse. Who would've thought he'd not only relish working with a Fed. *Hell*, he was eager to see her each day.

She was easy to work with, didn't expect special treatment, could hold her own in every situation he'd seen her in so far and she was like a cherry on top of a hot fudge sundae, the part that made your mouth water in anticipation of enjoying the taste of her on his tongue from first to last lick. And lick he'd done, slow and deliberate, worshiping every silky spot of her flawless flesh—in his sleep.

Shae sucked a breath, trying to stall his favorite body member's growth. The old boy had been getting a workout—up—down—up—down. It was hard keeping control of a penis raring to go with the merest vision of Reggie, whether in person or in Shae's mutinous mind.

He'd become obsessed, and had begun rehashing his long-standing personal rule of not bedding women he worked with. His rod insisted they worked for different organizations. Technically, they weren't co-workers. When he had full reasoning capacity, he admitted they were partners. His rebellious body argued the point inspecting the dazzling brunette.

Shae took leave of his senses in her presence—and in his dreams. The gal was what wet dreams were meant for.Reggie's bouncy curls shone in office lighting, teasing his eyes.

"What now, Agent Casse?" He winked.

"Close up, Montgomery; we've got places to go and chores to do." She retrieved her laptop, and strutted toward the door, obviously assuming he would follow.

Why not humor her?

"What, pray tell, are we headed for?"

Without a backward glance, she waltzed through the hallway and out their back door to the parking lot. She clicked open and jumped into her dark classic hot rod. "Get in, Montgomery. You'll thank me for this later." She gunned the engine and whipped the vehicle from its resting spot, barely giving Shae time to jump into the passenger seat. He buckled his seatbelt, as she spun out of the lot and onto the main drag.

"Don't suppose you want to share background on this assignment."

"You'll see soon enough. It's self-explanatory. Don't whine, Montgomery. It's not becoming of a handsome dude."

Handsome?

Nah, she's joking around. I'm not falling for it.

He might as well wait and see.

Moments later, Reggie and Shae were browsing the Men's Department at the local mall. Surprisingly, Shae hadn't fought her on it, but had played along. He was too good looking to wear nerdy clothing she'd seen him in.

"Golf shirts and khakis are for old farts, Montgomery. You bought that monster truck so you'd fit in."

"It's not exactly a monster truck, but I see how you'd call it that—a wee thing, like you."

She snickered.

"You think I dress like an old codger?"

She laughed. "You need to dress so you don't stand out like a Japanese tourist at a pizza convention in a Jewish Sabbath service. Prepare yourself, Montgomery. Winds of change are blowing through. Reserve the verdict until we're through."

"What's wrong with my clothing?" His hand slid adorably down the front of his navy shirt subconsciously then tugged on lapels of his blazer.

She envied that hand as it slid across those obviously rock hard abs rippling too-shiny fabric of his three-button, collared pullover. She couldn't hold back the titter, but a finger came to her mouth trying to hide it. "Nothing we can't fix. Get your plastic ready, Montgomery. We're making a dent in your balance. Time to replace those sorry-assed shoes. You need boots and sneakers."

Shae groaned but didn't argue then swung toward a display of shorts to hide the urge to drool caused by the vulnerable expression on his chiseled face.

Damn, why did he have to be so freaking hot?

The guy was mourning loss of a future he'd pictured with his ex and nursing a broken heart. He was the farthest thing from being ready to pursue a new relationship. It didn't stop her mouth from watering at the sight of him.

Unknowingly, he'd been driving her starving libido wacky. She knew better to screw around with a man with a broken heart. Nothing would come of it other than hers joining the ranks of the damaged.

Shit. She had the most pitiful timing.

She ruffled his short mop playfully. "Now you just need to grow your hair out."

He shook his head. "I'm growing it now."

They'd selected several pairs of jeans and a handful of shirts worthy of a country boy. As they climbed back into her car after stowing bags in the trunk, she turned to him. "Got dinner plans?"

"Nope; and I'm starved. Where you want to go?" His eagerness gave her heart a jump and jolted pheromones straight to her sex. Muscles in that delightful location flinched in anticipation.

"Let's eat at my place. I'll drop you at your truck. Pick up beer and I'll supply the grub. We can eat and watch the Wildcats on the tube."

"Seriously? You cook?" His eyes widened to dark, glistening pools, seeming to like the idea. What man didn't like beer, a full stomach and sports?

"Why does that surprise you?" She smacked his hand good-naturedly. The jolt of lightening from the contact took

118

her by surprise. She whiffed in a gulp of oxygenthen focused on the drive.

He snickered as his faced the highway. "You're on the road most of the time. You said yourself you never spent much time at home, even before returning to Sweetwater. I figured you'd be lost in the kitchen."

She shrugged and tilted her head sideways for a second without looking into those eyes, though they seemed to draw her in like they were asking questions every time she faced them.

Reggie wasn't used to fellas digging into her psyche as much as Shae Montgomery had over the past few weeks. She hadn't minded.

Their conversations had gone deep and long. Reggie had spilled her guts to him, talking about things in her past and present she'd never considered sharing with any living soul—except maybe Sage.

Shae showed up wearing a black tee shirt and jeansshe'd selected,carrying a twelve pack of Reggie's favorite beer. He looked mouth-watering.

Lynda Rees

"Nice call, Montgomery. You make a winning impression." She'd only known him a couple months. He knew her well. A gal had to appreciate a guy who paid attention, not only to what was said, but your preferences.

He mock-modeled, prancing in a circle for her pleasure. "I look good. Right?" He teased, wiggling his hips.

She shoved him toward the kitchen good-humoredly.

"Nice apartment, Casse." He glanced around at tasteful furnishings of the suite she'd chosen to occupy, three rooms and a bath.

"Thanks, but this isn't my stuff. Riley and Levi Madison live in the big house you passed and insisted I stay with them. I decided this would be less imposing on them than living in the mansion. I can come and go as I please. It's temporary—until I purchase a home of my own."

"Security is tight. I passed two gates manned by uniformed guards in order to get here." He plopped where she indicated on the cushy, tan, suede sofa.

She laughed. "Yeah, I forgot to warn you. Mane Lane Farm is a multi-billion-dollar business. Their steeds are worth millions. So is their sperm. Also, Levi's parents live with them in the main residence, whenever they're in Sweetwater. With Garrett Madison a Senator, he requires protection. He brings Secret Service operatives, but Levi maintains a strong team on staff."

He nodded, watching her sit a tray of food on the coffee table in front of them. "I've read newspaper articles about events that have happened here, so it's understandable." He surveyed the tray of food. "We're having hors-devours . . . for a meal?"

She plunked into the seat beside him and handed him an open bottle of beer. "Yes, the place has been involved in more than one crime. I'm sure you never read about some of

120

them. They've managed to keep all but murders out of the press."

He eyed her with a brow high and pointed at the food. "You call this grub? I thought you were cooking."

She snickered then slid to point out the fine points of her offerings. "This is the best bakery bread money can buy. This farmers cheese and these chunks of gourmet, organic goat cheese were manufactured by Sage Gordon and her partner Rose Casson. These fresh vegetables are from Sage's farm. These thick, juicy slices of roast beef came from Levi's kitchen. His maid helped me pack them for dinner, and she gave me two large slices of chocolate cake with fudge icing and a container of homemade vanilla ice cream."

His eyes lit at the mention of dessert. His tongue snaked out and licked his lower mouth, before it disappeared beneath sparkling white teeth that gripped his bottom lip. "Chocolate cake is my favorite."

Damn, she nearly melted, unable to take eyes from them. Maybe she did. Her panties suddenly felt creamy wet.

She'd feed him chocolate cake every day, if she could watch that magic trick his tongue did. Her shoulders rose and fell slightly, masking the quake going on inside her body. She retrieved the remote and clicked the television on.

"Play your cards right, Montgomery, if you want it," she whispered unsure whether she was talking about dessert or offering herself as dessert. Visions of that tongue doing delicious things to her naked flesh flashed through her ridiculously hungry mind. She deeply inhaled oxygen hoping it would cool her insides. "The game is on."

Attention turned to the basketball game. Rooting ensued as they imbibed in several beers and most of the food. She'd relented to his request for mayonnaise in order to make a sandwich of the goods on her snack tray.

Shae's hand reached for the last piece of meat, as hers did. Fingers met. Sparks riddled up her arm, shattering any inhibitions she'd still pretended to have. Eyes met and locked. She retrieved her hand.

Shae picked the morsel up and broke off a piece. "I'll share." He offered the tidbit to her mouth, never releasing the lock on her eyes.

Her lips fell opened with a pant. Feeling her nipples harden against the satin bra, her shoulders eased back. Her breast rose. The pebbles were anxious to reach as closely to his chest as possible and tingled with urgency for his touch.

He laid the piece on her tongue. She tasted his finger, as it lingered a second longer than necessary. She licked lips and enclosed the bite chewing slowly, sensually without losing eye contact. Every ion of her being was engaged in the mental exchange happening in their gaze.

She swallowed and wished her mouth had been around more than a piece of roast beef. Her tongue licked her lower lip, as though it had a mind of its own.

His lips opened, eyes trained on her mouth. A tiny snicker on his face proved he didn't miss his impact on her. He placed remaining meat on the tray without breaking visual connection. His hands went to her jaw. Long, slim fingers tenderly caressed her cheeks. He bit his lower lip, staring at hers. He moaned.

"You have no idea what you do to me, Reggie." His head bent. He nipped the spot beneath her ear.

She shivered at his heated pant against her body. "If it's anything like what you do to me, you're burning to a crisp inside." She shivered

He traced tiny snippets along jawbone to chin. Then he began again at the start, this time moving downward to her collarbone.

122

Her hands traced his broad shoulders, rolling across arms bulging from shirt sleeves. She tested rippling muscles flexing on his back and pulled him toward her. Her breast rose, reaching for his; and she cursed layers of fabric separating her tingling pebbles from his skin.

"Umm, yeah; I want you more than I want my next sniff of oxygen." His palm cupped one breast, and his fingers plucked the hard center. Jolts rocketed through her, and she wiggled in her seat. Her back arched.

She pressed her front against his hard chest. Shae convinced her he needed her in a way she'd never been desired. The attraction was mutual. No reason to fight it. She wanted him as much, maybe more. Shae reached for her top button, and Reggie thought she'd died and gone to heaven.

RING!

Shit.

Shae grimaced and drew away from her, reaching for his phone from his waist. "I'm sorry. I've got to take this." He huffed a deep breath and clicked the phone on, bringing it to his ear.

Lord, she'd never been jealous of a machine before.

"Yeah, you did the right thing. I'll be there in twenty minutes." He rolled eyes toward the ceiling with disappointment on his face. He twisted, adjusting the bulge in his trousers.

He hung up, rolled his head forward and rubbed his nape. Facing her with a bitter smile, he placed a single fingertip to her lips. "I'm sorry, Reggie."

For once he didn't call her Casse or Agent Casse. That was huge.

"I've got to go away for a few days." He stood, clearly reluctant and strode to the door.

"No worries." She knew better than to press, given the businesses the two of them were in. He'd share what he

123

could, and she wouldn't ask more. He'd do the same for her. Lives depended on their discretion.

It did nothing to abate gnawing worry, like she did already. He wasn't out the door yet, and she already missed him. Things had changed between them. She'd never longed for any man, much less worried about one. Shae was different—and she was glad.

He drew her into those bulging arms and pulled her against him. Remains of his waning erection pushed against her stomach above her waist.

She looked into those dark pools of emeralds and was profoundly lost. She wanted this man, not just for a fantastic romp in the sheets. She desired Shae permanently in her life.

Shae kissed the top of her head then tilted her chin with a finger so their eyes met. Every fabric of her being urged him to stay—something she would never voice.

His lips sought hers. At first the kiss was soft and exploratory, as though they were learning new territory. His taste melded with hers, and they became one. As it deepened, she pressed against him, trying to connect with as much body mass as possible.

He lifted her with ease. Her legs wrapped his middle. Fire from her crotch blazed against his stomach. His revived rod jerked against her bottom. Desire to have the staff inside her nearly caused her to climax.

She sucked his tongue with vigor, mimicking what she craved from his insistent joint. She didn't recognize the moan her throat emitted into his voracious mouth.

"Make love to me before you go." Her words came out garbled from her occupied lips.

He drew back and smiled broadly. "I wish like hell I could. I must go. Hold down the fort." He sat her gently onto her feet.

She doubted her legs would hold her molten frame, and wobbled against him. "No time?"

He slowly rocked his head. "No, not now; we'll continue this when I return." He pecked her nose with a wet kiss and turned the knob.

"Hurry back," she whimpered, not sounding or acting anything like her.

He tweaked her nose and was gone. "Bet on it."

Lord, what has happened to me?

CHAPTER 16

Sebastian Bryant was talking to the head librarian at the fundraiser and reopening ceremony for the Sweetwater Public Library. As he moved away and accepted a glass of champagne from a passing waiter, Chloe approached.

"Good evening Mr. Bryant. I'm Chloe Roberts, a real estate agent for The Roberts Agency."

He shook the hand she offered. "Nice meeting you, Ms. Roberts."

"Please, call me Chloe. You've done a wonderful thing for the community. I wanted to take this opportunity to personally thank you for funding renovation."

"It's my pleasure." He didn't appear eager to develop their conversation.

Chloe took charge of her agenda. "You own a property across the street from my office on the corner Main and Second streets. Are you planning to sell?"

Taking a surprised shuffle back a step, his hand went to his throat. Rapidly blinking he deliberated her a few seconds. "I'm not sure, Ms. Roberts. I have vast holdings in many cities. If I own facilities in Sweetwater, I'm unclear what they are. I leave real estate acquiring to my investment firms."

Clearly the man didn't know specifics or he was hiding something. "You own interest in more than one property in the area. Your conglomerate holds title to the storefront building I mentioned, and you have interest in a local distribution center."

Lifting eyebrows, he gave her a close-lipped smile. Appearing to tighten grip on his wine glass, his body visibly tensed. He glanced around at patrons then returned a steady gaze her way.

"My conglomerate? My dear Ms. Roberts, it appears you know more than I about my assets. I'm not involved in day-to-day dealings of my ventures, so have no idea what intentions for the facility you mentioned are. Now, if you'll excuse me, I must speak with the mayor." With a slight nod and head high, he strolled confidently away.

Jaiden approached Chloe. "I saw you speaking with our library benefactor."

Chloe smiled with a closed mouth and nodded. "A lot of good it did. I'm trying to get the listing for a storefront near my headquarters. He brushed me off." She shrugged and sipped her wine.

"I'd be careful prying into his affairs. One of his interests is the freight depot Simon Bedford managed."

Chloe's eyes widened. "The dead guy Sage, Reggie and I found with the young girl?"

"Yes, one and the same. We haven't figured out who murdered Bedford yet. Until we do, I'd steer clear of Mr. Bryant, if I were you. More than likely he has nothing to do with the killing; but if he does, it would pay to stay out of his business."

Her stomach soured. "He acted perturbed I was aware of his finances. I don't know the man personally. It could be a normal reaction for him." Many people preferred keeping financials private. A person with vast reserves and wealth should be accustomed to visibility, given most were corporations requiring regularly divulged status.

Jaiden placed a hand on her forearm. "Or you might've made him nervous, if he has anything to be concerned about. Be safe, Chloe. Let us solve the murder before digging further into something you might regret."

Wyatt approached Mayor Kenneth and Mr. Bryant, eager to learn what he could. "Good evening, Mayor, Mr. Bryant. There's quite a turnout for the celebration." Wyatt motioned to the crowd.

Mayor Ken smiled and lifted his wine goblet. "Yes, I'm pleased with attendance."

Bryant smiled congenially. "Nice to see you, Sheriff Gordon."

"Let me personally thank you for financial support of the library. It means a great deal to citizens of Sweetwater." Wyatt studied the wealthy patron's face.

With a gracious toast toward Wyatt, Bryant smiled. "My pleasure; I'm happy to fund a worthy cause."

Timing seemed right to broach what was on Wyatt's mind. "We've discovered your title to a certain building on Main Street and are concerned about your intentions for it."

Sebastian Bryant sat his champagne glass on a passing waiter's tray and crossed his arms. His jaw and his smile appeared fake. He shot a glance at the mayor then back. His voice elevated. "You may be right, Sheriff. Ms. Roberts approached me earlier informing me of the same thing. I understand her interest. What's yours?"

Wyatt liked getting straight to the point. "Townspeople and business owners are concerned you might be purchasing property to erect a mall."

Bryant blew out a puff of air. Brows furrowed. He pointed a finger as he spoke in a flat tone.

"I personally have no plans for any sort of construction in or around Sweetwater. That said; I stay out of everyday operations of my stock firms. If you have concerns, I suggest you reach out to the managers." His head tilted upward. "If you'll excuse me, I have another engagement. Thank you for coming today; it's been a pleasure." His head bowed, and he turned toward the exit.

Ken and Wyatt nodded at the gentleman's back as he left the room humming with attendee chatter. Wyatt looked at his old friend. "It's been enlightening. Mr. Bryan may not have directly given me what I want; but he spurred my interest in his assets."

Ken snickered. "I don't think that was his intention."

Wyatt laughed. "I'm sure you're right, Ken."

CHAPTER 17

Cariday had arrived at the sheriff's office and told the front desk he needed to see Deputy Sanders. The officer escorted him into the bullpen to Leo's desk.

"Deputy Sanders, I need to tell you something important."

"Sure, Mr. Cariday, let's go somewhere private." He led Cariday to an interrogation room. "Want a drink?" Leo asked then sat when Cariday took a seat and shook his head. Leo laid his phone on the metal table. "I need to record this."

"No problem."

Leo clicked the device on. "This is Deputy Leo Sanders speaking May thirteen to Mr. Jeromy Cariday. Go on, Mr. Cariday."

"Man, I don't know what to do. I overheard a conversation I wasn't supposed to hear earlier at the warehouse. I went into the can. Before the door slammed shut, some dude in the back stall shouted, probably into a cell phone, '*What the hell are you doing? Hart, you'd best get your shit together. You're responsibility for protecting inventory. You hired that pile of manure, lug head. Your life and his are on the line. A new shipment is coming Monday. Do your fucking jobs. Or I'll find someone who will.*' They weren't discussing potato chips—know what I mean?" Cariday pawed sweat from his brow.

"Did he hear you come in?" Leo grew concerned for the witness.

"No, I don't think so. I eased the door shut and went to the break room until the john was free.

"Did you see who was speaking?"

Cariday shook his head. "Nope, but I recognized him. It was Mack Bennett. He's Bedford's replacement. I heard someone refer to him as a *company man*, whatever that means."

"Listen, Deputy, I've got no death wish, but I had to tell you what I heard. It sounded sinister and important. That dude is into some heavy shit. God knows what he'd do to me, if he knew I heard him." Cariday wiped sweat from his brow with the back of his hand.

"Did you know this Mark Bennet before he became your boss?"

Cariday nodded. "Not personally, but I've seen him before. He stopped in occasionally to talk with Bedford. They always went outside to break tables or into a conference room to chat, so I never overheard their conversations. He didn't talk to anyone but Bedford."

"What do you think they're up to?"

"Not certain, but whatever it is it's not good. He acted superior to Bedford when he stopped in—before Bedford's death. I could tell Bedford was intimidated. I get the idea Bennett's some kind of ringleader."

Leo rubbed his chin. "How is he with the warehousemen?"

"He's all business and keeps to himself, except when he's directing operations. He's a hell of a lot easier to work for than Bedford was." Cariday chewed the inside of his jaw. "You won't tell Bennett I told you this. Right?"

"No, your secret's safe with me. I'll protect your identity, at least until we get to the bottom of this. You may be called on to testify, when we go to trial, if there's any connection between Bennett and a crime."

Cariday stood as Leo did. "Thanks, Deputy. I feel better already."

Leo wished he did.

Justin returned to his post behind the bar at the Ten Mile House and checked everyone's drinks. He sat up new bottles for the truckers seated at the end of the bar.

Wyatt waived at Justin. "I'm just stepping outside. I need to get something out of my vehicle. Be right back."

"I'll have a cold one waiting when you get back." Justin reached into a cooler.

Wyatt exited the tavern. It was easy spotting the truckers' ride. It was the only vehicle in the place besides Justin's pickup truck and Wyatt's cruiser. The semi stuck out like a sore thumb.

Good thing he arrived after the drivers. If they'd seen his cruiser in the lot, they never would've been freely talking. The jukebox had been crooning one country tune after another.

Wyatt and Justin had been preoccupied with their own conversation. Wyatt tried to curb his lawman inclination to eavesdrop when out socially. At times it was a good he didn't—like today.

He neared the large van and photographed the trucking information on the driver's side door, including website, official numbers authorizing him to haul contents inter and intrastate and company name he hauled merchandise for. In back of the trailer, he shot the rear door which had details about the cargo van. Then he stepped back far enough to take a photo of the complete length of the rig.

Pocketing his phone, he returned to the bar. The truckers seemed to be engaged in a debate about whether a certain truck stop waitress would sleep with them for under fifty-dollars. Evidently, their discussion of earlier had taken a more pleasant turn. Wyatt continued keeping half an ear toward the men, but they left after finishing their last drink.

"You know those fellas?" He nodded toward the door they'd walked out of.

"Not really. They stop in occasionally when passing through town. I think they pick up cargo at a warehouse here. I don't know which. Why?"

"Ah, just something I heard one of them say."

Sure as hell, Wyatt was going to learn a lot more about those guys—at least the one who'd overheard a discussion about criminal activity in Wyatt's town. It sounded like a drug deal going down. Wyatt was going to find out.

One call to the logistic headquarters, he'd know names, addresses, phone numbers, email addresses, what they were hauling and where it was loaded and delivered. They'd be lucky if Wyatt didn't dig up every ex-girlfriend, unhappy cocktail waitress and truck stop clerk they'd made acquaintance with, along with the dudes' jock strap sizes. Wyatt didn't condone shit going down in Sweetwater.

CHAPTER 18

Reggie sat at her desk pouring over information she'd researched online, hardly able to focus. Shea's scent had lodged in her nostrils the evening they'd spent together, keeping him fresh in her mind. Had his phone not rang with an emergency, she'd bet money they'd have shared her bed that night.

What would've become of them then? Would they be able to work as a team having slept together? Would one round of rousing bumping uglies satisfied their cravings? Would a night of getting it on ruin their working relationship? Would one round with Shae satisfy her yearning? Or would sex with the saucy marshal be so intense, like a drug, she'd become addicted?

One thing was for sure. Shae Montgomery had wanted her as much as she'd desired him. His erection against her

135

middle had made her cream for him. She hadn't stopped since that night—even though he'd been out of town two days now without a word. Visions of their fierce need burned deep in her core and beggedfor satisfaction.

The door opened. A tall, slim woman with cropped, blonde hair waltzed in as though she owned the place. A designer suit fit her svelte curves to a tee. Her handbag probably cost what Reggie earned in a month. Nobody said public service was lucrative.

The stranger glanced around with a scowl on her perfectly made up face. Not surprising—their utilitarian work space wasn't designed for show.

"May I help you?"

"I'm looking for Shae Montgomery."

"Mr. Montgomery is out. Are you looking for insurance? I can connect you with an agent who can help you."

The female glared, as though Reggie was an idiot. "No, thank you. When will Mr. Montgomery return?"

"I'm not sure. He's been gone a couple days. He could return today or anytime in the next few days." The strange female had peaked Reggie's curiosity, though she could do without the snooty attitude.

The gal rolled her eyes with what looked like resolve. "I'm Mr. Montgomery's fiancé, Lydia Rosenthal. Please give him a message when he calls in."

"I doubt he will. He'll likely show up when he returns."

He puffed out exasperation. "Fine—when Mr. Montgomery returns, tell him I'm waiting at the Sweetwater Inn. I hope I can tolerate that small-town hostel until Shae gets home. He forgot to leave a key to our new place." She appeared to look Reggie over then seemingly dismissed her as insignificant. "Can you manage that?"

Reggie saluted. "You've got it." Her blood was boiling. Good thing the snotty woman strode out in a snit. Reggie was itching for a fight. Her fists were dying to hit something.

She slammed the top on her computer, wrote a hasty note and slapped it on Shae's empty desktop and stomped out of the office. She needed an evening at the gym pounding a punching bag and visualizing Shae Montgomery's face on it.

"Fiancé my ass."

CHAPTER 19

Reggiesat across from Wyattin his office. Leo and Jaiden accompanied them.

Leo tented fingers in his lap. "I hate doing this without Shae."

Reggie's blood pressure spiked. "Forget it. He's gone on marshal business. Who knows when he'll return? We can't wait. Let's review evidence and see if what we know goes together, or if there's more than one crime happening in Sweetwater."

Wyatt leaned against the back of his chair. "She's right. We've got a lot of loose pieces. Let's play out the puzzle or puzzles. Shae can get up to speed when he returns."

Jaiden took the lead and started writing on Wyatt's whiteboard. "We have an upstanding citizen, well known for supporting local needs. Sebastian Bryant has donated heavilyto the library, helped fund adult education classes. He's a widower, doesn't get involved in local activities and is a loner, a private man. His shaky finances tie to the warehouse where our murder victim worked, but we don't have enough to link him to criminal activity."

Leo rubbed his chin. "True. Bryant could be planning to bring in mall business, which isn't a crime, but is concerning to residents. He could be involved in the murder, directly or indirectly, but no facts are substantial to consider him a suspect. We've ruled out employees, based on alibis. The wife is questionable, but not likely. It's difficult to believe she killed her husband. She's no better off with him dead than alive. Of course, it could be a murder of passion. There should've been a struggle, had she caught him with the hooker, pants down and attacked him."

Wyatt ran a hand through his long, silver locks. "I believe we have enough to assume the warehouse is being used for illegal activity—between what I overheard at the Ten Mile House and Cariday's snooping at the warehouse. It could be drugs, illegal knock-off jeans or nearly anything. It might have nothing to do with Bedford's slaying. Something fishy is happening and on Monday, from what we've heard. I'll go to the judge for a warrant. We're going to set up a bust when whatever shipment they're expecting comes in."

Reggie flipped through a file. "Yes, I'm happy to assist, especially if it's a drug bust. Wish we had more about the sex ring. Maybe we'll learn more when Shae gets back."

Leo waved his arm. "I'm curious about another thing. It could be connected, be something totally different, or it could be nothing. The building across Chloe's office has seen strange activity and is owned by Bryant. The connection is too strange to totally ignore. Entrance to the upstairs and parking facility is clearly visible from a cubicle in The Robinson Agency building. I've confirmed with Ava Roberts. It's okay with her if I work from there for a few days. I'd like to do that and see if I can gather intel."

Wyatt nodded with pursed lips. "Great. Bryant has been no help. Watch, keep notes and take photographs. It could be the owners are renovating, preparing to tear the facility down or preparing it for resale. Whatever is happening there, I want to know. We're going to find out for ourselves what

Bryant or his minions are up to. Lord, I hope it's not a mall coming to Sweetwater."

While Wyatt worked with the team to develop an attack plan for the Monday bust, Leo posted his behind at an unoccupied desk inside The Robert's Agency. In the next two days, he took photographs of vehicles and personnel entering and leaving the facility. By week's end he had much to report. Meeting again in Wyatt's office on Friday morning, he readied to brief Wyatt, Jaiden and Reggie.

Wyatt sipped a cup of coffee. "Was it worth working off site?"

Leo nodded. "Yep, I believe it was."

His partner appeared anxious. "So spill it, red." Jaiden laughed, shoving redheaded Leo playfully.

Reggie nibbled on a bagel with cream cheese and salmon and sipped a strong Earl Grey tea, enjoying being in Sweetwater near people she knew well and loved. Life was slower and easier in the small, rural town; and people were more casual.

She wasn't involved in the controversy over expansion on Main Street, but was happy to assist with what sounded like a drug bust at the warehouse. She missed Montgomery more each day, both professionally and personally.

Might as well get used to heartache where he was concerned, since what had started between them had taken a detour during his absence. He'd obviously made contact with his ex, and he and Lydia had resumed their love affair. She dreaded watching the loving couple canoodle after he returned, but she did wish he'd return in time to participate in Monday night's raid.

Leo stood to write on the white board. "Comings and goings in the building in question were interesting and not what I expected. I figured construction work was going on. I now believe it's something entirely different."

He laid a stack of eight-by-ten photographs on the desk and splayed them out so the group could view them all. "I spent not only days in the office, but also evenings until midnight or one a.m. Jaiden relieved me from time to time, so I could take a break. These men were spotted going in and out, sometimes alone. The big dude here," he pointed to one, "was periodically accompanied by a female—different one each time."

Jaiden pointed to a muscle-bound, burly guy about six-foot-four and middle-aged. "I've researched them and ran them through facial recognition. Leo pulled finger prints from their vehicle doors and license plates numbers. I ran them through the system. This dude is Conway Perkins, convicted felon who robbed a liquor store and spent two years in prison. He owns a string of laundromats and drives this non-descript sedan." She pointed to a photo of a grey four-seater car.

Reggie chewed her bagel and leaned to view the photographs.

Leo tapped the white board, where he attached the photo of Conway Perkins and picture of the car beside his name.

"Each time Perkins left with a young girl, he later returned with her. I saw him with three different females. The girls appeared inattentive, as though they might've been drugged. They were dressed risqué for young women."

"Holy crap." Reggie sat at the edge of her seat and laid the rest of her bagel on a paper plate. This was getting interesting.

Jaiden pointed to a photograph of a good-looking man with shoulder-length dreadlocks pulled into a ponytail at the nape of his neck. His onyx skin glowed in the shot; and he wore expensive, stylish clothing and dress shoes. He was shorter than Perkins, looking to be about five-foot-two or three. His neck sported a thick, gold chain. "This is Cecil Hart. Hedrives the fancy, black pickup truck. His criminal record consists of minor drug charges for possession. He did a month in the Bonnyville jail."

You could've heard a pin drop. Wyatt slid to the front of his seat and placed hands on his desk. Reggie's inhale was audible. She closed her eyes a second, with a silent wish for Montgomery's return.

Leo nodded, as they eyed him. He laid a fresh batch of glossies in front of them. "These are pictures of the girls accompanying Conway Perkins in and out of the building. I couldn't get a clear shot of their tattoos, but it's obvious each girl had one."

Wyatt took the photographs in hand. "I don't see one of Willow."

Leo shook his head. "No, I didn't spot the girl Sage met while I was on watch.

Reggie took the photos form Wyatt and reviewed each one closely. "Anything else?"

Jaiden pursed her lips. "I checked the national hotline for the girls. They're all on there. The phone company confirmed there are no land lines in the building, but both men have cell accounts. They may be using burner phones as well."

Reggie nodded. "It's likely they use burners for customer contacts. When we take these guys down, if we can confiscate the phones, we can tie the numbers to sex for sale advertisements in the dark web with the girl's photos. I need a copy of these shots with the girls on them to have our people start searching for the ads immediately."

"I printed this set specifically for you." Jaiden pushed a folder filled with photos to Reggie.

Wyatt nodded. "Criminals aren't usually smart—except top guys, maybe. Good work team. This isn't what we expected you'd uncover. It's better."

"Hot damn, this is exactly what we need. It's the missing link in our local sex trafficking case." Reggie's heart throbbedat a familiar hum as her brain went into battle mode. *Fuck, Shae should be here.* "I want the bastards running the show. It sounds like Hart and Perkins are the stock and trade managers. We take them down, free the sex slaves they're running then work Hart and Perkins over for leads. I'm after whoever is pulling their strings—not just a couple two-bit pimps."

"Right; first things first; we need to do this right. I'll get a warrant for phone records and to tap the lines. Chances are it's a dead end, and they keep confidential discussion to burners. Best be on the safe side. They don't know we're on to them. Who knows? We might get lucky."

Leo nodded and took a seat. "Yes." He placed a couple more snapshots on Wyatt's desk. "These men were seen going in and leaving a short while afterward alone. I believe them to be Johns."

Reggie spun and stomped her booted foot on the floor. "Damn it to hell and back." These middle-aged, balding, paunchy guys are purchasing sex from children. This is the freaking brothel we've been looking for."Her palms itched. Professional calm inside her was tamping down the urge to be frantic.

As much as she'd like to take those two down immediately and pistol-whip the assholes, she wanted more. They could provide inroads to the big guns of the operation. She was determined to get whatever intel they could provide and make a clean, well-packaged case for the prosecutor, so the brains of the operation got put away for a good, long time.

Wyatt bit his lower lip rocking his head for a minute while Reggie fumed. "It appears so. We need to be careful." His head was obviously spinning, as he tried cooking up a plan.

Reggie leaned hands on the desktop and faced her dear friend. "Wyatt, I don't just want the sex buyers and sleazy pimps. I want the brains behind this operation."

"Damn straight." Wyatt nodded standing then pacing.

Reggie slumped into her seat. "I'll alert Carla Orson from NCMEC. She'll be able to help us, once we set the girls free."

Leo tented his fingers and cringed. "We need a strategic plan to get to them."

Jaiden piped up. "What would you say to me going undercover as a troubled teen hanging out at the mall between here and Bonnyville? I can dress young and wear something that makes my neck tattoo stand out. With a bit of eye makeup and a back pack, I could look like a fifteen or sixteen-year-old."

Wyatt studied her a few seconds. "Yeah, it wouldn't hurt. It's early. Get on it and spend the day and evening there. Any luck, maybe you can make contact with someone casing the joint."

"Sure, boss. I'll spend today and tomorrow there." Jaiden glanced at Leo.

"I'll get the owner to let me set up as a maintenance man, so I can keep an eye on Jaiden. She might need backup."

"Good idea. I'll find out who the buyers in Leo's photos are. After we bust these perps, we need to pay them a visit as well." Wyatt stretched his long back. "In the meantime, we need to complete strategy for the drug bust at the warehouse on Monday."

Damn it. Shae should be here.

CHAPTER 20

Sage finished with a delivery. Her phone rang as she jumped into her van. Recognizing the meek voice, her heart stalled. She took a calming breath. This conversation could mean life or death to her young friend.

"Mrs. Gordon?"

Barely hearing the child, Sage's heart started pounding against her ribs so hard she feared they'd break. "Yes, this is Sage Gordon. Willow, it's good hearing from you." *Keep it casual. Stay calm.*

"You, ah . . . you said I could call."

"Yes, anytime, and I'm glad you did. How can I help you, sweetheart?"

"Why do you want to help me?" Mistrust filtered the question.

"Willow, I've been in bad situations and needed help. It brought home to me how sacred life is. Whatever your problem, I'm here for you."

"I'm in trouble, Mrs. Gordon. I'm scared and want out . . . before it's too late." She sniffed.

"Willow, I'll do everything in my power to save you and get whatever you need. Can you meet me?" Sage drew in a long, slow breath and closed her eyes in silent prayer. *Please, let her trust me.*

"I don't know. They're always watching. I'll try. Can you meet me in the alley beside the drug store? I'll try to get away in a few minutes." Willow's voice quivered, as though she'd been crying.

Hope filled Sage's lungs as she breathed in welcome air. "Absolutely; I'm heading there now and driving the Parsley, Sage, Rose, Mary & Wine delivery van. I'll wait for you. Be careful, Willow." *Thank you. Thank you. Thank you.*

Another sniff and the line disconnected.

She hit the gas and spoke to the hands-free phone attached to her dash. "Call Reggie." A few beeps later, Reggie's cheerful tone fired Sage's determination.

"Hey, Sage, what's shaking?"

"I need your help. Willow called. She's scared to death. I convinced her to meet me." Sage explained where she was meeting the girl.

"Try to persuade her to leave with you. Tell you you'll take her to safety. I'll reach out to Carla Owens from the National Center for Missing and Exploited Children. She has resources to get Willow care she needs."

"Okay, but I promised I'd be here for her. I'm not handing that girl off to a stranger—at least not until she's ready."

"I hear you, Sage. I would expect no less. We'll get her medical and psychological attention. Carla will help determine a location where she can continue to heal— somewhere they won't find her. You can walk through every step with her, if the two of you want. I promise."

A boulder lifted from Sage's shoulders. She twisted her head, releasing a cramp in her neck. Now all she had to do it convince Willow to come with her. "Thanks, Reggie. I was sure you'd know what to do."

"You want me to be around for backup when you meet her? Someone could be tailing Willow."

Sage's lungs jolted, and she expelled a gust. "Absolutely not, but I appreciate the offer. If Willow has any idea I brought someone along, she'll run. I might never get this chance to save her again. I've got to do this on my own."

"You're armed. Right?"

Sage's hand automatically touched the weapon in her under-the-bra holster. Its firmness reassured her she was up to the task. "Always, hey, I'm almost there. I need to hang up. I don't want her to see me on the phone, and maybe think I'm informing some who might harm her."

"Okay, be safe. Do you want to take her to the hospital or my office?"

"Neither. I'm taking her to my house, at least until we figure out where she needs to be."

"I'm not sure it's wise, but I know better than to argue with you. I'll contact Dr. Barnes. Clay has offered his expertise to NCMEC. I'll ask him to come to your place, when he finishes his shift. Carla and I will meet you there."

"Wish me luck."

"Lemon Sage Gordon, you make your own luck. You reached out to this young woman. You're an incredible person, and I love you."

The compliment surged Sage's determination and was exactly what she needed. "Love you too, Reggie. See you soon—I hope." Sage clicked off and drove slowly into the alley. She parked so the driver's side was against the throughway and the other close to the drug store wall. The storefront fronted Main Street. That way the truck, building and door would best shield from view Willow when she arrived.

Now the wait.

149

Nearly half an hour later the passenger side of her van popped open. Willow had approached from the street side, so Sage hadn't spotted her coming.

The girl hopped up into the seat. She glanced at Sage then stared for a few seconds at the wing mirror on her door, as though checking to see if she was being followed.

"Hi. I'm glad you decided to meet me." Sage hoped to ease into the hard conversation they were about to have. What's going on, Willow?"

She eyed Sage, glanced into the back. Willow's hair was a tangled mess, and dark hollows formed around her eyes. She was even thinner than when Sage saw her last.

"I'm alone."

Willow nodded then stared at her hands. Fingers linked on her lap and thumbs fidgeted. "Sorry to be a bother. I didn't know where else to turn."

Sage tenderly touched Willow's stringy, greasy hair, brushing a tendril from her sweating forehead. Willow flinched but didn't pull away. "You're no bother, Willow. I want to help. Tell me what's going on."

"I'm a . . . scared. Something bad is about to happen— already has; but more is coming. I have no idea what, but it's not going to be good. I don't know what they have planned, but they're all nervous and screaming at each other."

"I see. How did you get away?"

"It's time for my period. I told Yolanda I started early and needed to go steal tampons from the drug store. I'm sure they're watching me. They're always watching. I hope they think I went into the store, and didn't see me get in your van."

"By *they* you mean people holding you? You're involved in a sex ring. Right? Are they prostituting you?" Sage's stomach was in knots, twisting and turning.

Willow refused to move her glance from her hands, as she timidly nodded. She back-handed a tear. "Yeah, so I can't go to the cops. I'd go to prison." She sniffed.

"Oh, baby, how old are you?" Reggie was right. Willow had no idea she was the casualty, not the felon.

Another sniff. "Fourteen."

"Willow, you're a child, a victim. You're not going to jail. You've done nothing wrong. You're innocent, the injured party here. The men who are holding you are the criminals." She tilted Willow's chin so she had to face her then nodded at the sad, questioning look on her face.

Willow's beautiful eyes were ringed with dusky shadows. Excessive mascara had smeared, leaving smudges in deep depressions surrounding them. Her pale skin obviously hadn't seen much of the light of day for a while.

"No, I went with Cecil on my own. He's my . . . boyfriend."

"Cecil?"

Willow nodded. "Cecil Hart. I met him at the mall near Bonnyville. He was good to me and bought me nice things. I love him and went to be with him. He takes care of me."

"By taking care of you, you mean he drugged and had sex with you—which is a criminal act on his part, since you're a minor. He sold you into prostitution for financial gain."

"I had sex with him because I love him." Her chin went up.

"Does he love you?" The child needed to understand her situation. She was clearly oblivious.

"He says he does . . . sometimes." Sage could hardly hear her words.

"Does he hit you?" Sage gazed at scattered bruisingon Willow's arms and legs.

Willow followed Sage's stare and nodded. Her hands clenched in her lap. "Only when I make him mad or do something bad; sometimes he has Shiv punish me."

"Shiv?" Willow nodded. "Yeah, Shiv is our bodyguard. He watches out for us. He's big, strong and carries a knife, sometimes a gun."

Sage nodded. "Does Cecil Hart live with you? Are you his only girlfriend?"

Willow shook her head. "No, I have my own room. There are others. I've heard them come and go in the hallway, but I can't open the door and meet them. It's not allowed. I hear things, though."

"Cecil convinced you to sell your body to strangers for money. Right? Do you see any of the cash? What happened to nice things he bought you and promised?"

She nodded and swiped a tear away. "He bought me a pretty necklace when we first met. It was a gold locket with a big red stone in the middle shaped like a heart. He said it was because I was Hart's girl. I don't know what happened to it. I guess I lost it. I woke up once and it was gone."

Obviously the dude dangled a fancy piece of jewelry in Willow's face to dazzle the child. He clearly took it back, probably when she was dazed. "By woke up, you mean you came out of a drugged stupor. Right?" Sage eyed her critically.

Willow nodded, without meeting Sage's eyes. "I have to help pay our expenses. It's not cheap to live, you know. Cecil said I have to pull my own weight, but he takes care of the money."

"It appears Cecil keeps the money and you don't benefit from it. You don't appear to be eating or dressing well. When was the last time you had a haircut?" Sage fingered the spiky red and bronze mess on Willow's head. Dark roots were about an inch thick.

"He brings me food . . . when I'm good, and Yolanda cut my hair a few weeks ago. I have my own room."

"When was the last time you relaxed in a hot bath?" Sage's palm rested on the child's scrawny arm.

"I don't know—a long time. Sometimes I get a quick shower, when Hart decides I need it. Mostly I get to wash up every few days."

"Who is Yolanda?" Sage gazed in her rear view mirror. No one strange had appeared, though Willow's eyes continually darted around.

"She's Hart's head girl. Yolanda took me shopping at the Thrift Store for clothes. She cut my hair and dyed it. She's kind of in charge of the girls, and she helps me get jobs."

"Jobs? You mean Johns?"

Willow nodded, staring at the dashboard.

"How does she help?"

"She took some photos and posted an ad on the internet."

Sage held back the urge to vomit. "You're scared and fear for your safety. Right?"

"Yeah, I hear things. I don't know what, but something big is happening."

"Okay, let's get you out of there before it does. Come with me, Willow. I'll take you somewhere Hart and his men can't get at you. Let me take you to safety."

Willow winced, and her eyes filled with moisture. Her hand went to the door knob then paused. Her feet shuffled against the floorboard, appearing to be about to flee.

Sage laid a hand on Willow's quivering forearm. "Stay with me, Willow. I'll protect you. I won't let harm come to you. Don't go back. Whatever they're into, it can't be good for you. Go with me before they relocate you somewhere I can't rescue you from. If you return to Hart, I'll never see you again. They'll hurt you . . . or worse." Sage gripped her arm without causing pain.

153

The child stared at her hand and visibly seemed to relax. She slumped into the seat and released the door handle. "Okay."

Sage didn't hesitate. She fired the engine and as she whipped out of the alleyway, Willow slinked deeper into the seat, as though hiding and not wanting to be seen by anyone watching.

CHAPTER 21

Sage drove the speed limit, afraid to spook Willow. She pulled the van into the driveway nestled into a thick tree line and ambled along the lengthy, gravel driveway to her home.

Willow jerked more alert, as they entered the private lane and sat erect. Her hand continued trembling in Sage's. Eyes wide, she scanned the property.

Black board fencing separated three pastures along both sides of the road. As they rounded a bend, fence separated grazing and hay land from a rolling lawn surrounding the modern, angled, rustic-cut log structure fronted with glass. A thick deck flanked the front. A huge, metal barn sat off to the right and opened into a corral on that side.

Willow appeared to swallow hard. Eyes wide, she blew out wind. "Wow, where are we? This place is gorgeous. Is it a resort or rehab facility?"

Sage squeezed her hand and pulled to a stop in the circle drive fronting the house. "Nope, this is my home—mine and my husband, Wyatt's. He built it and lived here before I met him. I moved in after we married."

"Wow, and you have horses." She nodded toward three geldings grazing in a pasture.

155

Lynda Rees

"Yes, we have three. The black one is Wyatt's. He bought me the palomino as a wedding gift. The third belongs to his daughter, Hailey."

"Gosh, I've never been around horses before. They're awfully big." The innocent child in Willow was peeping out of the hollow shell she'd become.

Satisfaction filled Sage's lungs as she pulled keys from the ignition and hopped out of the vehicle. When Willow continued sitting in the cab, Sage rounded the front and opened the passenger door.

Two dogs came yapping and running toward her. When they neared the vehicle, Sage put a hand up. "Stay." The twosome ceased barking and placed their hind ends on the ground. She breathed easy, happy their animals were well trained.

Willow's eyes watered. She edged back.

Sage pushed a hand toward her. "It's fine. They're tame. They won't bother you unless you signal you want to pet them. As for horses, yes; they're big but are also well trained. They love attention, and none of them bites. If you want, I'll help you learn to pet them as well."

Willow hesitated then placed her hand in Sages and hopped from the van. Sage waved toward the patiently waiting dogs. Both wagged tails, sitting happily.

"Willow, the German Shepherd is Tuffy. I adopted Tuffy after he was injured as a New York City Police Dog. He is my hero and saved my life once. He's my rescuer as much as I am his. The cocker spaniel, Belle is Tuffy's best friend and is Wyatt's dog from before we met."

Willow's grip began relaxing as Sage made introductions, giving Sage hope this might work. "Would you like to pet them?"

Willow removed her hand from Sage's and knelt. "I would. Is it okay?"

156

Sage eyed the dogs. "Okay."

Tuffy stood with his tail continuing to wag. Belle followed suit. Willow held a hand out to be smelled. The critters politely whiffed her scent then circled her. Tuffy faced her and laid a pad in her hand.

Willow giggled. Optimism surged through Sage's lungs. The child was innocent, regardless what she'd endured.

Willow plopped onto her knees and allowed kisses from Tuffy and Belle, as she stroked their silky hair. Her laughter was like seeing sunshine for the first time after a week-long spring deluge. Sage referred to that period as Mud Season.

When Willow had obtained her share of welcoming, she stood. Sage massaged beneath the jawline and ears of the canines then kissed the top of Tuffy's head. "You are good dogs."

She turned to Willow. "Let's get you settled."

Willow looked around with brows scrunched. "Here? You want me to stay at your house? I figured you'd take me to the police station, a rehab center, hospital or foster care center." Her head jutted forward and disbelief coated her words.

"No way; I promised to help you through this and to protect you. I'm going to do it until you get on your own two feet."

Willow shook her head dubiously. Sage snatched her hand and led her up a few stairs to the immense deck then through French door. She didn't resist.

Eyes wide, Willow surveyed the great room with its massive island, stone countertops and stainless steel appliances. She gazed through the seating area. Cozy suede sofas flanked a gigantic, rock fireplace in a corner. Walls were rough-cut cedar, and heavy American Indian-print blankets rested across tops of the sofas and two matching chairs.

"This rustically decorated room is my favorite in the house." Sage's arm swiped toward the area.

"You live here?" Willow's mouth fell open. Sage nodded. Willow's awe was evident in her eyes. "It reminds me of a lodge we stayed at once in Gatlinburg before Dad died. We don't travel, since he's gone—no money."

"You like it?" Sage asked.

"I do." Willow almost smiled.

"Me too. We spend a lot of family time here." She led to a small hallway on one side and pointed to a door. "This is the guest bath. Feel free to use it anytime." She opened the next door. "You can use this room."

Willow followed her inside. "It's beautiful."

She ran a hand across the cushy, pink, microfiber comforter. Its shade matched silky pink curtains on windows facing woodland and past a black, wood fence. She eyed the dresser, which held vials of colognes and girly knickknacks.

Sage opened the closet. "You look about a size one. What size shoes do you wear?"

"I don't remember. I think a seven." Willow's brows knitted. "Why?"

Impaired memory was a symptom Sage was aware of, of drug abuse. She'd read literature Reggie had given her, after discovering Willow was in the grips of a human trafficking ring.

"I think Hailey left a couple pairs of size seven boots and shoes in here. She's outgrown them. Hailey is tall and slim like her daddy. I think she's in an eight-and-half by now."

"This is Hailey's room?" Willow's eyes popped again.

"It is, but no fear. She's away at college. She only lives part-time with Wyatt and me, when she has time off from studies."

Willow nodded understanding. "I . . . can't take her room."

"You certainly can. Hailey would be happy to have you stay here long as you need to. Make yourself at home. Use whatever you want from the perfume and makeup she left here. He usually brings her new stuff when she comes home anyway. She won't mind."

Willow sat on the bed tentatively and bounced. "It's really nice. I can't believe you're doing this for me."

Sage pulled out a pair of turquoise leather boots with embroidery on the sides. "Here you go. You can have these cowboy boots if they fit and you like them. She tossed them on the floor by the bed at Willow's feet. "Ah, hah, here we go." She reeled around and stood holding out a pair of white Niki gym shoes. "These will do. I might find another pair or two you can wear." When the child didn't reach for the slippers, Sage smiled. "Here, take them. Try them on."

Willow nodded, without meeting her eyes. Her words were a muffled mumble. "Thanks."

Sage sat beside her on the bed and slid an arm across her bony shoulders. "First things first. We need to get you checked out physically. I hear a car coming. It's probably Clay Barnes. He's a close friend and a surgeon at Sweetwater General. He's coming to examine you and determine what care you need."

Willow jerked and shook her head. "I got no money. I can't afford no doctor."

Sage smiled and stroked her narrow chin. "It is fine, Willow. Clay has volunteered his services to help people like you who need medical attention."

She began coughing frantically and wheezing, appearing to at the beginning of a panic attack. "I'm not sick."

She pushed a greasy lock from Willow's forehead. "You don't have the flu or anything, Sweetheart; but you were taking illegal substances and have been involved in sex for

159

hire. We need to ensure you haven't contracted some kind of disease and learn what we can do to get you off the drugs."

Willow's head dropped, and she stared at her fingers, picking at cuticles on her chewed-short nails. "Won't this doctor turn me in?"

"No, Willow. Clay is here to help you—like me. He has no other motive."

"But don't doctors have to turn in druggies?" Her shoulders trembled beneath Sage's arm.

"You're a child, Willow. It wasn't your choice to get hooked on drugs. It was a criminal act by this Hart, who took you in. Even if you took illegal substances willingly, it's Hart's fault—not yours. You're not to blame. The same goes for prostitution. You're innocent, Willow. We're here to protect you and help you heal from your ordeal."

Her head perked up, and her hand slapped across the tat on her neck. "I went with Hart because I love him. I sold myself to help him—and so he could pay for my drugs and my keep. It's expensive to buy food, a place to live and drugs—especially on the street."

"I realize that, Willow. You were coerced by Hart to become a slave. You did it willingly because he made you believe him. He lied to you, Willow. He doesn't love you. He only cares about money you bring in. He gave you food, but barely enough to keep you alive. He betrayed you, Willow. I realize you feel faithful to him, but it's because he brainwashed you—psychologically and with the help of whatever chemicals he gave you. You have no reason to be loyal to Hart—or any of your keepers. Do you know what drugs you were taking?"

The girl shrugged, and her head tilted. "I don't know all of it, or what it really is. I heard words like Peace, Clarity, Lover's Speed—Hart called it that when we made love the first time. Once he called it Ecstasy. Shiv mentioned Adam,

Eve, Molly and Uppers. Like I said, I don't know what they are."

"Did you snort it, swallow it or was it injected?" There were no visible tracks on Willow's arms. Sage's stomach was doing summersaults. She took a cleansing breath to keep from screaming.

Again, the shoulder-head tilt, but Willow looked away. "When I first got there, after I ate some and watched TV with Hart for a while, he told me to swallow something; and we'd have a really good time. I did and don't remember much about what happened next. I must've been out a few days. When I woke, I was dirty and stinky. During the time I was woozy, in-and-out of sleep, I vaguely recall some sweaty, fat, old man humping me." She appeared to swallow a baseball sized gulp as she paused. "Another time, I'm not sure it was a dream or real, a bald man who smelled fancy was rutting against my back then flipped me over and finished. He was skinny. I . . . think it was real. I had bruises where his bones hurt me."

Sage fought the urge to faint or rage at the walls. She stood silently, praying inside she could help Willow. "Did you take drugs when you first had sex with Hart?"

She nodded. "Yeah, I swallowed some pills. He said it would make it extra special. But I had needle marks on my arm when I finally came out of the haze—before we first made love—at least I think it was the first time we did it."Willow blinked a few times, appearing to cease defense of Hart for the time being.

"You hungry?" Sage stood.

"No." Willow shrugged. "I . . . I need to get out of here. They'll come for me. I don't want them to hurt you." She stood and glanced at her arm. A small scar marred her porcelain skin.

Sage stalled her escape with gentle hands on her emaciated shoulders. "You've come this far, Willow. If you go back now, they'll punish you for running and ship you somewhere I can't find you—sell you to another pimp. Or they'll kill you. Stay. See this through. Let me help you."

Willow nodded and slumped onto the bed.

"When did you eat last?"

"I don't know; maybe yesterday . . . or the day before. I think I ate peanut butter on a slice of bread."

"That's it. I'm fixing you some food. After Clay examines you, you're going to eat a good meal. Try the shoes on. I'll be right back with Clay." Sage closed the door quietly behind her. She listened briefly, hearing no movement inside. Then she went to let Clay in, since he was waiting at the glass doors.

"How is she?" The tall, blonde physician asked. His broad grin showed off sparkling white teeth and made him even more handsome. His short-cropped hair did nothing to detract from his approachable appearance. No wonder Deputy Jaiden Coldwater was nuts for him.

"Irritable, anxious, on the verge of panic, paranoid and generally scared shitless. I explained you were coming, and she nearly had a meltdown. I had to keep her from running. It's good the windows in Hailey's room are high off the ground. I wouldn't put it past her to try to escape. She wants help, but is terrified what's going to happen to her. I keep trying to reassure her, but it doesn't last more than a few minutes at a time."

His hand went to her shoulder. "You're doing a beautiful thing, Sage. Be patient. I know you will. She's not faced the worst of it yet. She's going to need you."

Sage nodded with lips pursed. "She's down here." She went to the master bedroom to retrieve some items then led him to Hailey's room and knocked on the door.

A timid, "Come in," was barely audible.

Sage swung the door open. She and Clay stepped inside. Willow lay in the same position she'd left her in. "Willow, this is my friend, Surgeon Clay Barnes. Clay is going to examine you."

"Clay, this is my friend, Willow." Sage placed clothing in her arms on the bed beside where Willow came to a sitting position. The shoes at her feet didn't appear to have been moved. "Here are a robe and pajamas. I wear a size five; so they might be a big on you, but they'll be comfortable."

Clay pointed to the silky mass on the comforter. "It's nice to meet you, Willow. Why don't you slip out of your things and put the robe on for now?"

Sage smiled. "Yes, that sounds perfect. After you and Clay are done and you've had some food, you can take a long soak in the bath. That will make you feel better. I want you to try the lovely shampoo and conditioner in the guest bathroom."

"Sage, I can't take your things." Her brow furrowed. A tear strolled down her ruddy cheek, and she slid a hand across the silk clothing as though it was precious.

"Nonsense, you most certainly can and will. I have others. This one seemed to be the smallest, so I chose it for you. If you refuse, you'll hurt my feelings. Please take them, Willow. I want you to have them."

"Okay, I'll wear them . . . after I'm clean. I'll wash them and return them to you later."

"Nope, I won't hear of it." Sage backed from the room. "They're gifts to my friend Willow."

Clay followed Sage as she exited. "Change into the robe. I'll wait outside the door. Tell me when you're ready, and I'll come back in."

Clay's patience with the frightened child was heartwarming. Willow was going to endure a lot of changes and intrusion during the next few weeks. Sage was grateful for Clay's understanding and safeguarding of the girl's privacy—as much as he could be.

He closed the door and turned to Sage. "Reduced appetite, irritability, anxiety, panic, paranoia, violent behavior and psychosis are some of the symptoms you may encounter with Willow. It depends on what drugs she's been on. I'll ask her when I examine her."

"That shithead doped her up and kept her in a fog for a few days. In the interim, he sold her virginity and youth to, I suspect, whoever paid the highest price. He gave her injections, probably to keep her controllable for a few days; but when she was awake, she swallowed drugs. She has no real clue what but heard terms Peace, Clarity, Lover's Speed, Ecstasy, Adam, Eve, Molly and Uppers."

"Shit, I was afraid of that. He's got her hooked on Meth. There are lots of names for it. Side effects are mild hallucinogenic episodes, increased sensitivity, empathic feelings, lowered inhibitions, anxiety, chills, sweating, teeth clenching, muscle cramping. She'll be at risk of sleep disturbances, depression, impaired memory, hyperthermia, addiction, reduced appetite, irritability, anxiety, panic, violent behavior and even psychosis. I'll explain the symptoms she's experiencing and will likely have during detox. If she understands, she'll better be able to deal with them. I hope you're prepared for what's about to happen. She's going to have a rough time for a while."

"Whatever it takes, I'll stay with her until she's stronger." Sage was committed to the girl and not about to run out on her.

A mild voice sounded through the closed door. Clay nodded toward the room. "We can talk more after I check her out."

Sage said a silent prayer. Clay disappeared into Willow's room. She went to make lunch for them. Willow would be more likely to eat if they joined her.

Finishing the last touches of their meal, rumbling of Wyatt's truck came through. Only in a rural town like Sweetwater would the sheriff drive a gold colored pickup truck with his designated emblem on doors and necessary light fixture on top for emergency calls.

Sage finished setting the heavy, rustic, wood table for four. She placed a fresh vase of flowers from her garden in the center. She'd picked them earlier, before Willow's call. While lunch cooked, she'd separated them into two smaller bundles, preparing one for Willow's bedside table and one for the dining area centerpiece.

Her handsome husband strode into the room. She rushed into his arms. A hand snaked into his silver mane, and she pulled him down for a leisurely kiss.

"Umm, something smells good. Hope there's enough for me." He cupped her cheeks and pecked her nose then slipped an arm around her waist and walked toward the stove.

"Of course; I knew Reggie would alert you what's going on and figured you'd stop by to eat with us—and to check on me." She winked, hating to alarm her over-protective husband and proud he seemed to be handling her latest escapade with tolerance.

"Yep, Reggie filled me in. Where is she?" He gazed around the empty great room.

"Clay is with Willow now. They shouldn't be much longer. Poor child hasn't eaten for a couple days. She's rail thin. I'm going to put meat on her scrawny bones, if I have to force feed her." She snickered and started filling soup bowls with fragrant beef stew.

He moved to stand behind her, slipping hands around her waist. His hot breath caressed her neck. She shivered

165

delightfully when it grazed her ear. "I have no doubt you'll entice the youngster to indulge. You're the best cook I know. Only Sadie Carson comes near to being as good a chef as my gourmet cooking wife." He nibbled her ear lobe, sending another tantalizing shiver through her body, straight to her core.

"What about Dovie? She's world-renowned for her cooking."

He shrugged, but didn't release her. "Sure, she's amazing. I enjoy French cuisine occasionally. Itearned Cabaret de Fuller a five-star rating. I prefer hearty meals you make— good old American grub."

She spun and kissed him briefly on the lips. The door opened and Clay came out.

"Hi, Wyatt, I guess you've heard about your houseguest." He strolled to shake Wyatt's outstretched hand.

Wyatt graciously greeted their surgeon friend. "Yep, how's our girl doing?"

"Decent. I'll tell you more, when she comes out. She's getting herself together now. That way I only need to go over her condition once."

Relief edged into Sage. Clay's easy attitude encouraged her to believe Willow might be okay.

"She had this in her arm. It had been crudely inserted, and she was told it was a tracker. It looks like a tiny piece of metal from a staple, if you ask me. I'll turn it over to Reggie. She can determine whether it's truly a tracking device or a fake to help make Willow manageable."

"These people certainly are devious." Wyatt opened a small evidence bag he pulled from his hip pocket. Clay inserted the bloody sample in his hand.

"No wonder she was paranoid." Sage could hardly believe what she saw.

The door creaked open. Willow stepped into the room tentatively then stalled realizing Wyatt had joined them. She glanced up and down his uniform and took a step backward.

Sage rushed to her side, wrapped a secure arm around her waist and ushered her to the table where the men stood. "Willow, I'd like you to meet my husband, Sheriff Wyatt Gordon." Feeling air rush from the girl's body, Sage squeezed her arm reassuringly.

Willow turned a shocked face toward Sage. "You're married to a lawman?" Her mouth hung open.

"I am. Wyatt is on your side, Willow. He and I are going to ensure your safety. He wants to support you as much as I do."

Wyatt's patient, lady-killer smile benefitted the frightened child. She eased under his soothing beam and sultry southern drawl. Those looks and voice could melt the heart of women of all ages.

"Hello, Willow; I'm extremely happy to have you as a guest in our home. I want you to know, you can rely on me as well as Sage. She's a good friend to have. I'd like to be your friend also. We won't let anything bad happen to you."

Clay interrupted, "What is that delightful smell? Sage, promised Willow and I lunch. I assume you're joining us, Wyatt."

Wyatt held a chair out for Willow. "Indeed I am. Willow, you're in for a treat. My wife's an excellent cook."

"Please, everyone sit. I'll bring the food over. It's nothing special." Sage winked at her husband, having prepared his favorite meal. "I made beef stew and homemade biscuits."

The threesome took seats. Sage smiled to herself, as Willow leaned as far from the men as possible. Sage placed plates with steaming biscuits and bowls of hearty soup on them. She served the men first then put a plateful in front of the girl and sat one beside Willow for herself. Before taking her chair, Sage brought a jar and tub with utensils, which she placed on the table.

"I bought this fresh honey and homemade butter from an area farmer." She faced the child, who sat staring at her food. "I keep goats and grow vegetables, fruits and grapes for wine, but haven't gotten into bee keeping. Maybe someday." She shrugged.

"Really?" Willow's interest lit her eyes, as she eyed Sage.

"Really, my partner and I tend goats, milk them and make goat cheese and farmer's cheese. When you're feeling better you can come to the farm with me, if you like."

"Wow that would be cool." Willow sat facing the bowl, hands in her lap, without touching it.

Sage started buttered her biscuit then passed the bowl of yellow creaminess to Willow. The men started eating, as though unaware of the ninety-pound elephant at the table. Willow watched them a few seconds, then put a pat on her biscuit and passed the container to Clay.

"Thank you, Willow." He waited until the girl took a testing bite of her meal then glanced casually at her with his spoonful poised midway to his mouth. "Would you mind if I discussed your condition with Wyatt and Sage present?"

Willow studied Wyatt's friendly expression then Sage's nod and mumbled, "It's fine." Willow had already started to act weaker than before. She seemed listless, and her stare was vague. A girl her age should be full of vitality.

"Great; they are concerned for you and will be assisting during recuperation."

Wyatt continued to chew the bite in his mouth but turned attention to Clay.

Clay laid his spoon down and addressed her directly, with clear expectations Sage and Wyatt were to take in his summary. "Willow you seem fine, with exception of malnutrition and drug addiction. I'll send cultures I took to the lab. We should have results in a day or two, but I see no visible signs of disease. You're starting to come down from your last dose of methamphetamine, which from what you and Sage told me, is the mainstay of your drug experience. Withdrawal is going to get worse before it gets better."

Willow must've liked the stew. She stared at her bowl and continued eating as though in a trance, making Sage wonder how much of what Clay explained she absorbed. It was good she allowed Sage and Wyatt to listen.

"You will have aches and pains. Your senses may become hypersensitive—touch, sound, taste, etc. You could experience heavy sweating and chills, muscle cramping, confusion and you may have trouble sleeping. You could have highs and lows, being elated then depressed for no reason. Anxiousness and depression are generally expected. It's possible to have impaired memory. You may hallucinate. These symptoms are normal and temporary. I'm telling you this so you'll be aware when any of these things happen. Understand, they'll subside; you're going to be okay."

The only reaction cluing Willow was listening, engrossed on eating tiny bites, was her head barely nodding as Clay paused—no doubt to give the girl time for his words to sink in. Too much too fast could be disastrous.

He took a bite of biscuit with a dab of honey on it. "Wow, Sage, these are remarkable." Clay spoke directly to Sage this time. "I'm leaving a mild sedative for her with you. Give her one whenever she has bouts of anxiety or depression. I'm also giving you sleeping pills, which are non-addictive, but will relax Willow enough so she can rest. It's important she stays hydrated and that she eats well. I'm sure that won't be a problem living with you. You're an amazing cook."

"Thank you, Clay. That's a sweet compliment. No worries. We're up to this." Sage gripped Wyatt's hand to her side.

169

She hoped her words were true. Willow's life was in her hands.

Clay turned back to Willow. "I'll stop in tomorrow and take your blood pressure. It's slightly elevated, which is to be expected, but not enough to put you on medication. The sedative should help calm you enough. I believe the BP will settle—at least after a few days."

Again, Willow nodded without looking at anyone. She'd eaten half the bowl and taken a couple bites of biscuit by the time the others finished.

Sage was elated. Drugs might've destroyed her appetite, but Hart's control of her food supply had no doubt shrunken Willow's stomach to a minute size. Willow might not have wanted to eat, but had been intrigued by the aromatic stew. She'd partaken more than expected.

With a little work on Sage's part, Willow would be eating normally soon. It might take a few days, because from what Sage had read about detoxing, she expected headaches and vomiting, as well as signs Clay mentioned.

Clay pushed back from the table. "I hate to eat and run, but I have surgery at three to prepare for. This was delicious, Sage. Thank you for lunch." He stood.

Sage followed him to the door. He shoved a couple small bottles into Sage's hands.

"Here are the meds I spoke of. Directions are on the bottles. Call my cell if you need me." The tall man bent and gave Sage a friendly hug. "See you tomorrow."

Clay glanced over Sage's shoulder to the two sitting at the dinner table. "Willow, you have my card, if you want to contact me. You're going to be fine. Goodbye, Willow and Wyatt."

Willow graced him with a weak, closed-mouth smile.

Wyatt threw a hand up. "See you later, Clay. Thanks for doing this."

"No problem." The tall physician waved and existed. Sage closed the door behind him. She went to remove dishes from the table.

Wyatt placed a paw across her wrist as she reached for a bowl. "You've got better things to do. I'll manage this. He stood and kissed her forehead with a sweet, knowing smile.

"Thank you, Darling. I appreciate it. I'll get Willow settled, and we can chat a minute before you return to work."

"No, I've got to run. I'll clean up here and get back to the office. I have a murder investigation going on . . . and other cases." A tilt of his head and raised brow told her more than words.

She nodded and tiptoed to kiss him. He cradled her in his arms and lifted her as he bent his tall frame. It wasn't a long or sensual meeting of the lips, but a warm, understanding caress, saying he was there for her and supported her every need. As they parted, his eyes articulated his appreciation for what she was doing.

"I love you." He pecked her nose and released her.

Wyatt stepped slowly toward Willow, who contemplated him with wary eye. He lifted a hand and placed it on her shoulder. Willow visibly stiffened, but didn't pull away. She sat quietly staring at Wyatt through hooded eyes.

"Willow, we're glad you're here. It was brave and wise of you to contact Sage. We'll keep you safe. You're an extremely strong, young woman, to have gone through hell you've faced. You can handle what is coming, and we'll help you—along with others waiting to do what they can for you. I cannot voice how proud I am of you for coming with Sage."

The girl's eyes teared, but she didn't attempt to hide them or wipe them away. "Thank you, Mr. Gordon . . . Sheriff."

"Please, we're living together. Call me Wyatt. My friends do."

171

Willow gave him a meek smile, without showing teeth.

Wyatt patted her arm gently. "I'll pick Ty up on my way home. See you gals this evening. Wonder what incredible, tasty delight Sage has in store for our dinner." He snickered and waltzed toward the sink with a handful of dishes.

Sage slapped his fine, firm buttocks with a bare hand and laughed. "I'm making baked potatoes and salad. You, my darling husband, are grilling steaks."

He chuckled, as he filled the sink with steaming water and squirted a dollop of dish detergent into the pan. "Can't complain about a big slab of beef, no matter who cooks it. A real man does like to grill, you know."

Sage walked close to Willow. "Grab your jammies. I put a pair of new panties on the bed. Bring them too. I'll start a nice bubble bath for you."

Willow stood and went to her bedroom. Sage entered the guest bath and poured luxurious bath soap into the oval tub. She turned the water on and when it got high enough flipped the jets on.

Feeling Willow's presence behind her, she turned and smiled. "Here you go. Get in, enjoy. Relax long as you want. Shampoo and conditioner are on the side of the tub. You can rinse using that spigot."

Sage pointed to the attached fixture and placed two thick towels on the table beside the bath. She took the garments from Willow and hung them on a hook above the hamper.

Clay had taken a bag with the clothing Willow had previously worn in it. It would, undoubtedly, be tested for evidence and DNA they might need to use in a court case once they prosecuted Hart and his gang.

"You should be comfortable in panties, pajamas and robe. We're going to be lounging around this afternoon, so you can rest. No need for anything more formal. When you feel up to it, we'll go shopping for clothing."

"I've got no cash to shop with."

"No worries; it'll be my treat." She smoothed oily locks off Willow's head. "It would be my pleasure."

"I can't ask you to do that. You've done enough." Willow looked like a blow up doll with a slow leak, wilting more by the minute.

"It would be my pleasure."

"What about dinner, when Sheriff Gordon gets home? I'll be in pajamas."

"No problem. You can have dinner in jammies tonight. Wyatt will understand." Sage noted Willow's reluctance to call Wyatt by his first name. She'd warm up to him in time. Wyatt had a way with the ladies—no matter the age.

Lynda Rees

CHAPTER 22

The afternoon had been uneventful, except the child had bouts of nausea, dry mouth, dizziness, confusion, itching and sometimes was barely able to breath. She had all this loveliness and possible constipation to look forward do. A couple bouts of quivering and vomiting had Sage holding Willow's hair. She'd experienced a couple bouts of heavy sweating; overheating then chills, but a mild sedative appeared to have helped.

Willow had picked at the meat and only taken a few bites, but downed the entire baked potato and half the salad. "I can't remember when I last ate vegetables."

"Well, get used to it. I'm a farmer. We eat lots of veggies around here." Sage smiled at Willow as she wiped butter off her toddler's cheeks and laughed. "I'll be damned if I know how this boy gets food in his ears."

Willow giggled. Ty grinned at the girl like a flirting teenager, showing off his baby teeth. "Wiwwo."

"I think he likes me."

Wyatt chuckled. "My boy adores pretty women."

175

"Like his father." Sage winked at her man.

Willow acted friendly, but wary of Wyatt, as they watched television in the evening. She went to bed early. Sage gave her a sleeping pill.

Far as she could tell, Willow had slept until she awoke and wandered into the kitchen wearing pajamas with Hailey's gym shoes. Ty was fed and playing with blocks in the living room floor.

Sage was making coffee. "Good morning, Willow. I hope you're hungry. I'm making Belgium waffles with blueberries and cream. Do you drink coffee?" Sage poured two cups and handed one to Wyatt, as he appeared wearing his uniform.

"Thank you, Babe." He accepted the cup and kissed her lips briefly then went to sit beside where Willow had plopped at the table. "Whether you're hungry or not, you'd be insane to pass up Sage's waffles."

Willow snickered but didn't answer. She turned to Sage. "No, I prefer milk."

Sage nodded and filled a tall glass then sat it in front of her. "Drink up. Waffles will be ready in a few minutes."

By the time fragrant squares of crispy delight were ready to serve, Willow had finished the entire glass. Sage brought the container and without speaking, refilled it. She took Wyatt's cup and poured steaming, black brew for him. She returned with a plate of breakfast for Wyatt. He poured syrup on the stack then sipped coffee with a grateful smile.

"Thanks, Babe."

Sage brought two more plates heaped with delicacies and placed one in front of Willow, the other at her seat between her husband and the girl. "I hope you like bacon. It's my favorite."

Willow stared at the mound of three thick waffles, layered with freshly made whipped cream and fruit. Beside them lay four crisp pieces of meat. Her head tilted upward as she inhaled, testing the aroma. Smell of bacon and sugar would do the trick and get the young gal's taste buds begging for satisfaction, if anything would.

"Did you sleep well?" Sage glanced at Willow then back at her plate.

"I did. I was out soon as my head hit the pillow. I don't think I stirred until I heard you rustling around in here."

"Sorry I woke you."

"It's okay. I'm good."

Sage reached a hand and patted Willow's arm. Then she pretended to ignore her guest and poured maple syrup on her food. "Yum, this is my favorite meal in the world." Without asking, she pushed the syrup container toward Willow. "Let's eat." Sage cut her food and stuffed a bite into her mouth.

Willow did likewise, and before long the meat had disappeared from her plate along with more than half the waffles. Sage ate slowly giving Willow as much time as necessary, not wanting to rush the child's meal. When Willow laid her fork down and pushed back from the table, a hand went to her stomach. "Wow, that was the best thing I've had in . . . I can't remember."

Sage chuckled. "Thank you, Willow. I appreciate the compliment. I love to cook. There's nothing satisfying as feeding people." Sage gave a quick wink Wyatt's direction.

Sage began clearing the table. Willow stood and carried her dishes to the sink. Sage wiped the table down and prepared a soapy pan of water. "Thanks, Willow. Why don't you join Wyatt? He has something you can help him with. I can handle washing dishes."

Willow looked like a child being sent to the principal's office, but didn't argue. She sat with a chair between herself and Wyatt.

"Thank you, Willow. I need your assistance with a case."

177

"I don't know how I can help." The baffled expression on her face was what Sage expected.

"A young girl was murdered recently in the home of a local businessman. She had a tattoo like yours with one star in the middle."

Willow's hand went to the heart on her neck, surrounding a star. "She must've been one of Hart's girls."

"Yes, we believe she was another victim, like you brought into prostitution by Cecil Hart. I need you to tell me about the tattoo." Wyatt rested hands on the table.

Willow glanced at the floor beside her then at her hands clenched in her lap. "Hart has girls. I don't know how many. He brings some guy in to tattoo them—us . . . when we first come. He told me if I loved him and was devoted, I'd let them mark my neck with his brand. It shows everyone I'm proud to be his woman."

Wyatt touched the table in front of her with a flat palm. "Willow, it's okay. Go on."

"I did it, thinking I was his only woman. Then he stopped staying with me. He said he can't sleep with me in his bed. He's got another room of his own. I've heard voices. There are other girls—women—Hart's other women. He slapped me around when I asked about them. He said I have no reason to be jealous and never to question him about anything. He loved me and I should trust him. The other girls didn't matter—but they do."

"I believe you're right. This was one of Hart's girls. She was slain by a John."

Willow looked like she wanted to toss her breakfast, but gulped air and swallowed hard then clamped lips together.

"That could've been you, Willow. How often did Hart hit you?" Tenderness in her husband's eyes nearly made Sage burst into tears.

Willow's head tilted, and her shoulder rose and fell. "I don't know—a lot. Sometimes he brought Shiv in to do it, while he watched. Shiv was worse. I think he liked beating me. I finally learned what not to do, and how to please Hart. I couldn't question him about anything or complain. I had to . . . be good with him in bed."

"I'm sure you're a quick learner." Wyatt blinked back what Sage knew were tears.

Who wouldn't be a quick learner, when their life depended on it?

"We'll get to Shiv. I'm interested in the design Hart marked you with and Hart first of all. Are all the tats the same?"

"No, some have more stars. I haven't seen the other girls, but Yolanda has five. She told me it's because she's Hart's top girl. I think she's jealous of the other girls, but she's afraid to question Hart too; so she doesn't show it much. The higher up you're graded on Hart's list, the more stars you get."

"What makes Yolanda special?" Sage admired steadiness and lack of expression on her husband's congenial face. She'd be a basket case examining Willow this way.

"She turns tricks too, but mostly steady customers she's been with a long time. Yolanda helped me get started, took me shopping—at the thrift store, cut and dyed my hair and took photos of me. She posted anad on a website to get business for me. I needed to work, to help support myself and Hart, so he could take care of me. He said I had to pull my own weight and help pay room and board—and drugs I needed."

"You realize you're only involved in substance abuse because he made you that way. He did it so you'd be easier to manage. Willow, I'm not sure what you understand about your situation. You are Hart's business inventory, a

179

commodity—you and the other girls—even Yolanda, to be used, sold, traded to reap the largest profit possible—or to be disposed of as he sees fit. He uses you women to make a living—illegally. You're stock to him, nothing more."

Willow looked Wyatt in the eye for the first time, blinking back tears that came anyway. "I heard him and Shiv talking about disposing of stock. They've been arguing loudly a lot more than normal. I got scared. That's why I called Sage. What did he mean by *disposing of stock*?"

Sage dried hands and moved to place them reassuringly on Willow's quaking shoulders. Willow blinked up at her, sniffed then returned focus on Wyatt.

He wasn't about to beat around the bush. Wyatt would give it to Willow straight. She needed to hear it.

"It probably means they intend to move or sell girls to the highest bidder. Slaves like you are bought and sold easily, moved in and out of the country and used for a variety of purposes. A few are sold to people who truly want children and resort to illegal means to get them; but those are generally babies and toddlers." Wyatt glanced at Ty, still playing in the floor. "This is rare and the best case scenario. Sometimes girls—or boys—are used by drug traffickers to carry illegal substances to other locations or in or out of the country. You might be forced to ingest them so you can pass security inspections at check points—airports or borders. Other times drugs are inserted into your body surgically, to avoid detection. You can be sold as slaves to do work and provide sex or peddled to another pimp and moved to a new district. It's a difficult business to identify. Your tattoo and that of the deceased girl are the first breaks we've had to pinpoint human trafficking operations in this area. You have power to rescue those Hart has preyed on. You can save not only yourself, but other girls in Hart's stable."

Willow's shoulders shivered beneath Sage's palms. Sage bent and kissed the top of her head, smelling honeysuckle conditioner and shampoo on her fresh hair. "You can do this, Willow. Help Wyatt, please—and help you," Sage cooed.

"I can't stop them. What can I do?" Willow's cheeks rose. Her brow furrowed. Tears of fear welled in her beautiful brown eyes.

"Where was Hart keeping you? Do you know where he lives? Do you know his full name?"

Willow's head rocked side-to-side. "We live in an old storefront building on the corner of Main Street and Second. The front windows are painted white, but we never use that entrance. We go in through a stairway to the second floor. My room is near the front, where Shiv has a couch near the door. I hear everyone coming and going and some conversation. It's muffled, so I don't catch much. Girls whimper or speak as they're moved in and out. Mostly I hear Shiv, Yolanda and Hart. Hart has a room there, but it's large and really nice. It's where he took me when we first met. I thought we were going to live there together. I woke up in my own room."

"It's not so nice?" Sage asked with no intonation in her voice.

"No, it's a twin bed, a lamp on the floor. Nothing else and it's not clean."

"I see, and Hart? Can you describe him?" Wyatt sat deeper in his chair.

"I don't know his name, but I think it's Cecil. He told me to call him Hart, and the rest doesn't matter. He's about my height, thin, with dreadlocks coming to mid-back that he wears in a ponytail. He dresses super snazzy. Hart's really handsome and sweet when he wants to me." Her face took a dreamy expression as she recalled her captor.

181

"I'm sure he is, when the purpose suits his needs. He has to look good and act nice to entice victims in. Once he has you in his grasp, he drugs and beats you, so you're pliable and will do whatever he says. I'd guess he pulls out the charm and acts loving when it works for him. Keeping you loyal and in fear makes you easy to control." Wyatt's voice didn't judge, only informed Willow of the facts. She'd make her own judgement.

Her gaze showed Wyatt wasn't wrong.

"You're no longer in his stable, Willow. You're free." Sage spoke as calmly as her frazzled heart would allow.

She whimpered. "I don't feel free. Scared, maybe."

Sage patted her shoulder. "You have nothing to fear. We'll protect you."

"Those people are not coming near you again, Willow. Mark my words." Wyatt's voice was emphatic.

Willow nodded.

"Tell me about Shiv and Yolanda." Wyatt clasped hands in his lap.

"Yolanda is tall, black and skinny. It's all I know. I guess she lives in the house too." She gulped a few deep breaths. "Shiv is there to protect us. He's armed with a gun but prefers his knife. It's big and ugly. I've seen it. He threatened to cut my throat with it, but beat me instead. I think Hart told him not to kill me, only scare me."

"Yes, no doubt into submission."

"Yes, and so I wouldn't question Hart—no matter what."

"We get it. What else?" Wyatt didn't move.

"I don't know much else. Mostly Shiv protects the house. Johns go through him as they come to the house. He drives me to Johns when I have to go to them. He waits around to make sure I'm safe and handles the money. Once I had to go to another city. He took me on a bus and made sure I didn't talk to stranger. It felt rude, when some lady sat beside me and tried to talk. He gave me a bad eye, so I ignored her and stared at the floor. I'm watched—protected, even when they allow me to go to the store to steal food." She glanced up at Sage, smiled and swiped a tear.

"Sage tells me you lied to get away."

"Yes, and I'm sure Shiv or Yolanda was watching. They can't see the storefront of the drug store from the house, so I'm pretty sure they didn't see me go past it into the alley and jump in Sage's van. I'm sure they came looking for me. They won't let me out of their sight for long. I had a tracking device. Dr. Clay took it out." She rolled her arm over to show Wyatt the Band-Aid.

"By now they realize you've run away. They're probably searching for you. More than ever, they're likely getting nervous with you gone. It sounds like they were already concerned about something. We have limited time to put a stop to their operation before they move it and can't be traced. What you're telling me is important. I want you to be proud of yourself for helping save those children. We're going to do everything we can to get you healthy, well and on your feet. You deserve a great future. We're also going to catch whoever is leading this ring and those running it."

"Hart too?" Her eyes teared.

Wyatt nodded solemnly. "Hart too—he's a bad man—the worst—and has done horrible things to you and others. He's responsible for that girl's death and God knows what else. You owe Hart nothing. He doesn't love you—only the money your body put in his pocket."

Willow meekly nodded.

"Do you realize your mother is looking for you?" Sage spoke softly.

Willow looked up with hooded eyes. "No, I figured she'd be glad I was out of her hair, or hadn't noticed I was gone. I can't go back. You haven't called her. Have you?" Moisture welled in her eyes.

Sage knelt, facing Willow and cupped her trembling hands. "It's going to be fine, Willow. We won't force you to return to a harmful situation. You are a minor. The law requires we let your legal guardian—your mother—know where you are. She's sincerely worried for you and has been searching day and night. Having exhausted search efforts in and around Bonnyville, about a month ago she started outward and landed in Wyatt's office with flyers. I saw the photo hanging on the billboard in the precinct and recognized you. The National Center for Missing and Exploited Children is also searching for you."

Willow gulped hard as her head dunked. She drew in a heavy breath and shoulders rose and fell. "I had no idea she'd care so much. She barely had time for me after Dad died."

Sage brushed a hand against Willow's cheek. "Apparently she loves you and noticed you more than you knew. She's frantic."

Wyatt leaned toward the females. "We haven't called her yet, but at some point we must."

Sage stood, continuing to hold Willow's hands. "How about we talk this through later? We have guests arriving soon, and Wyatt needs to get to the office."

Willow nodded with a shrug. Wyatt took the hint, stood and took Sage by the shoulders for a brief kiss. "Call if you gals need me."

"Thank you." Sage hated the fell of him releasing her. The day was about to get juicier.

Shae strolled into the office like he'd only been there the day before. Reggie looked up from her desk with a scowl.

"How's it going, Casse?" He rounded his desk.

Reggie retrieved the note and tossed it onto his desk then went back to her computer screen trying to ignore the scent of him. She'd craved that fragrance since their last night together, and it drove her mad.

She snorted. "I didn't miss you, Montgomery, but someone did."

In her peripheral vision he read the card, shook his head then headed to the door.

"Running away again, Montgomery?" *Or running to?* Snootiness had its hold on Reggie, regardless whether she had a right to jealousy.

"I'll check with you later. I've got news." He winked as though he didn't care he'd broken her spirit.

Her heart sank further into the depths it had been treading water in. She spoke to the door closing behind his tight behind. "I'm sure you do."

Reggie had thought they'd made progress, had something going for them as a potential couple. The dumbass knew she'd assumed he'd left town for an assignment. He could've mentioned he was going to reconcile with his ex.

She should've known better to think she might find true love, like her friends had; or that she might find some semblance of normalcy in her own life.

Reggie and Carla entered the door Sage held open. A puny, fidgeting teenager slumped on the couch in front of the rock fireplace, picking at her cuticles.

Sage's brilliant smile and attitude made it sound like a social call. She was one smart cookie. "I'm so happy you two could join us today. I've made my special white chicken chili for lunch."

"Thanks, Sage; somehow I figured you'd feed us." Reggie pecked Sage's cheek as she accepted the warm hug. "You remember Carla Orson, don't you?"

Sage shook Carla's hand. The chunky, middle-aged woman could've been a soccer mom, dressed in a casual velour track suit with her long, brown curls pulled into a ponytail. Her sunny disposition and fierce love for children made her perfect for her chosen field.

"Welcome to our home, Carla." Sage led the women to where the child was seated. "I'd like to introduce you both to my houseguest and friend, Willow. Willow, this is my dearest friend, Reggie Casse and Carla Orson. Reggie is an FBI Special Agent, and Carla heads up the local branch of the National Center for Missing and Exploited Children. I've asked them here today to speak with you. They're going to help me take care of you, until you're able to do it for yourself."

Carla sat on the other end of the sofa, leaving an arm's length between her and Willow. Reggie took a seat beside Sage on the second divan facing them.

"I'm pleased to meet you Willow. It takes guts to do what you've done, and run away from your captors. I admire your strength." Reggie relaxed into the seat.

Carla laid hands nonchalantly in her lap. "Yes, Willow; we all do. You're a brave, strong young woman. Like your friend Sage, we're here to help you. Feel free to ask us anything."

Willow's brows furrowed as she scanned the women. "Why are you all so concerned for me? I'm nobody." Mistrust was clearly written on her pale face.

Reggie took the bull by the horns. "I became an FBI agent because I wanted to fight injustice. What has happened to you is the vilest kind of criminal act. You are an innocent child who has suffered abuse and exploitation. I want to put an end to that—for you and others."

Carla nodded, appearing unflappable. "Yes, Willow, I joined the NCMEC for the same reason. I was an abused child, sexually assaulted and brutalized by a family member in my own home. I was fortunate enough to find help and decided to do everything in my power to help other children do the same. We realize you're going through physical trauma at the present. Drug withdrawal is difficult, regardless how it's managed. Keep in mind it is temporary. Before long, you'll be healthy and strong, without need for drugs. Soon, you're going to need to deal with long-term effects of your situation. I can help with that. My organization provides victim and family support to enable you cope with the traumatic experience. It's going to require courage and determination, which you've proved you have. We assist with emotional support; provide referrals for community agencies and health professionals that offer assistance. I can connect you with peers going through or having experienced similar trials and can assist with reunification."

"I can't afford all that. I have no money. Hart kept the cash I earned." Willow's eyes blinked several times, and her lips slightly pouted.

Carla shook her head. "No, Willow. There is no charge. My organization is funded by government and private donors. We're here for you, Willow—no matter what." She handed Willow a business card with her name, job classification, her direct line number, *NCMEC, 1-877-446-2632 ext. 6117* and website *MissingKids.org* printed on it.

Willow stared blindly at the card and sniffed loudly. "What is reunification?" She eyed Carla with a frown.

"NCMEC has a network of trained parent volunteers who have been impacted by the sexual exploitation of a child to counsel others experiencing the same. We can provide guidance and support to you and your family."

"My mom don't know I'm here." She glanced at Sage who nodded, then back at Carla.

Reggie took the cue. "Not yet, Willow; but the law is clear. You're a minor. We must alert your legal guardian, which in your case is your mother. She's concerned for your safety and seems to be desperately searching for you."

Willow appeared to be chewing the inside of her jaw. "That's what Wyatt and Sage said. I don't want to go back there."

Reggie wasn't sure the child was buying the story about her mother. That was a problem for another day.

Carla continued to act composed. No doubt, she'd been through this scenario many times. "No one is going to force you to return to a situation that won't allow you to heal. We'll work together with you and your mother, to determine how to manage your recovery and, if you choose to in the future, transition back to your family."

"She can't make me go back?" Willow ducked her head as she spoke.

"No, dear; no one is going to force you to do anything from now on. You have the power in this situation. It's good you're a courageous young woman." Carla reached and patted Willow's frail hand.

Reggie moved to sit at the edge of her seat and clasped hands together, elbows on knees. "Together, we'll get you through this. Carla's organization and mine, the FBI, will work together to get your photographs and advertisements off the dark web."

"Yolanda said she posted one photo on the internet." Willow seemed to study Reggie's face.

"So far, I've found a dozen shots of you on as many websites. My team is doing a thorough search and working with hosts to get as many of them removed as possible. We have less control over some than others, depending on the country location of the server; but it will be an ongoing process we will not stop."

Willow's head rocked back. She inhaled loudly. Her eyes rounded and mouth fell open. "You think my mom has seen them?"

Reggie shook her head. "Doubtful, unless she frequents pornography and sex-for-sale sites."

Carla faced Willow. "You have legal rights that have been infringed by many. I can put you in touch with legal representation to assist you with seeking retribution from parties involved—when you're ready. First, we need to get you healthy, strong, and on the road to full recovery."

Reggie took the opportunity. "My team will be working with The Marshal's Services and Wyatt Gordon's team to catch the criminals who did this to you, Willow. You've met Sheriff Wyatt, Sage's husband. I'd hoped to introduce you to my counterpart in The Marshal's Services, Marshal Shae Montgomery. He is otherwise detained today." Sour bile

189

flowed from her stomach, through her esophagus and across Reggie's taste buds. She swallowed firmly to get rid of it.

Sage shot Reggie a questioning look. Reggie winked at her. She'd fill Sage in later in the latest episode of *Reggie Screws Up Her Screwed Up Life Once Again.*

Damn men, anyway.

Shae had texted Carla and Reggie while they ate lunch with Sage and Willow, telling them to meet him at Gordon's office. She'd texted him back that Willow was safely at Sage's home. When the women arrived, Shae, Leo, Jaiden and Wyatt were assembled in Wyatt's glass-lined cubical.

"Glad you ladies made it before we began. Marshal Montgomery has news." Wyatt shook their hands, and they took two empty seats.

Reggie groaned inside at having to sit across from Shae. She'd have a hell of a time avoiding his gaze. *Why did he grow his hair out*, like she'd suggested. Her fingers itched to skim through its silkiness; and he smelled so freaking good, she could nearly taste him on her lips.

Shae nodded. "You're aware as a U. S. Marshal one of my duties is to oversee WITSEC enrollees. I've been protecting a man relocated to Sweetwater. He was working recently at the estate of a local businessman and witnessed what he recognized as criminal activity. He should know. Criminal instincts run deep. Anyway, I left town for a few days to take him into protective custody, until he was assigned a new identity and escorted him to his new home location. He provided this taped interview, giving details of what he heard and saw. It appears to be relevant to the current child sex ring we're investigating and connects a prominent citizen to a trafficking organization."

He'd been working after all, at least part of the time. Reggie focused on the recording Shae played, without meeting his eyes.

A male voice in a New Jersey accent told how he'd been landscaping at the residence of Sebastian Bryant. "The first thing I noticed was one evening as I finished mowing the lawn. Several sleazy dressed, young women were ushered through the service entrance from a black van. I went to piss in the servant's restroom. I went into the galley area where maids were preparing for a party. I overheard two men arguing in another room, when I stepped back into the kitchen area to get a drink.I never seen them fancy girls again."

The next thing he saw was the morning after the warehouse manager was murdered. "I heard about that girl and dude getting murdered on the morning news a couple weeks later. Later that day, I was working at the same suspicious joint. Two agitated looking thugs rushed into the house through the front entrance. They left their damned fancy, black truck blocking my work truck in. I couldn't get the fucking mower out. I went inside to see if I could find them so's they could move their vehicle. The head housekeeper told me I'd best not approach those lunatics. She'd called 'em dangerous, and advised me to wait until

191

they left. A door opened somewhere within hearing distance and a loud voice boomed. 'Get the hell out and never come here again. You know better. You dumb shits can't even keep your own noses clean. I should have you put down like the rabid dogs you are.' Now, I'm no stranger to that kinda talk. I ain't no fool. I backed my truck out without doing my job, called Marshal Montgomery and went home to pack my bag. It was time for me to get outta Dodge—if you know what I mean."

Shae shut the recording off. "I immediately instigated procedures to reposition him. These are the two men my witness saw." He laid photographs of Conway Perkins and Cecil Hart on the desk.

"Hell, this is fucking awesome. This ties Hart and Perkins to Bryant. They're in it together, and now we know who to boss is." Reggie didn't try to hide elation. "Perkins was identified by Willow as Shiv, the Protector. She identified Hart as her pimp. They're running sex for hire using under-aged children. This ties the trafficking game to Bryant. Now we know how he earned the dough he's got invested in real estate and other holdings. I'd guess many of his assets are being used for illegitimate business. At least this one and probably many more are used for illicit trade. My people will check it out. We've pinpointed those locations we believe he owned that could be involved. I want a massive sting to take them all down at once. We need to get all these bastards. No one walks out of this shindig without a party favor—I prefer handcuffs myself."

Wyatt snickered, as did Shae.

Leo bit his upper lip then spoke. "We now know who the local king pen is. If this is a national or regional ring run by a single person, it might be Bryant; or there could be someone above him on the food chain—someone more powerful."

Wyatt's head bounced. He sucked his upper lip in. "Wewon't know until the guy is in custody, and we can put the screws to him."

Shae bit the side of his bottom lip. "My main concern is taking down Bryant and possibly missing out on catching whoever is pulling his strings. If they're nervous, we'd best act quickly."

Reggie twisted her neck to release tension. "We need to rattle Bryant's cage."

Wyatt pursed lips and nodded then leaned back in his over-sized, leather chair. "I've got enough to subpoena their phone records and trace their lines. Maybe we'll get lucky. In the meantime, Deputy Coldwater has been on sting with Deputy Sanders for backup, working the mall near Bonnyville. We learned from our recently rescued victim, as we previous assumed, the pimp is scoping that area for possible abductees. It's where he picked Willow up."

Jaiden's chin went high. "Yes, sure enough, I hung out there Friday and this morning. A good-looking dude approached me. He was all charming and sickeningly sympathetic and concerned for my abusive home life. He offered to take me away from my brutal daddy and make my life a bed of roses with him as my *boyfriend*."

The beautiful part-Choctaw, part-Irish, ex-Texas Ranger-turned Sweetwater deputy's pert nose snarled. Her voice braced with contempt. Jaiden Coldwater was well known for ferocious defense of downtrodden, especially women and children. They were lucky having her on this case.

Leo nodded and placed a photograph on the desk. "I posed as a maintenance man and kept eyes on Jaiden. I spotted the guy long before he approached Jaiden. He was prowling around the facility appraising potential targets. He watched Jaiden from afar several times before making contact. I was sure he'd spot her. He's the same guy I photographed going into the building across from Chloe's real estate office. His name is Cecil Hart—Willow's pimp."

Wyatt tented his fingers. "Willow confirmed the murdered prostitute was one of Hart's girls. She didn't personally see her but recognized the tattoo as Hart's."

Reggie leaned forward and viewed the photo. "Yes, Willow identified him as her *boyfriend*. She confirmed the building you're speaking of is where she was kept." Reggie snickered at Wyatt. "So much for your theory the new owner intended to sell the property or tear it down and put in a strip mall."

Wyatt shrugged and blinked.

Leo sneered. "Yep, guess Chloe won't be getting that listing."

Wyatt regarded Shae then turned to Reggie. "We filled Shae in on the girl."

Wyatt knew her too well. He'd obviously picked up on her avoidance of Shae's gaze.

Reggie nodded her thanks to her dear friend. No doubt, Sage would fill him in on *Reggie's lost before found love life*, once she updated his wife.

Got to love the Sweetwater grapevine.

"This is great work, people." Reggie chewed her lip. "We need to act before something worse happens or these guys skip out. They're influential and extremely careful. If they move, we may never catch them. Willow said Hart and Perkins were on edge and arguing. It must have to do with the dead John and Chloe's and Wyatt's interest in the property they're using as a crib."

Jaiden turned to Reggie. "Hart tried to convince me to leave with him this morning. I told him I had something I must do, but I'd be back this afternoon."

"Awesome." A plan formulated in Reggie's mind. She sat straight to explain her idea to the rest.

Lynda Rees

CHAPTER 23

Jaiden plopped her backpack beside her on the mall pavilion bench and slumped into the seat. She sighed heavily and twisted her neck with a visible cringe. A hand went to her extremely made up face, as though neck pain made her recall a traumatic incident that her cheek bore evidence of. She pulled out a bedazzled, purple phone and began absently playing a game.

Before log Cecil Hart slid onto the seat beside her. "Oh, baby, what happened?" He cooed, gently touching her bruised cheek with a cool, manicured finger.

She pocketed the glitzy telephone and shrugged, gazing at the floor. "Pa wasn't happy when he got home, finding me gone and breakfast not ready. He noticed I took the five dollar bill off his dresser, so I could come here earlier for coffee and those special donuts I love." She glanced toward the food bar where they'd met early that morning.

His face exhibited what appeared as genuine concern. The dude was a talented actor. "Damn, girl, if you were mine that bastard couldn't touch you. I'd protect you so no one could hurt you." Hart's arm slipped around her, and he pulled so her head rested on his shoulder. "Come away with me, Jaiden. Be my girl."

197

She gazed into his bright, obsidian eyes questioningly. "Really?"

"Sure; I can take care of you. You'll never want for anything."

She blinked back tears recalling her devoted, loving father. Tears came easy, since he'd only died a couple years back. "Why me?"

He pulled away enough to look her in the eyes. "Why? Because you're amazing, and I love you."

She swiped tears with the back of her hand. "Pa said I'm ugly, and no man would ever want a half-breed freak." She sniffed and shuffled feet.

Jaiden had dressed to look the part of a disgruntled teen with raven hair in a messy top knot. Booted feet accompanied a too-short, tight skirt and slutty crop top exposing her tight abs.

Hart seemed to buy her awkward youngster act. He pulled a box from his leather jacket pocket. "I bought you something."

The jeweler's box didn't appear new, but might fool a young person. Jaiden allowed eyes to widen, showing delight as he opened it and pulled out a shiny red bauble on a gold chain.

"It's a heart like your name." She gasped.

His wide smile displayed straight, white teeth contrasting with his glistening, coffee-colored skin. Well-groomed and snazzydressed; Hart presented an enticing package, well suited to lure unsuspecting souls into his trap.

Jaiden played along, allowing him to secure the necklace around her neck, wondering if it was the same jewelry he'd given then taken from Willow, once she was drugged into unconsciousness.

"Oh, Hart, it's beautiful." Her hand caressed the pendant lying against her collarbone. It felt like a noose ready to strangle her, but she hid emotions and continued playing the role.

"I'm glad you like it." He took her hand. "Let's grab food and to eat in peace at my place. What do you want for lunch?"

She noted he hadn't given her an option to not join him, by distracting with a different choice. She snatched her backpack and allowed him to tug her toward the food court.

"I've never had Chinese, but it smells so good."

"Chinese it is." He didn't slow their pace toward the area of the mall emitting enticing aromas. Hart ordered several dishes then paid cash from a thick wad of bills pulled from his pants.

Jaiden made her eyes widen at the sight; and he hid a quick, smug look as it came across his face. Hart escorted her outside to a black, shiny truck.

"Wow, is this yours?" She asked as he helped her climb inside.

He rounded the vehicle and climbed aboard. "Of course." He fired the engine, watching her reaction.

She wore a sad face. "Pa had a new truck . . . but some guy stole it in the middle of the night and returned it to the dealer, when Pa didn't make payments." She ran a hand across the clean dash.

Hart snickered. "No one is taking mine. It's bought and paid cash for." He patted the wheel and took her hand, holding it until he pulled into the empty lot behind what resembled an abandoned building.

"Where are we?" She forced surprise into her eyes, though she'd known their destination.

"Home; don't worry. I like the outside this way. It masks what I've turned into a beautiful home safe from nosey eyes." He hopped out. When she didn't follow, he waltzed around and opened her door.

199

Sure you do—and a stable full of young girls living in appalling conditions in other rooms.

Hart helped her to the pavement and tugged her toward the staircase leading to the second floor. She tried to keep up the persona of a frightened teenager showing hesitancy, but let him coax her to enter.

A bulky, tall, middle-aged man lounged on a grungy sofa in the dimly lit hallway. Willow had referred to him as Shiv, but Jaiden knew is true identity. He flicked off the television screen on the wall and sprang to his feet.

"Hi, boss." The reference was for Jaiden's benefit. Doubtful he called Cecil Hart boss regularly. It was part of the act.

"Jaiden this is Shiv. He's my—our—bodyguard. He keeps us safe and watches out for my investments."

She swallowed bile the remark caused and stayed in character. "Wow, you must be successful." Her tone showed she was impressed.

"Definitely," Shiv responded.

"Shiv, this beautiful creature is my girlfriend, Jaiden."

She forced a blush to her cheeks.

"Pleased to meet you, Miss Jaiden." Shiv played along in what was surely a well-rehearsed game they'd acted out many times.

Hart pulled Jaiden to the end of a corridor past several closed doors. One was marked with an ancient, dusty EXIT tag above it. She and the others had studied schematics of the building before she'd gone to the mall to make contact with Hart. So she scoped out the location and found it to be as expected.

He opened a door to an elaborately furnished, immaculate room with a king-sized bed to one side and a stainless steel and quarts kitchenette to the other. An L-shaped leather sofa in the back faced a gigantic television screen attached to a wall.

"That Jaiden is one cool cookie. It's not easy keeping a sound head in an undercover situation." Reggie listened to her com as she, Shae, Wyatt and a host of deputies and FBI agents poised in position.

Leo had been watching at the shopping center and trailed the couple to Hart's crib. He slipped into his assigned spot. "That's my partner."

Wyatt's smooth, southern twang came through the equipment. "Jaiden is one determined protector of the innocent. She'll do whatever necessary to catch these assholes."

Their earpieces provided access to Hart's continuing to woo Jaiden while they ate. Everyone waited for Jaiden's signal.

When Hart offered her pills to enhance their lovemaking, she hesitated. "I don't know. I've never done drugs."

"Seriously? Not even with friends?" He pushed the idea like it should cause an actual teen to feel ashamed, like she alone had missed out on the world's greatest pleasure.

Reggie was impressed. "This dude is good."

Shae spoke in a low tone. "Yep, he's a professional dirt bag, expert at brainwashing."

"I don't have friends," Jaiden's voice whimpered.

Hart pressed Jaiden toward the bed, but stalled at the loud slam sounding from the hallway. The FBI stormed the back entrance. Shots rang out.

Shiv wouldn't go down easily, but was quickly subdued. A bullet wound seeped red flow on his tee shirt, as Reggie and her team burst in.

Hart flung his apartment door wide and pulled a weapon from beneath his shirt. Shae and Wyatt faced him, guns drawn and pointed at his direction. Wyatt, Shae and Leo had accessed the staircase. The internal exit Jaiden and Hart had passed on the way in led to a storage room behind the first floor storefront, where the FBI had breached earlier as the lawmen prepared to storm the building.

Hart's face greyed. He flicked his pistol to hang from a thumb and put hands in the air. Wyatt retrieved the firearm and turned Hart around as. Shae frisked him for other weapons. Wyatt turned Hart over to Leo and Shae, and strode toward Reggie and her crew.

Facing Jaiden, Hart's mouth widened. Jaiden stood feet apart, handgun targeting his chest. "You're a fucking cop?"

"You bet 'cha, Lover Boy. Deputy Jaiden Coldwater at your service."

Leo spun Hart around and winked at her. "You want to do the honors, partner?"

She slapped handcuffs on the fancy black man. "Now I'm taking you for a ride, Cecil Hart; only you're not going to like where you're headed. She read him Maranda Rights and shovedhim into the corridor, where his cohort was being pushed out the rear doorway by one of Reggie's people.

Reggie and Shae began clearing the first of several closed doors. A scrawny girl, looking to be about twelve, huddled in the furthest corner of a metal-framed, twin bed made up with a stained, dirty sheet. A ragged blanket clutched against her bare chest, terror in her eyes.

Reggie lowered her shooter and approached the child. "It's okay, Hon. We're here to free you. The girl took Reggie's outreached hand with her shaky one and stood. Reggie blinked back tears.

With no top and only panties, bare skin exposed welts formed across the child's back and arms. Dark circles pooled with moisture seeping from her hollow eyes. From the odor, she'd not been allowed to bath.

"I'm FBI Special Agent Reggie Casse. Let's get you out of this dump." Reggie pulled the nasty blanket around the child's frail, underfed body and smiled, noting the girl's neck. As she walked the girl past Shae she whispered, "She must've been a recent acquisition."

Reggie issued the captive into the corridor where a kind-faced officer took charge. "This gentleman will get you to the hospital so you can be treated. You're safe now."

With a meek nod, the young woman followed orders.

Reggie nodded to Shae. He unveiled what waited behind door number two.

Reggie, Wyatt and Shae sipped coffee in Wyatt's office. Wyatt leaned back into his chair. "Jaiden is staying with Carla and the kids at the hospitaluntil they're released. She'll accompany them to the safe house Carla arranged."

Reggie sat her cup down. "Not a bad day. We saved six girls, a boy and Yolanda from worse than certain death."

Shae's eyes remained on Wyatt, obviously avoiding hers. "Carla's made arrangements for their treatment, including removal of tattoos. She'll help them reunite with families, if possible. She says most can—eventually. Some prefer never to. It depends on circumstances."

Wyatt grimaced. "Yolanda is nineteen. Far as we can tell, she's been in the trade for five years and with Hart and Shiv since before they located in Sweetwater. She's going to be a tough nut to crack. Devotion to Hart makes her not want to talk. They're all loyal to a point, except the newest one."

Reggie shook her head in awe. "I swear. I teared up when I saw that dear child's neck and realized she hadn't been branded with Hart's mark yet."

Wyatt nodded and picked his cup up. "Leo's guarding Shiv—Conway Perkins at the hospital. They dug the bullet out of his shoulder and are keeping him overnight for observation. Then he's ours. We need to get him to talk."

Reggie agreed. "Yes, we need Perkins and Hart to roll over, so we can take down the top guy's. Unless we nab those running the show, they'll simply start over again elsewhere with a new pimp and guard. Hart and Perkins are going away for murder and a long list of despicable crimes. Our CSI team is going over weapons seized."

"Reggie and I will interview each of the kidnapped kids once we get them into a stable situation. We might learn more from them. Willow's testimony will help, and if we can get Perkins and Hart to spill their guts, we should learn enough to go after the top men."

"It needs to happen quickly. Once they learn we've raided their stable, they'll shift gears and be harder to catch." Wyatt scooted backward.

"We've got our work cut out for us; but we're serving up a dose of sassy justice to those shrewd scumbags." Reggie grimaced.

Wyatt splayed hands on his desktop "Much as I hate taking attention off this case, we've got to finalize schematics for the drug bust at the warehouse. Information says the deal is going down on Monday. I want that drug ring out of my county."

Reggie had offered assistance for the drug case, as Shae had. So they switched gears and rehashed the strategy formulated earlier, making necessary changes and looking at every scenario so it would be a successful shakedown.

CHAPTER 24

Reggie curled into her cozy blanket, glass of wine in hand. A bowl of chocolate chunk ice cream sat on the table beside her along with the remote. A sappy love story played on her television. She hated perpetuating the prototype, but it was Sunday and her first opportunity to administer to her broken heart.

She picked up the chirping phone. "Hi, Sage. What's up?"

She welcomed balm of her best friend's understanding voice. "I haven't seen you in a few days. A lot has happened. I figured I'd best check on you. How are you, Reggie?"

"Good as can be, I guess. Exhausted—mentally and physically."

"I expected as much. Not only have you been busting ass on the crime scene, you've been through the wringer personally."

She hadn't found time to fill Sage in. How did she know?

"What do you mean?"

"Wyatt said you and Shae are on the outs. I thought the two of you were getting tight. What happened?"

"Good old Wyatt; he knows me well. I didn't get a chance to bring him up to speed on a personal front. You can fill him in later."

"So, spill it." Sage's tone dared.

"I seriously thought Shae and I were creating something beautiful between us before he was called away—I thought for work. It turned out it was for a job. He must've been contacted by his ex while he was away and spent time reconnecting with her. She showed up here before he returned ready to move in with him—so much for a relationship with Shae."

"I'm sorry, Reggie—truly. You're too young to give up on love. I had hopes Shae was the guy for you."

"That snippy bitch put an end to my ditzy fantasy about being in Shae's arms. The notion of her long legs wrapped around his waist burns my ass. I tell you, Sage, I'm thinking of giving men up for good. Vibrators are highly underrated." Reggie took a long sip of her wine.

"If he's hung up on his ex, you're better off without him. Do you hate him for dropping you for her?"

Reggie had to mull on it a second. "No, not really; he obviously loves that skinny bitch. More power to him. He has a right to happiness. It is better I find out he's in love with her now, rather than later."

Sage's voice sounded sympathetic. "No way; there's someone special out there just for you. Life's not a spectator sport. You've got to suit and saddle up to win the race. Reaping great rewards requires risk. You're no quitter and fearless. Don't forget it. Think of Shae as a practice run. You'll find the right man for you. Don't give up hope."

"So what? I keep putting my heart on the bullseye and let every man I'm attracted to take pot shots at it?"

"That's one way to look at it. I prefer to think of it as a teaching experience. You learn with each failed encounter, how to perfect a relationship. When you meet the right fella, you'll know how to make it work."

"Sage, it makes sense when you put it that way; but it's sounds like a grueling way to live."

"Believe me, Reggie, when you meet the right guy, it will be worth it."

"I want to believe you, Sage. Right now I need to soak up indulgent calories and sappy tears. Shae made no promises. I can't hold it against him. He's doing what his heart needs. I'm taking the evening to do what mine requires—dessert, alcohol and chick-flicks."

"Fine. But get over it and get on with life."

"I know I'd better. If not you'll do me like I did you."

"You mean after Cade was killed?" Sage chuckled. "It takes a good pal to tell you to your face you stink and to get off your ass and take a shower."

Reggie sniggered. "Yeah, well, you did." A change of subject was in order. "How's Willow?"

"She looks like a wounded baby bird, weak and terrified and dying for someone to place her in a safe nest. Deep in her soul she's a fighter.She's getting past withdrawal symptoms and growing stronger each day. She's begun therapy with a specialist in recovering victims of trafficking. Her head's been positioned somewhere out there in the big old sky, doing a lunar orbit. She's going to come down to earth soon. Starship Willow has a long, rough flight ahead of her before landing. Avoidance is a safety mechanism. It's kept her from falling off the deep end. She'll be fighting ghosts the remainder of her life; but sessions seem to be doing her good. Carla Orson is a God send."

"Good to hear. I can imagine being around you and Wyatt is helping her too. Taking her in was a heroic thing to do. I admire the incredible limitlessness of your heart, Sage. You're one in a million. We're lucky you're in our lives."

"I'm the lucky one. I wouldn't be the independent person I am today if it weren't for you; and I never would've met Wyatt. Ty's the best therapy Willow's getting in our house. He's smitten with our house guest. She adores him."

"Speaking of the sexy hunk in your bed, how did he take it?"

"He's one-hundred-percent behind my decision, though he wasn't happy I went to pick her up without backup. In hindsight, I should've called him. I was afraid if I hesitated even for the short time it would take to bring him in on it, she'd flee and I'd never see her again. I had to take her in. I'd never go back on my promise to stand by her.She's starting to warm up to Wyatt, but remains wary of men in general—for good reason. Kids like Willow have trust issues."

"She's making progress. What about her mother?"

"Carla contacted the mother. Of course, the woman wanted Willow to come home. After attending family counseling Carla set up for her, she understands what Willow has endured and will need to recuperate. The mom finally consented to allow Carla and the experts to manage Willow's care, and to give Willow as much time as she needs to face meeting her again. That doesn't mean Willow will have to return home. More than likely she'll be relocated to a safe location, where she can continue therapy and recover. Living anywhere near where she was held captive would provide constant triggers that could cause setbacks. If things go well, someday she and her mother may develop an entirely new relationship. I hope so, for Willow's sake. Everyone needs to belong."

Reggie might have a shattered heart, but she was lucky. Her parents and grandfather were alive and retired, living in Phoenix. She had the closest one could get to brothers in Wyatt, Levi and Justin. Sage, Riley and Corrie were sisters from other mothers; and Reggie was looking for her own personal nest in Sweetwater. No man owned her heart—at least none who wanted it, but Reggie was where she belonged.

As if Sage read her mind, she asked, "Any luck finding a house?"

"Maybe. You know Anthony Russo, Chloe's grandfather?"

"Yeah, sure. He's notorious for his past gangster life and connections to the infamous Cleveland Mob. I heard he bought Gavin Pierce's property."

"He did, and he made a deal with the bourbon recipe owner to produce it at the distillery in Sweetwater."

"The one Pierce constructed on the farm before he was killed?"

"One and the same; he's been rambling around that big, old, antebellum mansion on the property since he moved here from Lexington. He told Chloe it's too large for him. She helped him purchase a unit in the condominium community where his wife, Angelica lives. He wants to be in Sweetwater to be closer to Chloe, her mother and his wife."

"That's great. Too bad poor Angelica suffers from dementia. I hear it's getting worse."

"Yes, it's progressive. He doesn't want to disturb her too much, by being in her home. Relocating Angelica to the mansion would cause undo stress on her condition. Being close by is the best he can do. Between him, Angelica's private nursing staff, Chloe and her mom, they take care of her needs."

"That's really sweet. They're lucky to afford such care and to be able to keep her at home. What's that got to do with you buying a house?"

It was a long story, and Reggie was rambling. "The mansion is finally rehabbed and vacant. He gave it and half the farm acreage to Chloe as a wedding gift. He doesn't like the mansion sitting empty. Chloe can move in whenever she wants, and she and Leo can live there together when they get hitched in December."

"Or sooner?" Sage sniggered.

"Possibly; anyway, Chloe won't need her house. She gave me a tour of it. It's perfect. I made her an offer, and she accepted. I'm buying a house." Elation bolstered her spirits at the concept and filled her lungs with cleansing air.

"See there, you have something wonderful to look forward to and to be grateful for. We'll celebrate. Let me plan a housewarming party for you. When are you moving in?"

"In a few weeks, closing date isn't set yet."

"Well, I'm going now. You get back to your boozing sugar fest and sappy movies. Hugs."

"Will do. See you later." She disconnected to sound of Sage blowing her a smooch.

One night of indulgence was all she was allowing herself. She needed to shop for furniture and household necessities— if work would let up long enough.

They still had the drug bust coming on Monday night. That gave her time to finish her misery party and go to be early. It wouldn't pay to go into battle with a hangover.

CHAPTER 25

Wyatt leaned against a filing cabinet. "The tap on Sebastian Bryant's phone and records from his service show nothing abnormal. We used a drone to place a listening device and a visual recording device on the window ledge of Bryant's home office—thanks to Reggie's resources." Wyatt nodded her direction.

Reggie stood at the coffee counter mixing a cup of brew. "Glad to be of assistance."

Wyatt spoke as he walked to his office. "Not only can we hear what is being said in the house. The contraption pinged a second line other than Bryant's cell service. He's using a burner. That line has recorded calls to a burner in the capital building on a regular basis. The one from the state building sometimes pings from a tower near Senator Basin's personal residence. That tells me those two are in regular contact and don't want anyone aware." Shae and Reggie trailed Wyatt in and took seats across the desk from the sheriff.

"Holy shit, a state senator?" Shae's brows arched, and his head rocked back and forth in awe.

"Listen to this conversation." Wyatt pushed play on a machine on his desktop.

213

The voice of Sebastian Bryant, upstanding citizen and generous donor, was familiar. "I don't care. I'm shutting down in Sweetwater. Some nosey real estate agent has been snooping through my financials and got Sheriff Gordon and the mayor in a huff. They think I'm planning to destroy their quaint, little town by plunking a strip mall on Main Street. That misconception won't hold water for long. It's time to move the operation elsewhere. If you're smart, you'll do the same."

"What would you have me do? I'm a public figure,"a second familiar voice argued.

"I don't give a rat's ass. Fake your death and get out of the country. It's not like you haven't fabricated a new identity or created a bogus passing before. You've become proficient at getting rid of competition. If it looks suspicious, hell, you're a United States Senator. The public will simply blame another murder on the Clintons." He chuckled.

"Good Lord, you've gone mad," the Senator crowed.

"It's over," Sebastian gushed.

Senator Basin's smooth vocals had been in the media, campaigning for Governor for the last few months. Today they were bursting with distain and plotting what sounded like pure evil. "You fools can't keep your own noses clean. Why the hell should I take your advice?"

"Look, you bastard; I'm getting the fuck out of here, while the getting's good. If I go down, you drown with me." Bryant's tone filled with contempt.

"See you in hell," the Senator spat.

"Back at you, you pompous prick." The line went dead.

Reggie's mind was cooking with the new information. "We've got to find a way to get these guys before they disappear.

Shae slumped in his seat and groaned.

Wyatt flicked a couple buttons then eyed them. "Now, listen to these two short recordings. The first is from Bryant's burner. The second is Basin's line."

First there was a click. "Yes?" Reggie didn't recognize who was speaking.

Bryant took control. "It's time. Take care of the loose end we discussed. Plan B is in play."

"Consider it done," the stranger answered. The line went dead.

Reggie studied Wyatt with brows raised. His response was to cue the next call.

"Hello," another stranger answered.

"Take care of that matter," Senator Basin directed.

"You've got it." Again, the line went dead.

"What do you make of that?" Wyatt asked the law persons sitting across from him.

Shae drew in a lengthy breath. "Those bad boys don't seem to trust each other, if you ask me."

Reggie snickered. "They're cleaning up loose ends that might tie illegal business to them. Or they've put hits out on each other. You think they've planted insiders in each other's circles? Or do they keep outside hit men on the payroll with access to the other?"

Shae rubbed his chin staring at the floor then looked at the sheriff. "Do we care?"

Wyatt shrugged nonchalantly. "Not sure—if it doesn't occur in my jurisdiction. Right now I have more immediate fish to fry." Wyatt studied Reggie as though trying to read her mind. "We'll worry about those two, soon as we put that drug ring out of commission. Leo and Jaiden have troops assembled and in place. You two ready to roll?" Wyatt stood and plucked his hat off a hook, securing it on his silver head.

Reggie stood, doing a mental check. She patted weapons at various locations on her person and touched her flak jacket. Black jeans matched a long-sleeved, tee shirt. Retrieving the navy slicker from back of her chair, she slipped into the coatthat boldly pronouncingFBI in large, white embroidery on the back.

Shae followed them out snapping closed his Kevlar vest over the long-sleeved, army green tee shirt matching his slacks. The protective garment's bold lettering on the front and back readPOLICE U.S. MARSHAL.

CHAPTER 26

A grey frost hung on the ground setting the evening's somber tone. Wind whipped from the west. The gorgeous night sky didn't care that something dramatic was about to go down. Tension dominated the moment.

Reggie glanced up. "The sky's so bright. I could reach and steal the stars."

Shae gave her a sappy look with brows furrowed, as though studying her mood before pulling down his night vision goggles. She should've known better than to say something sentimental like that.

"Warehouse hours are six a.m. to ten p.m. Monday through Friday. Mack Bennett is the new manager dock worker, Cariday, referred to as a *Company Man*. Bennett just locked the front door behind the last second-shift worker." Wyatt's twang spoke softly into his com.

"It's time, folks. The ball should be rolling. Synchronize watches—ten-fifteen." Reggie directed her team, Wyatt's and Shae's from her position behind the facility. Troops were set in invisible spaces surrounding rear loading docks.

Shae's mellow Midwestern tone rolled through their coms. "There's a semi parked along the access lane. Lights are off, but the driver remains inside. Looks like our man."

Seconds later dock door number one slid up. Mack Bennett's frame was visible in half moonlight. He flicked a flashlight on and shone it at the tree line shielding view of the semi-truck. Lights flicked on the van and it began rolling through gates that slid open as he approached, obviously controlled by Bennett from the facility.

The delivery truck rolled slowly past the drop lot through another gated area into the loading and unloading space then came to an easy stop near the open port. Mack Bennett took the few steps down from the dock and stepped behind the truck. The driver hopped out to join him.

A previously unnoticed panel van with no logo on its sides rolled from the drop lot area, which Bennett had also unlocked access to. The white delivery van parked adjacentto the bigger vehicle. Its driver joined the other two.

One man unlocked the container door, and the panel van driver slid open the side door alongside the cargo trailer. Bennett and the men spoke, waving hands and using stern voices. The teamster pointed toward the cargo area of his trailer.

The semi driver climbed into the container and pushed out several cartons to the back edge. The van driver and Bennett hauled the first two to the distribution center and place them on the dock. They began loading the next two boxes into the smaller van.

Reggie's direction was clear in ears of those waiting for her signal. "Let's shake some action. Post time."

A horde of darkly dressed lawmen decked in protective gear and night vision equipment sped on silent feet, toward the delivery in process.

Reggie's voice rang loud in the cool night air. "FBI, stop what you're doing. You're under arrest."

Perpetrators pulled weapons. The van driver ducked behind his vehicle. Screams thundered from the container. Rumbling reverberated inside, as though inhabitants scrambled for cover. The semi-truck driver hunched behind a wheel between the van and his lorry.

Shots fired toward approaching officers. A man went down. A second snatched his protective garment and dragged him to safety. Men and women scurried to get clear shots, as gunfire filled the beautiful night.

The van driver was hit and dropped his weapon. An agent kicked it toward another who confiscated it. The first flipped the injured guy over and cuffed him.

"You'll live," a female voice gruffly told him.

Reggie placed herself against the front bumper of the semi-cab, out of range of fire from the persistently shooting driver. Shae took the opposite front fender, aiming toward Bennett. Reggie shot as her target came into view. The man went down with a scream. Shae's prey shrieked an obscenity just before Shae's bullet pierced his skull.

Reggie replaced her magazine. She glanced across her shoulder. Shae turned toward her.

She sensed impact before hearing the round. She felt as though her chest had been run over by the forty-foot freighter she used as cover. Her back slammed concrete. Her head lobbed forward then made contact with pavement. Eyes rolled back into her head. Blackness erased the vision of Mack Bennett's face looming above her.

Reggie's eyes flicked open. Brilliant light forced them closed.

"She's awake." Wyatt's voice broadcast relieved.

Footsteps sounded. Sage's soft lilt was like balm on a burn. She took Reggie's limp hand. "You're going to be fine, Reggie. We're here for you."

She drifted into a dream state. Shae's face smiled, and his soft lips touched hers. "I thought I'd lost you." He sniffed. "I'm glad you're okay."

She didn't want to wake. The dream was too perfect, too real to swap it for consciousness.

A sharp objectstung Reggie's arm and pierced her peaceful rest. Eyes flicked open with a few bats of the lids to clear sight. A nurse exited the room.

Sage sat reading a magazine nearby. An IV machine with a half-empty bag of clear liquid poised between them. To the other side, a monitor calibrated body status. Cords were taped to her person in various places, and a finger was secured into a clip.

Sage glanced up then stood. "Good, you're awake."

Reggie winced, as she tried to adjust positions. "What the fuck happened? My head feels like the Reds used it for batting practice." Her hand went to one temple.

Sage took the hand with a needle taped to it. "You have a concussion from smashing it against concrete."

"My neck feels like rubber, unable to support the weight of my head."

"Yeah, Shae said your skull rocked up and slammed back with amazing force."

Reggie tried painfully nodding. Her hand flew to examine her chest. "Ouch; I was shot."

She ripped the ugly hospital version of a nightgown down. Her chest was a massive purple and green bruise but no puncture at the point of impact.

"You're probably sore from bullet velocity hitting your Kevlar vest. Good thing you were suited up."

221

She blinked at her friend. "I'd never attempt a stakeout without proper gear. That son-of-a-bitch, Mack Bennett, came out of nowhere, the warehouse manager who replaced Simon Bedford."

"You saw his face?"

Again she tried nodding before realizing it, and searing fire shot from her neck through her cranium. "Shit fire and throw away the matches. This sucker hurts." She clasped her skull with both hands.

Sage snickered. "I see injury to your topknot didn't damage your personality. You're still the same spitfire I know and love." She shook her head. "Reggie, you gave me a horrible scare. I'm so glad you're going to be okay. Clay said your headache and neck pain will subside in a few days. He's prescribed muscle relaxers to get you through it. Your chest is badly bruised. No ribs are broken. You'll be colorful for a while, but there's no permanent damage."

"What about Bennett and the rest?" Her condition wasn't life threatening. She could focus on work.

"Shae killed Bennett. The way Wyatt described it, the guy came to finish you off. Shae walked straight at him and fired. Montgomery's one smoking hot, courageous gun slinger, if you ask me. You have to have serious *Gump* to strut toward a dude pointing a gun in your face."

"Shae Montgomery has quality stones on him." Thank goodness her partner made it home to Sweetwater in time for the bust. She'd been right about trusting him. Shae had her back."What about the others?"

"The driver of the van was arrested and identified as Jerome Cummings. Shae wounded the semi driver. He is under hospital arrest until he can be released. His name is Hayden Hunt. Rose and Riley came to the station to look at photos of arresteesfrom the distribution center and whore house. They recognized Hayden Hunt and Jerome

Cummings as the men with the hooker at the off-track betting lounge. Yolanda was the girl with them."

It hurt to think too much. Reggie's brain was on overdrive. "So the drug ring is connected to the human sex trafficking operation? It makes sense, with Sebastian Bryant's partial ownership of the shipping facility."

"Yeah, it's a perfect set up, giving Bryant's men access to warehousing, shipping and easy circulation of drugs and captives."

"Captives? I thought I heard voices inside the container."

"Yes, not only were they hauling a massive drug supply. They were shipping captives."

"So they were providing their own drugs to turn prisoners into addicts; and theysupplied this and other areas with illegal substances and slaves."

"Yes, the FBI put another Special Agent on the case to take over for you, with your injury. They've taken down seven other sex outlets owned by Bryant's holding company across the Midwest, like the one you busted here."

"Great; yes, we'd pinpointed buildings we figured could be involved in the operation."

Wyatt entered the room and came to stand beside Sage, giving her a peck on the lips. "I see our girl is alive and well." He bent and kissed Reggie on the cheek.

"I'm alive. Not sure how long that will last. I've got a killer headache." She grimaced. "Sage was filling me in on results from the sting."

He nodded. "We got more than we bargained for. We confiscated fifty pounds of marijuana and twenty kilograms of methamphetamine, crystal meth. We're charging the two arrested with intent to distribute, possession, possession of illegal firearms, drug and human trafficking and anything else I can come up with." Satisfaction on Wyatt's handsome face gave Reggie a sense of pride.

"So they're definitely involved in the child abduction setup? I was just telling Sage. I thought there were voices coming from inside that trailer during the takedown." She winced as she spoke.

Wyatt nodded. "Yep, there was a fresh shipment of kids inside. Not sure if they were being dropped off in Sweetwater, or destined for other areas. We notified Carla, and the NCMEC is working to identify them and get them needed care. We'll interview each of them once they're stable, to learn if they have information that can be used during prosecution. We saved those ten children from fates worse than death."

Relief washed through Reggie's limbs. She allowed it to bring peace to her heart. She might not have the love she dreamed of from Shae, but she was doing a righteous job she loved. Her career was immenselyfulfilling. It had to be good enough payoff.

She held a hand up. Wyatt slapped it. "We make a hell of a team, old friend."

He smiled broadly. "We sure as shit do, Reggie. You rest. You've earned it."

Sage kissed her cheek. "Now you're out of the woods, I'm heading home for a shower. I've been here two days."

Reggie snickered and kissed her dear friend, comically waving a hand. "Yeah, you stink."

Sage tweaked her nose. "Not the first time you've told me that. Smell yourself, girl. It's been a couple days since you showered, too. You can bathe soon as you're up to getting out of bed. Ring your bell. Your nurse will assist you."

They chuckled. Wyatt shook his head, rolling his eyes.

"Oh, fuck, don't make me laugh." Reggie grimaced and waved them out.

CHAPTER 27

A few days later, Reggie waltzed into the Sheriff's office. She strutted to the coffee table and mixed a cup of brew.

The tall, handsome sheriff leaned his behind against the bar and watched as he sipped his own. "How you doing, gal?"

She shrugged. "Still taking muscle relaxers for my neck. My head's better and brain is clear. I'm released for duty and resumed my role." She took a sip of the strong, dark magic and let its spell warm her insides.

She followed Wyatt to his cubicle. "My man filled me in, but I want your take. Where do interviews stand?" She sat in one of Wyatt's guest chairs.

"Driver Hayden Hunt confessed to movingcontrabandinto Logistical Excellence and other facilities owned by Logistical Excellence. Heowns a small fleet of trucks for hire. Most are leased to other drivers, but he keeps the one we confiscated for this special purpose. Hunt handles moves in and out of this warehouse and others your team shut down—both kids and drugs. He rolled over. Shae's put him into witness protection until he testifies in a future trial, once we arrest all players."

"How did you get him to talk?"

227

"Shae advised him the ring will have him killed in prison, if he lives through this. They won't want him lingering with information he could use against them in the future. Shae explained these perps are not devoted. Most people who have wronged them end up dead. He showed Hunt a string of victim photos—a hit-and-run car accident; lethal overdose of a guy with no history of drug abuse and a couple prison shanking's. Hunt nearly crapped himself in the interrogation room. He talked to protect himself and get a lesser sentence. If they all get put away, he's got a better chance of living through this. That scrawny tool is going to atone for his sins. He's going down for human trafficking, pandering, drug possession, possession of narcotics with intent to distribute, kidnapping and accessory to murder one."

She cackled and slapped her leg. "What about Bennett? That dude looks no more the outlaw than I do, with his growing beer belly, partial receding, grey hairline. He could be someone's grandpa."

Wyatt chuckled. "He might be. Mack Bennett seems to be the top man, below Sebastian Bryant. He's going down, but won't testify. It seems he's aware there's more than Bryant at the top of this ring and is afraid of someone—I assume the senator. We're still working on him, but so far, he won't give up info on the leader."

"What about Cecil Hart and Yolanda?"

Wyatt winced. "Yolanda Green is a tough customer. She's a well-honed prostitute. Cecil Hart has taught her well and established undying trust in her pimp.She won't give him up, refuses to talk. We've told her she's being prosecuted for human trafficking and accessory to murder, along with the rest, unless she cooperates."

"She's not old. She must've been a kid when Hart slid his fangs into her."

He nodded. "Yolanda was about to age out of the foster care system, when she was brought in. She doesn't have a clue what normal life is. Even the psychologists from the NCMEC haven't been able to get through to her."

Reggie nodded staring at the wall then turned to Wyatt. "And Cecil Hart?"

"Hart has been arrested for drug charges in the past, but never done more time than a few months in the Bonnyville jail. He's not anxious to spend life in prison for aiding and abetting a criminal, pandering, human trafficking, possession of drugs for purposes of distribution, and accessory to murder one. This time we've got that *perv* for something serious."

"So you've confirmed who murdered Simon Bedford?" She chewed her bottom lip.

"Yep, good old Shiv is our man. Forensics uncovered Bedford's DNA under the shaft of Conway Perkin's pig sticker. Bedford's little sex party with the child hooker got out of hand. Bedford strangled the girl. Hearing her scream, Perkins rushed in. Bedford started acting belligerent. Perkins slit Bedford's throat."

"I get that, but why didn't the dumb ass ditch the knife? Surely he had to realize no matter how well he cleaned it, evidence could remain on the murder weapon."

"Criminals aren't necessarily smart—not when their specialty is muscle. The dude is strong but isn't carrying a heavy load on his neck. He's got a lot of hefty charges against him. Conway Perkins did two years in the pen for robbing a liquor store a few years back. He owns a string of laundromats in Bonnyville, living in a suburb with a wife and two kids. He appeared to all who knew him from his personal life, as a normal guy. His role was to keep the girls secure, drive them around and watch after them. Sometimes he took Yolanda to the laundromat to do laundry. Nothing required a full deck upstairs."

Reggie snickered. "Hard to believe anything got laundered from that joint; every stitch I saw in that fleapit was filthy dirty."

Wyatt pulled out a photo of the murder weapon. "What do you think of this baby?"

"That's some blade. It looks like a Bowie Knife."

"Yeah, it is, made by the man himself. Perkins held onto it because of the historical value. He paid a pretty penny for it years ago and didn't want to part with it."

"Doesn't pay to be sentimental." Didn't she know it?

Wyatt sniggered and nodded. "Being a convicted felon, Perkin is spilling his guts about everything he knows, trying to work with the DA to get a shorter sentence. He's going down for murder one and charged with pandering and human trafficking. He killed Bedford intentionally, brought a lethal weapon into the house with premeditated malice and forethought. No way isn't he seeing a minimum of life in prison. Even if he's eligible for parole after thirty years, he'll likely not live to see it. He's already fifty-nine years old."

"Good to hear. I can't find it in my heart to feel sorry for the dude. Maybe his testimony will get him some special perks in the joint." She sipped the last of her coffee and sat up straight.

A deputy entered Wyatt's office. "Sheriff, you'd best turn the tube on. You'll want to see the latest news." The man left them.

Wyatt's brow rose. He flicked on a small television above a credenza on the side of his desk. He and Reggie studied the screen.

A news reporter came on. "Senator Trevor Bason was discovered this morning by his wife, who had been traveling. Upon return to their estate in Frankfort, she found her husband succumbed to carbon monoxide poisoning in his automobile parked in their garage. Senator Bason's death is believed to be suicide. Now, more on the weather."

Wyatt shut the television down and turned to Reggie. "Son-of-a-bitch."

"Exactly—I don't give a rat's ass what the media says. That dude was murdered."

"You pursuing it?" He studied her face.

She shrugged. "Why would I? His death puts him out of my box."

Wyatt snickered and pursed his lips. "Next on our agenda—get the bastard Sebastian Bryant. We stormed his house, but he'd already left. No one at the mansion provide useful intel on his whereabouts. He's on the run. We're following the money trail. It's virtually impossible to leave no digital footprint. We'll locate him."

"Yeah, my guys filled me in. We've got eyes on every airport, bus and train station in the area. The Bentley is missing, so he must've taken it. I've no doubt we'll locate him in that flashy car. His face is all over the media, and we've calculated a radius he'd be able to drive to on a tank of gas. He's going to have to refill, if he intends to continue to run in a vehicle.If he's smart—and he is—he'll ditch it for something less obvious. We're watching reports for stolen cars, but he could have one stashed in a location we're not aware of. His many properties are being combed by our men for clues. We'll get him. It's a matter of time. We're studying inside a radius looking for destinations he might seek refuge. I'll keep you in the loop." She stood to leave and extended a hand.

Wyatt stood and shook it. "Likewise; and Reggie, glad you're back."

"Thanks, pal; it means a lot."

Lynda Rees

CHAPTER 28

Reggie sidled into The Ten Mile House, anxious to spend an evening drinking with a friend instead of sitting in her new home missing Shae. She'd become expert at avoiding him, and he was easy to evade. His role with WITSEC had him traveling considerably.

"How's it hanging, Justin?" She snickered at the busy bartender, racing from one end of the bar to another, setting drinks up for customers. The barroom rumbled with chatter and country music from the jukebox.

Justin waved and nodded, jokingly. "Shaking a leg—the only good one I've got."

She slid onto one of the two barstools available. She gazed over her shoulder and nodded toward several people she recognized at tables.

Beside her sat a tall, Native American man. Raven hair draped his broad back nearly to his waist. She smiled. "Save this seat for me, cowboy?"

Calvin Coldwater nodded with a broad smile. "I did. Rose said you're joining us tonight. She's on her way. We can move to a table when she gets here."

She took a long draw on the icy, amber bottle Justin placed in front of her. "Fine with me. So, tell me why the two of you haven't popped out a baby yet? You've been married a couple years. I'm sure my dear friend has been humping the hell out of that gorgeous body of yours." She cackled.

Cal bit his lower lip with a snide sneer. "You scare the hell out of me, Reggie. You'll never change. Why don't I tell you about my horses while we dance? That's a safer topic than my sex life. I'll leave juicy stuff for you and Rose to chat about." He spun on his stool, took her hand and drew her to the small dance floor, where two other couples moved to the beat.

Cal was an amazing dancer, so she didn't resist. She was willing to listen to him expound on his latest hopeful for the triple crown in horse racing.

The idea of Cal fearing her tickled Reggie's fancy. The Seal and had been called upon more than once by the Navy for operations since his retirement, and he must've saved thousands of lives during his active career.

Shae was happy being home in Sweetwater. Walls of the tiny apartment had recently begun to feel as though they were converging on him. Hating to sentence himself to an evening licking his wounds alone, he opted for a beer at The Ten Mile House.

Reggie had been avoiding him since he removed his lawn mowing enrollee to another WITSEC-created identity and location. He wasn't sure what she was pissed at him for, but he'd screwed up somewhere along the line.

At least the enrollee was providing testimony that would help convict Sebastian Bryant. Too bad Bryant was still in the wind.

They'd been too busy with Reggie's injury and his WITSEC work for Shae to press her. At some point, he had to corner the woman and clear the air.

Not being with her was driving him to distraction. He thought about her every waking second—and dreamed of her every night. The bitchy, filthy-mouthed, insubordinate, sexy,

Lynda Rees

spicy, fiery female was in his blood. Funny thing was, he didn't mind. *Hell*, he thrived on it.

He'd finally found the one for him—the estrogen-driven human who completed him, made him strive to be a better person, and unlocked drive in him to live life to the fullest. He hadn't known he possessed such vigor for living. He was hopelessly and completely under Reggie Casse's spell. God help him. He didn't want a cure for the ailment.

At least he could drown sorrows in a few beers. Maybe he'd get a good night's rest—alone—if he found solace in alcohol. Life looked different staring at the bottom of an amber bottle.

He paid the Uber driver and strolled to the entrance of the log building. Music strained through glass on the thick door. His hand went to the knob, and his eyes gazed inside through the glass panel. His hand froze.

Reggie was on the dancefloor with a tall, dark man. Broad shoulders were blanketed with coal black hair. Muscular arms gripped her gorgeous body too closely for Shae's comfort. Her generous breasts draped against the unfamiliar fellow's rippling chest, pressing fabric of his western-cut shirt. Her eyes glistened in iridescent light. She smiled up at the handsome face.

Shae finally let go of his grip and forced eyes from the happy couple canoodling on the dancefloor. He spun and stepped away from the doorway.

A young woman with a purple streak in her dark, bias-cut hair strode toward the entry. "Excuse me." She side-stepped Shae who had nearly ran into her.

"Sorry," he muttered in a stupor.

"Aren't you going in?" She smiled congenially.

"No . . . no, I ah . . . forgot something . . . I need to do." He walked toward the road.

Barroom noise grew louder then quieter, as the door opened and closed with the woman's entrance. At the roadside, he leaned his butt on the concrete mound supporting a neon sign touting *The Ten Mile House* in bold, red lettering. He flipped his phone out and called another ride.

Lynda Rees

CHAPTER 29

Reggie had taken to working at her new dining room table instead of the office Shae had set up for them. She couldn't evade him forever, but she was going to as long as possible.

Her cell rang. "Hi, Joe, good to hear from you. What's going on?"

"Big news—the guy you've been looking for, Sebastian Bryant, has been located."

Her breath caught. "Do you have him in custody? When can I interrogate him?"

"Sorry, Reggie, that won't be possible. Bryant and another man were killed today in the crash of a private airplane over the Rockies in Idaho. We haven't identified the other gentleman, but it's definitely Bryant. A duffle bag filled with cash was recovered from wreckage. The flight plan for Kamloops, British Colombia, was made in the name of a pilot, who died during the last year. His license hadn't been updated in the system to show him deceased. It appears they were posing as vacationing fishermen flying toward Canada and experienced engine trouble."

Her stomach plummeted. "I'm sure that wasn't Bryant's final destination—probably somewhere we couldn't get extradition from. He must've been taking a jagged trail to avoid detection. They were probably going to change planes or fuel up."

"I'd say you're right. I'm sending you the link to the crash site investigation and what we got from Bryant's remains."

"Thanks, Joe. Catch you later."

"See you, Casse."

Shit.

Reggie read reports on the links Joe sent her then called Wyatt to update him. "I so wanted to nail Bryant to the cross for his crimes. He didn't deserve the easy way out. At least rotting in hell, he can't bring harm to other children."

"Thanks for the update, Reggie. Does Shae know yet?"

She groaned. "Doubtful. Guess I'll go tell him."

She had no choice. She had to face Shae—for business.

Keep it professional.

The ridiculously sexy man glanced up from the bland desk in his non-descript office and made her heart flip-flop. Why the hell had she convinced him to buy new duds and grow his buzz cut out. Jeans hugged his lean muscles, and arms bulged from short sleeves of a sinfully clingy, black tee shirt showing each ripple of his torso.

She was doomed.

Taking a cleansing breath, she quietly closed the door behind her.

He quirked a brow. "Agent Casse, good of you to make an appearance." Like her, Shae was a professional and well-practiced at keeping emotion out of his expression.

She sat at her station and spun the seat to face him. God help her. The good-looking man had a hold on her she couldn't break. Her stomach was gurgling like she'd swallowed hot lava, and her chest was so tight she could hardly breathe.

"I've got news on Sebastian Bryant."

"You mean the crash?" He looked her up and down.

She felt naked under his gaze. Ignoring hormones bouncing from place to place trying to manipulate her brain waves, she sniffed and focused on the tiny line beneath his left eye.

Why did scars make people more interesting? Survivors had marks, badges of courage, proving they'd made it through trauma.

"Casse, you okay?"

"Yeah, sure; life's full of bumps and bruises. No one gets out alive."

He chuckled. "Got that right, but you gave me a hell of a scare at the warehouse raid."

"I'm surprised you cared. You never showed up at the hospital."

"I did but got called away to secure the witnesses. You were comatose. I'm not surprised you don't remember."

He'd been there? She'd dreamed of him, like she often did. Surely he didn't actually say those words while she was out.

"Sorry, I must've been unconscious. You heard about the airplane crash?"

"The Marshal Services contact in that area updated me. We've got one less bastard to put away."

"Guess so. We've got enough to do, packaging this case for prosecution."

"Agreed." He turned toward his computer.

She opened hers and began searching a database. They spent the rest of the afternoon working quietly. It was the most uncomfortable afternoon Reggie had experienced. She'd rather be shot at than sit side-by-side in awkward silence with Shae.

He'd sure as hell fucked up somewhere. Reggie was professional and cold with him.

The woman was hot as a blazing barn filled with hay. Yet she could produce icicles on his testicles with a simple gaze or tone of voice. Reggie Casse was a thousand-piece puzzle with missing pieces. He couldn't figure her out.

Grateful to finish his last report for the day, he was ready for a break.

Should I invite her along? What do I have to lose?

"I'm meeting Wyatt for a brew. Want to come?" Oh shit, slip of the tongue. That should get a spicy response from her. He closed his laptop and walked toward the door.

She pushed back from the desk with both arms. "Nope, thanks. I'll pass. Tell Wyatt I said hi."

Her lack of playful, sexual banter shocked and disappointed him. She wasn't over whatever ailed her.

Her scowl grazed him from top to bottom, making his skin itch. His balls took refuge far as they could tuck themselves inside.

Without another word, he turned and fled. If he didn't get out quickly, his frozen cock would crack and fall off from her stare.

"For the life of me, Wyatt, I don't understand why she's pissed. Reggie has been frosty as a well digger's ass on a January morning. I thought Reggie and I were creating something special. Guess I was wrong; but, man, she's the one who moved on." Shae took another sip of his cold one.

Wyatt tilted his chair back onto two feet with hands on the barroom table and studied Shae. "You're sweet on Reggie."

"Duh, a blind man could see that. Hell yeah. I'm really into her—a lot of good it's doing me. She's angry and acts like she wants to smack my mom for giving birth to me. You've known her most of your life. Can you shed light on Reggie's mood?"

Wyatt snickered and put his seat down. Picking up his bottle, he pointed the neck toward Shae. "I feel you, man. I've been there. Sage and I had a rocky start. I believe Reggie is into you, too, but I could be mistaken. Who can tell with women? You sure pride isn't holding the two of you back? All I can say is hang in there. Figure out what's eating her and attack it. Reggie's worth the fight."

"I'd tackle a freaking mountain lion with a butter knife, if it would get me in her good graces. I have no clue what I'm up against and not sure it matters. She's tossed me to the curb for another guy already. I saw them dancing together. He's one hell of a good-looking stud. Not sure nerdy old me can compete."

Wyatt took a sip then deliberated Shae. "Sorry, man. I hadn't heard about her new flame. I was under the impression she was crazy about you. She sure as hell acted like it—at least before you took off on that work jaunt. She's been kind of squirrelly since then. There was a lot going on in a short period of time, with the brothel thing then immediately taking down the warehouse operation. I figured it had to do with work then afterward, with her injury."

"Glad her wounds healed. Not sure mine will. Being on the outs with her is killing me. I'm not sure I can stick around Sweetwater and watch her with her new love. I'm thinking I'll ask for a transfer, once we get this case wrapped up."

"I'd hate to see you go, Shae. Don't make rash decisions."

CHAPTER 30

Wyatt's office was packed with people—Sage, Wyatt, Willow, Reggie, Shae and of course, Wyatt. Reggie took a seat where she wouldn't have to look Marshal Montgomery in the eye.

"Thank you for coming, Willow." Reggie smiled at the young girl. "You look to be doing as well as Sage said you were. I'll be damned if your skin isn't glowing. I like the new style and color."

Willow fingered her silky looking hair. The child had come a long way, and looked nearly normal now.

"Thanks, Agent Reggie. Sage took me to her hair dresser. I love it. I feel great, thanks to Sage." She reached across to the next seat for Sage's hand. As her head turned, purple bruising showed where she'd recently had the heart tattoo removed from her neck. Soon that reminder of her horrendous past would be gone for good.

If only internal scars would heal so quickly

Sage beamed. "Willow's done the work. I'm just here to help her."

"We need you to hear a few recordings. Let us know if you recognize anyone." Wyatt played the audio from

247

Sebastian Bryant's call with Senator Bason. Then he played the two calls from Bryant and Bason to unknown voices.

She listened intently, leaning toward the recording device. With a blank stare she met Wyatt's eyes. "I've never heard any of those men's voices—that I recall. The first one sounds vaguely familiar, but I can't place it."

"Take a look at these photos. Do you recognize any of these men?" Reggie splayed an assortment of perpetrator pictures on the desktop—the three deceased and the ones arrested.

Willow pointed to the black woman. "This is Yolanda. This is Hart." She pointed to Cecil Hart's shot then to Conway Perkins. "This is Shiv."

She silently sifted through photographs until she came to one. Her hand withdrew as though she'd been burnt. Blinking several times, she stared and quivered.

"I . . . I . . . ah . . . I've seen this man before. I wasn't sure if it was a dream or if it really happened. This is the guy I told you, was humping me when I was dazed, after I first went with Hart. He's the first one who took me. I'll never forget his sweating, bulging eyes as he rutted on top of me." Her finger went back to the photo of Sebastian Bryant.

Reggie laid a gentle hand atop the girl's trembling one. "Don't worry, Willow. You're safe."

Willow's eyes teared, as she met Reggie's. "That's the voice I knew on the recording, right? It's distinctive and sends shivers down my back. He didn't say much when he was . . . with me. He didn't have to. I had a feeling . . . like he was a very bad man. I envisioned him as a silent tiger. When he roars, you'd best run for your life." Her head bent, and with several blinks tears rolled down her cheeks.

"No worries, Willow. We rattled his cage, and he was on the run. He ran out of time. Karma got to him before we could. The evil man and his accomplice are gone for good.He'll never hurt anyone again."

Is Karma a hit man?

Shae wanted a coffee from the bakery and one of their special, sugary, fried donuts before going to the office to face tons of paperwork. He parked on Main Street beside the pink and purple painted confectionery. Sugar filled damp morning air. Bright sunlight shone, as he stepped onto the sidewalk in front of glistening plate glass windows.

He gazed at a display of the day's featured desserts on lace topped trays. Maybe he'd have one of those nut-covered, thick brownies with chocolate icing as dessert, to go with his tuna salad packed lunch.

Gazing past the display, he spotted the owner sitting at a table in a small space beside the donut section, reserved for meetings with customers. She had created a delightful marketing array for her customer, including a selection of cake samples and several wedding cake toppers. A book splayed open between them. She pointed out a recommendation on a page, to the woman across from her. The back of the female caused Shae's breath to catch in his throat nearly choking him.

Damn his sweet tooth.

Shae's feet stalled in place. Body froze. He gaped at the image, wishing he hadn't craved sweets.

Shae couldn't un-see what he'd witnessed. Reggie choosing a cake for her wedding would forever be branded in his mind.

Son-of-a-bitch.

She's really into that dude—so into him she's planning a life together. He's quicker to the draw than I could ever be. Shae had been licking his ridiculous wounds and had wasted what time she'd given him.

What a dumb fuck.

He'd sensed Reggie's clicking time bomb—baby fever. No; women referred to it as their biological clock ticking. He'd felt much the same every time he'd seen Wyatt's and Sage's toddler, Ty. The child was a dream-come-true. Shea couldn't get enough of the boy, when he had the opportunity. Watching Reggie hold the baby brought tears to his eyes and made it impossible to speak. Did he have baby fever, too?

Shae had found plenty of time to come to grips with his needs. He needed Reggie—the woman he'd never dreamed of but couldn't live without. He needed a home, stability and family—hopefully his own offspring like Ty.

He was racked with images of Reggie lying in a bed holding his child in her arms—their child. In Ty's presence in those dark, fathomless eyes of hers conjured up a smokiness nothing else put there. Visions of her filled his brain and heart. He wanted to dive into those eyes and never come up for air.

Shae rushed to his truck and sped away.

Too late.

CHAPTER 31

Wyatt scribbled his signature on the contract then bent to kiss his wife. "Got a meeting, I've got to go. You ladies can handle the rest of this. See you later." He winked at Reggie and Chloe then slid the screen door closed behind him.

Chloe pointed at locations for Sage to sign paperwork she'd previously explained in detail to the threesome. "I can hardly believe this asset was freed up so quickly and the Federal government took your bid. What are you ladies going to do with the property?"

Sage signed the last spot then shoved the stack toward Reggie. "Thanks to Reggie and Shae pulling a few strings, the building was released for auction soon as all evidence was collected. They convinced authorities it would dilapidate further if left unmanaged for the normal, lengthy period of time confiscated real estate sits before auctioned off."

Reggie nodded and began writing her signature on lines Chloe had marked with stickers. "Our plans are a significant benefit to the FBI's and U. S. Marshal's ongoing investigation of human trafficking in the I75 corridor. It was a compelling argument."

Chloe tilted her head with a serious expression. "What exactly are your plans?"

Sage beamed. "We're going to remodel the facility so it looks nothing like the rundown structure it is now. The storefront will look inviting and will become a small daycare operation. The remainder of the first floor will be an industrial kitchen, dining area, laundry space and comfortable lounge. Half of the parking lot in back will be dug up. Grass, flowers and trees will be planted, and a pathway will meander through it. There will be inviting areas to sit and enjoy the outdoors, and a section will be devoted to a children's playground."

"That sounds awesome." Chloe frowned, as though confused. "What about the upstairs; and what are you using most of the property for?"

Reggie pushed forms to Chloe. "We're turning the building into a shelter for women and girls. We'll take in runaways seeking refuge from abusive environments and victims rescued from trafficking—like Willow."

Sage perked up at reference to the youngster. "We're naming it Willow House and are planting a huge, weeping willow tree in the back corner, near the parking area by the alley."

Chloe smiled broadly and laid a hand atop Sage's on the table. "That's wonderful and so generous of you both. It's a fitting use of the structure. How is Willow faring?"

Sage nodded. "We think so. I miss that girl terribly. She's become family to Wyatt, Ty and me." Sage glanced at her son playing happily in the floor with his tractor. "Willow's doing well and making friends. She's taken a job at a coffee house and learning to bowl and roller skate with new pals. After a few focused classes, she passed her GED test and enrolled in community college in the town she's living in. She and her mom had phone contact, but agreed not to push for direct interaction for a full year. At that time, it's up to Willow whether she wants to reconcile with her mother. It's important nothing triggers a relapse, which is why she's been relocated to a distant town."

"I'm sure you miss her."

Sage shook her head with a frown. "We invited her to visit Thanksgiving and Christmas, but it's doubtful she'll be able to handle returning to Sweetwater that soon, if ever. If she's not up to it, Wyatt, Ty, Hailey and I plan to visit her between the holidays. Hailey is anxious to meet Willow and likewise."

Chloe slipped the contract into her briefcase and gathered her pens. "Willow's a lucky young woman, having you in her life."

"I'm the lucky one. Helping that child has been a highlight in my life. I never could've saved her without Reggie's help." Sage reached for Reggie's hand and squeezed it.

"Family is where you find it. We're sisters from other mothers. This sister will always support you, Sage." Reggie returned Sage's squeeze.

"It sounds like a massive undertaking." Chloe hefted her briefcase onto her lap and took a last sip of sweet tea, obviously preparing to leave.

Sage scooted her seat back. Reggie released her hand, so Sage could see her guest out.

"It is. I've hired a great contractor to manage renovation. Once the property is in operation, guests will live in the second floor. Rooms will be converted into efficiency units with space for living and bedroom. Several shared bathrooms will take up some space. They'll have run of the kitchen, lounge and yard. Children of guests will have access to free daycare at the storefront facility, but each of them will be required to take shifts working there. They'll be given special training for that work. Cooking classes will be given in the kitchen periodically. Rose and Cal Coldwater will give a self-defense course. We'll see they get into GED training classes at the community center. I worked a deal with Sweetwater Community College for scholarships for girls who work hard and qualify."

Chloe looked in awe of their plans. "Wow; it sounds like a lot of work. How will you manage?"

"Rose and Jaiden plan to volunteer, as will I; but I will hire a capable person to be the '*house mom*' for the center. We have lots of community support. I've secured the Mayor's support. Your mother is a major donor, as are Riley and Levi Madison, Corrie and Justin Henderson and Adelle and Senator Madison to fund running Willow House Foundation."

Chloe stood and strolled toward the door. "Willow must be excited. Will she attend the Grand Opening?"

Sage followed her and opened the kitchen door for her friend to exit. "She is touched and happy to hear the place she was prisoner at will be turned into something positive to help others like her. It's doubtful she'll come for the celebration. It will probably be too soon."

Chloe kissed Sage's cheek and waved a hand Reggie's direction. "Congratulations ladies. Soon as we get to closing on this deal, you're downtown property owners. I'm sure I'm not alone in the sentiment. You two are officially my heroes."

Lynda Rees

CHAPTER 32

Shae prepared himself for facing Reggie, seeing her vehicle parked in her designated spot in the lot. He'd missed her presence in the office, but not the scowl she wore every time they'd been in the same room, since the shit hit the fan with their case.

Each day he'd arrived at their shared space with a cup of iced, sugar-free, caramel macchiato hoping she'd show up. Each day he'd been disappointed. Today that icy cup in his hand had a home.

Shae shut the door quietly behind him. The vision in a navy suit accented by a chartreuse tank top didn't bother to look up. Sitting the cup beside her right hand, he went to his desk. "Enjoy, Sunshine."

He turned in time to catch the roll of her eyes. She picked the drink up and stared at it with a tilted head. "That's thoughtful of you, Montgomery. How did you know I'd come in today?"

He shrugged and turned to open his computer, as though he hadn't tossed nearly a dozen containers of the sweet confection into the trash when she'd failed to arrive.

"I didn't—just hoping." His chest burned under her scrutiny, but he refused to look her in the eye. One ray of the old Reggie in those profound, impenetrable, coffee-colored peepers and he'd be lost.

After some time, she spun and resumed working. She patted a stack beside her drink. "Carla Orson dropped off a fresh batch of missing children flyers. I put a set on your desk."

"Thanks; we no sooner shut down one trafficking operation, and another fills the gap and takes over." He began going through the photographs. "None were children from the last raid."

Sadness filled her voice. "I know. It's frightening and sad. I'll run them through the FBI's facial recognition software when I finish this report. This stack is for the bulletin board." She laid a hand atop another pile.

Shae stood and reached for them. His hand touched hers, and his chest tightened at her warm, silky skin. She jerked away. Her head spun away from him, toward her desktop.

Did he imagine sparks between them, or did she trigger his heartbeat to a flashing stop?

Shae took the fliers and strolled to the board. He had previously removed shots of children liberated in their recent bust. He secured each new one to the corkboard.

"This damned board is mocking us. We no sooner empty it and it's filled again."

"It's scary how prevalent human trafficking is these days." She sighed heavily.

"Unfortunately, it's exceedingly profitable and not about to end anytime soon."

"It seems you're right." From his view of her straight back, she lifted a hand toward her cheek, as though wiping a tear away.

Damn, he loved this woman. He had as much of a chance with her as a snowball in hell. She was already in the wedding planning stage of her new relationship.

Reggie had nearly lost it when Shae took the fliers from her desktop and touched her. She had snatched her hand away reflexively from the spark physical contact caused.

They were co-workers. Whether he deserved it or not, she could at least be cordial—especially when he'd treated her to her favorite drink—without being sure she'd show up. Had he done it before—when she'd been hiding out in her new home?

"Are you feeling better?" Shae returned to his desk, sat and paused, facing her.

She shrugged. "I'm fine—off the muscle relaxers. I've had a lot on my plate, between catching up with paperwork from the case, moving into my new house and recovering from being shot."

"At least the shooter targeted your chest. He was close enough to make a head shot, assuming he was a good aim. You'd have been a goner." He visibly winced.

"Thanks for putting him down, when he came in for the killer round."

"No problem, Casse. It's what partners do." At least he still thought of them as partners.

Too bad he'd reverted to her surname. Her first name rolling over Shae's tongue was one of the most sensual sounds she'd heard, making her cream and flutter inside.

"I'm lucky you have my back." *Take the rest—my breasts, my lips and naked flesh. Hell, take it all, Shae.*

She bit her lip so she couldn't beg.

After one of the most uncomfortable days of his life, Shae had endured enough. He could stand it no more. The woman had moved on with her life. She'd been civil all day, but something had changed between them. Maybe she was embarrassed and afraid to broach the subject. Someone had to do it.

Shae spun toward her, leaned back into his swivel chair and braced nape of his neck in linked palms. "It's time to clear the air. I can't stand tension between us. It keeps building. I've had enough."

She swiveled to face him. Her gut went into battle mode. "What are you talking about?" Her professional mask gave no clue to what ran through her mind.

"You seem angry with me. What's eating you?" He trained on her reaction.

"Why? If I am, it's not your concern." Soon as words spit out, she regretted them. Why the hell did she have to be so damned snarky? He was making an effort.

"You could be right, but you've had a burr under your saddle since I returned from my trip. You understand I can't talk about work, unless it's a joint operation. Did I do something to piss you off?" His sparkly, brown eyes penetrated her skin, apparently trying to read her mind.

She couldn't control the green-eyed monster. "If you can't take the heat, stay out of the fire."

His feet flattened on the floor, as he sat up straight. Hands moved to his thighs. "What's that supposed mean?"

"Nothing; forget it. How's domestic life treating you?" She didn't want to know, but couldn't resist pushing the needle in further.

"Better than you." He shook his head with his mouth open, grabbed his laptop and stormed toward the door.

As he exited, before the door slammed behind him she got one more lick in. "Guess you made the right choice."

"Son-of-a-bitch—what is wrong with me?" She spoke to the walls in the empty room, as her eyes filled.

Shae couldn't stand it. Greasy takeout and a six pack of beer did nothing to drown his sorrows. Walls were closing in around him in the long-term, hotel rental. He needed to find a permanent home.

If he was going to ask for a transfer, it wouldn't be in Sweetwater. Shae wasn't about to hang around and watch Reggie and her new fella fall all over each other in public, as they planned their nuptials.

Mad as hell, he needed to understand why she was so pissed. She was an FIB agent, for God's sake. She understood the job took him away without notice and sometimes for extended periods. Hers did the same. If the shoe was on the other foot, he'd be gracious about her absence. It was no reason to put a total stop to their budding romance.He'd done nothing but fall head-over-heels for the spitfire.

Shae tossed the remote and picked up his phone. A few minutes later he was at the entrance to Reggie's new digs. He wasn't totally bombed, but he was tittering on drunk-as-a-skunk. At least he wasn't slurring words . . . yet—he didn't think.

He banged the brass thing in the center of her door. Shuffling from inside, then Reggie threw the ornately carved wooden entry wide.

"What's up?" She looked at him with one brow cocked and arms crossed.

A glance down showed his shirt halfway untucked and wrinkled. A blob of pasta sauce stained the lapel of his blue, button-down shirt. He expelled a huff of air.

"I'm sorry to bust in without calling. I had to talk with you." He prayed internally she wouldn't send him packing.

She stood back and waved him inside. He handed her the wine bottle he'd pulled from his refrigerator. "Peace offering."

She rolled her eyes and waltzed to the counter. "Not sure you need more of the bubbly."

Pulling out an opener, she screwed the squiggly end into the cork. It was a tight one. She twisted mightily with one hand and held the icy bottle in the other. Strain showed as tension grew on her face.

He reached for the wine bottle and corkscrew. Their fingers touched. Electricity that sparked in him every time he made physical contact with the fabulous female shot up his arm and bounced through is brain, leaving him addled. He inhaled deeply.

Scent of magnolias and cherry blossoms whiffed into his nostrils. A heady sensation swelled his chest as it rose and fell. Then itmeandered downward beginninga familiar reaction in his groin, he experienced each time he was with Reggie.

She jerked the flask from his grasp and blinked peculiarly. Brows arched and eyes widened. She shut her response down and grew stone-faced, making him wish more than ever he could read that brilliant, wacky mind of hers.

"I've got this." She spat the snide remark.

"Okay, Take Charge Casse, where's your pal?" He glimpsed around the room, surprised to find her accompanied only by the televised Red's baseball game.He retreated to the far side of the kitchen counter, putting space between them after her reaction to their brief, physical contact.

She frowned. The cork finally gave way with a pop. "I'm alone." She filled two goblets and shoved one to his side of the counter.

"Thanks." He sipped the refreshing red liquid. "The clerk at the liquor store told me this one has Sage's organic grapes in it, from Parsley, Sage, Rose, Mary & Wine."

She glanced at the label before refrigerating the remainder of the recorked bottle. "Yes, it's one of my favorites. It was thoughtful of you to bring it. Care to get to the meat of why you're here?" She strolled to the sofa and took a seat in the corner. Her bare feet came up to curl beneath her bare legs.

Unable to breath at the vision before him, speech would've been impossible. He plopped at the opposite end of the couch and faced her. He could barely think straight with hormones pinging through his system. Pulse raced, and he finally gulped in a swig of oxygen. Lightheaded, not from alcohol consumption, he struggled to keep his head from exploding.

His stupid eyes kept darting to the crux between her legs. Shorter-than-short shorts pressed her womanhood making an impression his lips watered to taste.

She'd obviously nixed the professional suit and bra. Opting for more casual wear, she still wore the flashy-colored tank top, but had clearly shed the bra. Silky fabric caressed each bump and crevice of her well-formed breasts. Material clearly defined perky nipples.

Shae bit his lower lip hard and gazed at the television, trying to stall blood flow to his penis. His freaking body was wrecking his capability to make sense. He'd never craved the taste of a woman so strongly.

She shrugged and turned her head toward the tube, sipping her drink. He must look like an idiot, and she was apparently giving him time to get his act together.

When he could think straight again, he swallowed the tennis ball-sized mound in his throat. "Casse, I realize you're angry with me. I'd like to get things straight between us, before I go. I owe you the heads up. I'm considering asking for a transfer on Monday. We've worked closely and well together and shared more than professional partnership.I wish you well and hope you find what you're after."

She swigged remainder of her wine—most of the glassful and puffed out a hearty exhale. "Son-of-a-bitch."

She turned away, sitting her glass down with a clang. Inhaling deeply, her delicate shoulders rose and fell. The angle gave him a view of her closing her eyes. Then she blinked them several times and turned to him.

"Shae, I'm sorry. You don't deserve my anger. You have every right to your happiness, wherever you find it." She shrugged, and her head tilted sideways for a second. "Too bad it didn't work out for you in Sweetwater." Her lips pressed together firmly.

He wasn't sure what to say. "Hmm . . . yeah . . . me too."

"Where are you asking to be moved to?" Her head slanted, and her brows slightly rose.

His open palms came up, and he grimaced. "It doesn't matter. I'll take whatever they've got open."

She eyed him curiously. "You all don't care where you live, long as it's not Sweetwater."

"What do you mean by you all? Is that southern slang for you? Yes; I don't care."

"No, I meant the two of you. I assumed you were moving to be near her work, wherever that is."

"Her who?" He squirrelled his nose up, clueless.

267

"Your fiancée Ms. Rosenthal, that's who. She moved in with you. Doesn't Lydia like Sweetwater's quaint, small-town charm? Please tell me it's got nothing to do with me. She was snooty when she came in the office. I figured she was that way with everyone. She's got nothing to be jealous of me for."

He chuckled. "No, she doesn't—I mean have reason to be jealous of you."

She looked like he'd slapped her. Her eyes welled with moisture.

He reached for her hand. She pulled it closer to her body, so he backed off.

Her voice was quivery as she spoke. "You don't have to be rude. We made no promises, but something special was happening between us when you were called away. The least you could've done when you returned was explain your reconciliation. It hurt, the way you treated me, like I have no right to feel rejected. I don't hold your getting back with Lydia against you, but I deserve your respect."

"Holy cow; no wonder you've been snippy." His eyes rolled ceiling-ward.

"I beg your pardon. Snippy?" Her brows rose, and she eyed him down her nose.

"Yeah, you've acted like I took a match to your favorite navy blue suit." He felt bad for the reference. Mocking her wardrobe was no way to get into her good graces. "I'm sorry, Reggie. I do respect you. I had no idea you thought I'd gone back to Lydia. Far from it—she came here hoping to mend fences. I sent her away."

"But she said—"

"I don't give a rat's ass what she said. It's over between Lydia and me. She has no reason to be jealous of you, because my rejection of her has nothing to do with you and everything to do with me. Her leaving did a job on my heart.

That's true; but time apart made me realize she wasn't the woman for me. Lydia didn't understand my career and hated what I do. She wanted me to change everything about myself to please her. When we were together, all I did was try to make her happy. I'm done with that. Guess I'll be a loner the rest of my sorry life, at least until the Marshal Services retires my ass."

Her face tempered as he spoke, and dreamy eyes softened with it. "Why would anyone want to change you, Shae? You're a hell of a man. Any woman would be lucky to have you." The words were like honey rolling off her sweet tongue—the one he ached to taste.

"I appreciate that. I sent her packing the day I returned. I could never go back to a faulty relationship. I'd rather be alone. Too bad no one else wants me." His head bobbed.

"Yeah, me too; I'll stick with the FBI until cataracts turn me into an aging, crappy shot."

"Sure, but you won't be alone." He smiled wishing her the best with her . . . he couldn't even think the word.

She nodded and beamed. "No, of course, you're right. I've got a great support system in this town, with my friends living here."

"You've got the wedding coming up. When is it, anyway?" He wanted to be sure he'd be long gone before festivities.

"Oh, yeah, they're getting married the third Saturday in December, the week before Christmas."

"They? I meant your wedding." He batted his eyes, confused.

"The only wedding I know of is Chloe Roberts and Leo Sanders."

He didn't believe his ears. "But I saw you at Simpson's Confectionaries picking out a wedding cake."

She cackled, slapped her leg and slid feet to the floor, not meeting Shae's eyes. Continuing laughter brought tears to her eyes. She sniffed and reached toward the end table for a tissue.

"What the hell is so funny?" Baffled, he frowned and observed the woman clearly having a good laugh at his expense.

Reggie blew her nose and wiped tears from her eyes. Those gorgeous peepers continued to sparkle with emotion and moisture, even as she finally settled down and faced him.

"Sage and I are putting on a wedding shower for Chloe. I was at the bakery to pick out a cake for the party. Mrs. Simpson was showing me the cake and topper Chloe chose for her wedding, so I could match design and colors. I thought you'd learned your lesson about making assumptions, Montgomery."

"What about you, Casse?"

She pointed a playful finger his way, and with a stern expression, cocked an eyebrow. "Now listen here. I didn't make that shit up. Lydia told me, you and she were shacking up. What the hell do you want from me, Montgomery?"

He gently tugged the finger to his lips easily transporting the woman toward him. He sucked the tip of the soft digit into his mouth then flipped the palm to kiss its sweet softness. Heat sieved from it through him, fortifying desire pushed down deep in his gut during their argument.

"I don't want to be alone." Heat welled deep in his belly, and blood flowed lower. He shifted in his seat.

Her brows rose and eyes widened. "What *do* you want?"

"Someone blazed into Sweetwater and stole my heart."

"Theft is illegal, Marshal Montgomery." Her eyes narrowed.

"I might have to take you in on charges, Special Agent Casse." His brow waggled, and his tongue slid along the single digit he held with his lips.

Her shoulders twitched, and her voice was deep and throaty. "We're bridging unconquered territory here, Shae."

"I'll take the risk. I like living vicariously on the edge of fire. Say my name again. I've never heard such a sweet sound." He sucked the finger inside completely.

"I've never been in love, Shae. It's doubtful I'll be good at it."

"We'll practice together." He flipped her hand and kissed the palm then began splaying tiny nibbles along the inside of her forearm. She shivered, and he breathed out a heavy sigh, bringing on another quake in the woman.

She didn't resist him, but scooted her behind closer, making it easier for him as he continued his search up the inside of her bare arm as slowly as he could move. His body wanted to race to taste every zesty inch of the fabulous, spicy female.

"So there's no man in your life?"

Her smoky voice eased across her tongue with an exhale. "There might be. Who did you think I was marrying?"

"That tall, musclebound, Native American dude you were cozying up to at The Ten Mile House."

Her head rocked back and she studied him oddly. "You weren't there."

"No, but I started to come in. I couldn't face the evening watching you carry on with that massive monster."

Her back stiffened. "For one thing, that guy is the soul of gentleness—farthest thing from a monster, though he's definitely powerful. Calvin Coldwater is a retired Navy Seal, a trained warrior. He trains horses for Levi Madison and is husband to my dear friend Rose. She was running late for

271

our night out, and Cal was showing me how to two-step. He's a great dancer."

Shea shook his head staring at the ceiling, but not releasing his hold on Reggie's arm. "No wonder you were laughing it up at my expense."

She chuckled. "You damn fool, why didn't you say something?" Her free hand took his chin, and fingers caressed his jaw. "I had no clue you thought I was seeing someone else."

"I don't know. I guess it's because I'm a damned fool. Reggie, it was killing me inside wanting you so badly and envisioning you in that man's arms. I thought you'd tossed me to the curb for a better model, without giving me a second thought."

Reggie freed her other hand. Both came to cup his jaws. "There is no better model. Your being with Lydia was eating me alive. No matter, I kept telling myself I had no right to be jealous. You're a free agent. We made no promises."

"I'm sick and tired of being a loner. I want a life with a picket fence, home, PTA and two-point-five children. I want to make promises and keep them. More than anything else, I want you, Reggie. You're the only damned woman I want screwing my brain up."

"Just your brain?"

"We can explore other options, if you're game." He winked wickedly.

She snickered and kissed his nose with a wink. "I have a picket fence, but I'm not sure how to produce a half-child."

He pulled the delightful, chortling spitfire onto his lap and snuggled her tight.

"It's an omen. We're meant to be. We'll work on the rest."

THE END

Dear Reader,

Thank you for reading, and I hope you enjoyed my book. It would please me a great deal if you would drop me a short line at these review sites. I value your time, so feel free to copy paste the same review on both, if you would please. Reviews affect readership and are more important to me as an author than you can imagine. Thank you for your time. I hope we become lifelong friends.

Links:

Bookbubhttps://www.bookbub.com/profile/lynda-rees

Goodreadshttps://www.goodreads.com/author/show/171874 00.Lynda_Rees

If you liked the book, you're going to love *2nd Chance Ranch*. Here's the first chapter to get you started.

2ND CHANCE RANCH

CHAPTER 1

Sweetwater Townspeople line Main Street welcoming home one of their own wounded in battle. The mayor waves from the front passenger seat of his baby blue 1957 Chevy.

The reigning hero sits on the rolled-down soft top, looking wan but elated.

Dory Farmer hadn't expected her heart to race at the vision dressed in full regalia. A white, flat-top hat covered his still blonde, but short cropped hair. His face was thinner than she'd expected, but still ruggedly handsome.

His dress jacket lined with chrome buttons down the front was pulled tight with a white belt. A mass of ribbons was displayed on the left side of his chest. Red stripes ran down the outside of navy slacks drapingawkwardly on abnormally thin legs.

Captain Chance Gibson had changed since he'd creeped out of town. Of course he had. The man had fought in a bloody war.

Dory was a different person, too. No longer the gullible, innocent who had fallen headlong for a high school basketball champ, she was a strong, capable, independent woman.

Life was good. She had everything she needed, though her friends constantly encouraged her to date and tried fixing her up. She had no need for a man and no room in her world for one. Life with her incredible son on the ranch she adored was a hearty meal. Men were simply desserts one indulged in occasionally—not to be taken seriously.

Did Chance notice her in the crowd? Their eyes never met, as he passed Dory and Lee watching from sidelines. Why should he recognize her?

Six years ago she'd been a fling—nothing more. Like all teenaged boys, his goal was to get into her pants. Once she gave it up, he'd gotten what he came for. She was nothing but a notch on his belt. He likely didn't remember her name.

"Can I go to the party, Mom?" Lee hopped from her knee bouncing side-to-side.

Her gentle hand swiped the adorable blonde hair. "You know better, young man. You're too young to parade around in a barroom."

"Okay; Ty said his mom is making my favorite walnut cake to the party.Can you bring me a piece?" He twisted sideways with that sly snicker that made her heart melt. He looked so like his dad and had the same effect on her. She could refuse him nothing and didn't whenever possible.

"You know it. Sage bakes the best pastries in town. I'll bring two slices. We can eat them for breakfast tomorrow. Sound good?"

His face lit up. Those deep, chocolate brown eyes gleamed. A grin spanned width of his square jaw. "Wow; that sounds amazing, Mom. Cake for breakfast. Yum." He rubbed his belly through his red-white-and blue tee shirt.

"Don't get used to it. This is a special occasion." She stood and folded their lawn chairs. Taking his hand, she led him to her pickup truck.

"Why not, Mom?"

"Cake isn't a traditional breakfast." She rustled his blonde hair playfully.

"It should be. Doesn't it have milk and eggs in it?"

"You've got me there." Logical and smart as a whip in a debate—like his father.

As she hoisted him into the passenger's seat and watched him secure the seatbelt, he studied her with a tilted head. "Is it special because the soldier was hurt?"

"No; because he returned home alive. The Captain is brave and strong. He saved three soldiers' lives." She shut the door and placed the chairs in the truck bed, hoping he'd change the subject by the time she slowly rounded the vehicle and climbed in.

GET YOUR COPY AT:
https://www.amazon.com/2nd-Chance-Ranch-Lynda-Rees-ebook/dp/B085X4JR6X/ref=sr_1_1?keywords=2nd+Chance+Ranch&qid=1585173456&sr=8-1

orwww.lyndareesauthor.com/2nd-Chance-Ranch/

ALSO BY LYNDA REES

Historical Romance:
Gold Lust Conspiracy

Mystery:
The Bloodline Series:
Leah's Story
Parsley, Sage, Rose, Mary & Wine
Blood & Studs
Hot Blooded
Blood of Champions
Bloodlines & Lies
Horseshoes & Roses
The Bloodline Trail
Real Money
The Bourbon Trail

Single Titles:
God Father's Day
Madam Mom
2nd Chance Ranch
Hart's Girls
7 Book Anthology: *Sacrifice For Love:*
Second Chance Romance, Lynda Rees

Children's Middle Grade:
Freckle Face & Blondie
The Thinking Tree
277

Lynda Rees

Find information about these books at website:
http://www.lyndareesauthor.com

ABOUT LYNDA REES

Lynda is a storyteller, an award-winning novelist, and a free-spirited dreamer with workaholic tendencies and a passion for writing. Her dreams come true, blessing her with a supportive family. Whatever crazy adventure Lynda congers up, her loving Mike is by her side. A diverse background, visits to exotic locations, and curiosity about how history effects today's world fuels her writing. Born in the splendor of the Appalachian Mountains as a coal miner's daughter and part-Cherokee, she grew up in northern Kentucky when Newport prospered as a mecca for gambling and prostitution. Lynda's work is published in cozy mystery, historical romance, children's middle-grade, advertising copy, self-help and freelance.

Author's Note:

Enjoy my work. I hope we become life-long friends.
Time for Romance!

Lynda Rees

Love is a dangerous mystery. Enjoy the ride!

Get the latest book deals, exclusive content and **FREE** reads by joining my **VIPs**. Email me for a **FREE** copy of *Leah's Story*.

Lynda Rees

Visit my website: http://www.lyndareesauthor.com
Email: lyndareesauthor@gmail.com

Lynda Rees